JUST NO

PETER UDELL

Copyright © Peter Udell, 2014

The right of Peter Udell to be identified as the author of this work has been asserted by him in accordance with the Copyright, Designs and Patents Act 1988.

All rights reserved. No part of this publication may be reproduced, stored in a retrieval system, or transmitted, in any form or by any means, without the prior permission of the copyright owner.

This book is a work of fiction. All the characters in this book are fictitious, and any resemblance to actual persons, living or dead, is purely coincidental.

ISBN-13: 978-1495273216

Cover design by Hallam Udell

'Alone, alone, all, all alone,
Alone on a wide, wide sea!'

The Rime of the Ancient Mariner,
Samuel Taylor Coleridge

'No man is an island,
entire of itself.'

Meditation XVII, John Donne

CHAPTER ONE

'What a beautiful face!'

She heard the whisper of a stranger who was standing beside her.

'What a beautiful body!' she whispered in reply.

'Which body?' asked the man, who was now clearly talking to her.

'Which face?' she replied, equally clearly talking to him.

They turned away from the Botticelli painting in front of them. He looked, perhaps reluctantly, away from the face of the victorious Venus on the left. Dressed in a long white robe fringed with gold, she lay with her right arm resting on a cushion. Her left leg was stretched out on the ground.

She looked away, also perhaps reluctantly, from the naked beauty of the young yet exhausted body of the vanquished Mars on the right. He lay fast asleep. His left arm and right leg were bent. His right arm and left leg were almost straight. They turned, instead, to face each other.

At once they burst out laughing, loudly and uncontrollably, at what they had said. This was, though they did not notice it, to the surprise of some of the

National Gallery visitors around them. It was, too, to the annoyance of others. And, before they had managed to bring their laughter under control, they looked fully at each other for the first time.

She did not, he noticed, have anything like the face of the goddess of love and beauty. She had neither the eyes looking coolly into the distance, nor the thin face. She had neither the high forehead, nor the nose that was slightly upturned, nor the chin that was a little pointed. Her freckled face was a little rounder than the goddess' face, with a forehead not quite as high, and with a nose that was straight.

Nor did she have the goddess' straw-blond hair, curling at the ends as it fell onto her breasts. For hers was dark brown, rich and thick and long. And it cascaded not onto her breasts but over her shoulders and onto the mauve trenchcoat she was wearing above her black drainpipe jeans.

Yet her face was, in its own way, both remarkable and memorable. It was also, he admitted to himself, more than a little attractive. He noticed especially her quiet green eyes. In these he thought he saw, or so he felt, a hint of pain or suffering or even damage.

In his brown suede jacket and his grey flannels, he had – as far as she could judge – little in common with the god of war. His hair was not brown with a hint of red. Nor was it long like the god's hair. It was almost black and very much shorter. His body did not have the perfect proportions of a Greek or Renaissance sculpture. As far as she could judge, though – and with at least as much pleasure as he felt when he looked at her – it was not too far short of that.

His face was long, angular, tanned, and with a nose that

almost deserved the description of prominent or aquiline. It had a depth of expression that the face in the painting, its eyes closed in deep sleep and its mouth slightly open, lacked. To her, or so she imagined, his brown eyes told a story he might find more than a little difficult to tell himself.

'Do you come here often?' he asked.

Then, though neither of them knew why, they burst out laughing again.

'Just now and then,' she replied. 'Usually then.'

'So what are you doing here now?'

'We all make mistakes.'

'Even you?'

'Especially me.'

He looked carefully at her. He was unsure whether to say to her what he had just thought. 'As when you're asked by a complete stranger to come and have a drink?'

'Being asked isn't the mistake,' she answered. 'The mistake's in agreeing.'

'So will you make the mistake?'

She knew she should think twice before agreeing. But she had already made up her mind: 'It's not that I will. I already have.'

'Name?'

'Joanna. But my friends all call me Jo.'

'Address?'

'Shepherd's Bush. Closer to East Acton than West Kensington. But not for too much longer.'

'Occupation?'

'School teacher. With three years of teaching primary school kids behind me. Not dedicated enough, though, to want to make a career of it.'

'Interests?'

'Reading whatever I can get my hands on. Novels. Plays. Above all poems. And, though you may think it's more than a little odd, the older the poems are the better. Anything, I guess, to escape from the real world. A bookworm if ever there was one. And far from ashamed of it.'

'Marital status?'

'Single. Very single. And with every intention of staying that way.'

'Age?'

'Old enough to know better than to tell a stranger. Even if he has just bought me a drink.'

'Twenty something?'

'Twenty plus: yes. And if *something* is five years – five and a half to be exact – you wouldn't be far wrong.'

They had left the National Gallery in the late morning of that Easter Saturday. They had walked past St Martin in the Fields. They had walked on to the east up the Strand. They had faced a bitter wind that seemed to promise sleet or even snow rather than sweet April showers.

Just past the Adelphi Theatre they had turned left into Bull Inn Court. They had entered a narrow alley whose gas lamps were still in place. A design in coloured tiles proclaimed *To the Nell Gwynne Tavern Saloon Lounge*. He had bought her a campari and soda. For himself he had bought half a pint of draught bitter.

They were sitting on low stools in a corner of the small bar. They faced each other across a little round table, copper-topped and with ornate iron legs. There were two windows looking out onto the alley. There were lamps hanging down from the ceiling. There was a mirror above the fireplace beside them.

The windows seemed, though, to let in little light. The lamps were dim. The mirror reflected the darkness of the tiny pub rather than the light outside.

The wooden floors were dark and bare. The wooden panels along the lower part of the walls and the wallpaper above were even darker. The ceiling was dark brown. The black cast-iron fireplace was framed in dark wood.

Because of all this, they could hardly see the old prints and photos on the walls. Nor could they see the old pots and bottles above the entrance. They even found it difficult to see each other, to capture anything of what their faces were saying.

'And you?' she asked.

'Name: Stephen. And that's what all my friends, even my closest friends, call me. Address: North West London. Or, more precisely, Kensal Rise. Closer to Willesden Junction than Maida Vale. Profession: lawyer. Or, more precisely, barrister. Practicing in chambers in Lincoln's Inn.

'That may help to explain why I talk the way I do. Sentences that are often grammatical to a fault. And often complicated beyond belief. But, at the other end of the spectrum, I use flowery language much more than I should. Though often, far too often, the flowers have gone to seed.'

'Which, believe it or not, is just what some of my friends say about me!' she exclaimed. 'And your interests apart from the law?'

'Books are high up on my list. Just as they are on yours. And I've got a weakness for lacing what I'm trying to say with what somebody else has said so much better.

'But as well as books, I'm a glutton for what I've always

called natural history. Animals and birds. Reptiles and fish and insects. Trees and flowers. To put it in a nutshell: anything that isn't human.'

'Age?'

'Thirty. Or, more precisely, thirty one. Born, so my parents told me, in the year of the Cuban missile crisis and the death of Marilyn Monroe. It was my birthday yesterday – Good Friday. I was, at least until we met, celebrating it by looking at some of my very favourite paintings.'

'Congratulations on your birthday! And do I congratulate you on being single or married? Separated or divorced?'

'If I were single or divorced you could congratulate me as much as you like. And in any way you like.' He lifted his glass and swallowed much more than a mouthful of his beer. 'But as it is you'd better just congratulate me on my birthday.'

She watched his face. It had, a moment before, been so full of smiles and laughter. Suddenly it became tense as he replied to her question.

His eyes moved from looking at her – even, she thought, staring at her more than she would have expected him to do. Instead they looked past her, into some distance in which her intuition told her she had no place.

Without thinking, she stretched out her hand and put it for a moment, lightly and hesitantly, on his.

'Another drink?' she asked. 'To celebrate your birthday.'

He nodded with a slight, almost imperceptible, movement of his head. His eyes were still looking, fixed and frozen, into the far distance.

'Stephen!'

She caught sight of him as he walked towards the wrought-iron gates of the school where she taught. It was close to the backstreets of nineteenth-century terraced houses and twentieth-century council houses between Shepherd's Bush and East Acton.

She was waiting for him here, keeping warm in a plum-coloured and oversized sweater, and in matching slacks. This was after she had been working for a few hours to prepare her classroom for the summer term.

He was, she noticed, looking every inch the lawyer, in a well-pressed grey suit and well-polished black shoes, a white shirt and a sober blue tie. He had a black bag slung over his shoulder. Quite unexpectedly, and almost in spite of herself, she felt her heart beating more quickly.

'Jo!'

He hesitated as he reached her by the gates. Should he kiss her, which is what he wanted to do? Or should he shake her hand, which he felt might be what she would expect him to do?

As in the few seconds before they met he could not make up his mind, he did both. He held her hands in his, but less tightly than he would have wished. He brushed her forehead with his lips.

'I wasn't sure you'd be able to find your way here,' she told him as soon as she had recovered from his unexpected – though far from unwelcome – kiss.

'Just for once I finished the work on the case I'd been preparing earlier than I thought I would.' He chuckled a little self-consciously. 'It wasn't too difficult to take the tube from Holborn to Shepherd's Bush. And it wasn't too difficult to walk the rest of the way. So I didn't have much of an excuse, did I?'

'Would you have wanted an excuse?' she asked.

His eyes looked long and hard, or so it seemed to her, into hers. Slowly, very deliberately, he shook his head.

'Would you have wanted me to have had one?' he asked in reply.

She, too, shook her head. She did it less slowly than he had done, but just as deliberately. She looked away from him. She tried, though unsuccessfully, to hide her face. For she felt it was beginning to burn with a blush she knew she would not be able to control.

'I thought it was schoolgirls and not schoolmistresses who blushed.'

'No. You're quite wrong. And in any case,' she retorted, 'we're teachers. We're not mistresses.'

'Though some of you, I'm sure, must be both.'

She blushed again, this time more furiously. At a stroke, she lost all ability to control her blushing.

'That's our own business and nobody else's.' She hesitated. 'But I have to admit some of us may be both.'

'You're being almost as pedantic when you're not working,' he replied, 'as I have to be when I am.'

They both burst out laughing as they had done when they had first met the weekend before in front of *Venus and Mars*. This time, though, their laughter helped to dissolve the tension they both felt.

'Let's go for a walk,' she suggested. 'To celebrate our second meeting.'

'Where?'

'Wormwood Scrubs is just a few minutes from here. It's what some of your former clients probably see more often than they'd like to. Or there's the towpath along the Thames at Hammersmith. And that's a bus ride away.'

'Yes,' he replied, knowing perfectly well he was not giving her an answer.

'But which?' she asked.
'You choose.'
'I already have.'
'So?'
'It's the river.'

'Tell me more.'
'What about?' she asked.
'About you.'
From the bus stop they had walked over Hammersmith Bridge, its faded green and gold paint brightened by the late-afternoon sun. They had climbed down onto the towpath on the south side of the river. They were strolling along it towards the west.
'There's not much more to tell.'
'Or is there much more not to tell?' he countered.
She looked to her right across the Thames. She focussed on the waterside row of old houses, and on the Blue Anchor and the Rutland Arms. Both reminded her of some of the pubs she knew from her early drinking days near Oxford.
She looked to her left at a bank of nettles between her and the black iron railings of St Paul's School playing fields. She looked above her at the horse-chestnut tree. She looked in particular at its new leaves, all so very green, and at its white flowers which were just beginning to open.
She looked down at the uneven stone and gravel path they were walking along. For a moment – and for the first time since she had met him – she was lost for a reply.
'There's always more we don't tell about ourselves than we do tell,' she replied defensively. 'We all select, sometimes ruthlessly, sometimes carelessly, what we offer

to tell. And that'll be as true of you as it is of me.'

'So what's on offer?' he asked.

'I've told you I live in Shepherd's Bush. I'm in an attic flat that's so small I couldn't swing a kitten in it let alone a cat.'

'And?'

'I've told you I teach. As I've also told you, I've been doing it for three years. I can see myself staying in teaching for a few more years. But I certainly don't see myself doing it for the rest of my life.'

'Keep going!' he urged her.

'I've told you I'm twenty five. A child of the late sixties. Born to the beat of the Rolling Stones' *Jumping Jack Flash*. Reached my adolescence at our local comprehensive school when John Lennon came out with *Imagine*.'

'And after school?'

'Finished my education, with Madonna in full flood, when I studied English at King's College. Only a few hundred yards along the Strand from the pub where we had our drink.

'And, to use your own words, that may help to explain why I talk the way I do. With sentences too grammatical and too complicated by a mile – which is exactly what you said about yours. With lines from plays and poems popping up from the recesses of my memory when I least expect them. Just as being a barrister may help to explain why you sound more than a little like a Victorian academic in full flood.'

He snorted as he pretended to register his frustration at her answer.

'Take out the padding and everything you've just said tells me little more about you than you'd put on an application for a passport or a driving licence.'

'It tells you just as much about me as you've told me about yourself.'

'Which,' he admitted, 'is next to nothing.'

She snorted in return, and decided to seize the initiative in their exchange.

'I've also told you for good measure I'm single. Though there's nothing very special about that.' She paused for a moment, then added with a flourish: '*I had rather hear my dog bark at a crow than a man swear he loves me.*'

'If you have to quote Beatrice, then I'm going to have to quote Benedick back at you.' He made a mock Shakespearean bow. To her surprise, he produced Benedick's exact reply: '*God keep your ladyship still in that mind, so some gentleman or other shall 'scape a predestinate scratched face.*'

She made a flamboyant curtsy. Now, to his surprise, she produced word for word Beatrice's reply: '*Scratching could not make it worse, an 'twere such a face as yours were.*'

They stopped, looked at each other. Yet again, they burst out laughing.

'We can't keep on laughing like this. Or,' he added, 'making so much ado about nothing.'

'How do you think you can put a stop to it?'

'Unless you stop me,' he replied, 'it's quite simple.'

They were standing beside some hawthorn bushes. The leaves on these were already open. Tiny clusters of flowers were already starting to appear.

Beyond them: the steep stone bank down to the river, which was now flowing downstream with the ebb tide. The first few feet of grey mud and drying stones were beginning to appear.

He stepped uncertainly towards her. He put his arms

gently round her, brought her closer to him. He kissed her softly. First, and briefly, on her forehead, as he had done outside the school gates. Then, less hurriedly, on each cheek. Finally, and at length, on her lips.

She, in response, lifted her arms and put one hand on the back of his neck, the other behind his head. She pressed her lips firmly and eagerly against his.

'Do you do this often?' he asked after their kiss had ended, and in a voice she found extraordinarily soft and gentle.

'Just now and then,' she replied, with the same words she had used when they first met. 'Usually, if the truth be told, then.'

Again they broke into laughter. Again they held each other and kissed.

Two children raced past them along the towpath on their bicycles, ringing their bells wildly and shouting shrilly at each other. A school crew struggled to row upstream against the tide, cajoled by a coach's voice blasting at them through a megaphone. A dog a few yards from them barked enthusiastically across the water at a couple of ducks that were swimming close to the bank.

They heard none of the sounds around them. They saw neither the two children, nor the boat crew, nor the dog, nor the ducks. They stood, aware only of each other, until he broke their silence.

'It seems to me,' he whispered, 'we crossed some sort of frontier just now.'

'Even if we did, there's still a lot of travelling to do.' She pointed at the surface of the river in front of them. 'We're like those two leaves over there floating down the river. One minute they're travelling downstream quite separately. The next they're moving closer. The next they're bobbing along beside each other. The next they're floating together.'

'And the next?' he asked her.

'Who knows what the currents and the winds will do to them? Who knows what storms will hit them?'

He nodded slowly and, perhaps, a little sadly as she paused for a moment to think how to complete her reply.

'And, to go back to what you said about crossing a frontier,' she added, 'in spite of all your efforts, all your questions, you still don't know as much about me as I'd have had to put on those applications for my passport or my driving licence.'

'Stop!' he demanded a few minutes later. 'Listen.'

They were on their way back to Hammersmith Bridge along the towpath. They were holding hands as they strolled along, sharing the same elation. Past horse-chestnuts and willows, poplars and sycamores, most with their leaves already open. Past plane trees whose leaves were just emerging. Past other trees whose leaves were still firmly encased in their buds.

On the other side of the Thames was a tight group of narrowboats, dark-blue, deep-red, ochre, burgundy. To the left of these was Dove Pier with its larger barges, higher fore and aft than amidships, and tied up to a jetty.

'Listen to what?' she asked. 'To the traffic? To the jets?'

'Neither. Just listen.'

She did as he told her. To her surprise and delight, she heard a bird singing from a high branch on the sycamore above them.

'What is it?'

'One of my most favourite birds,' he replied. 'Yet, though skylarks and nightingales have had poems written about them, blackbirds like the one up there have, as far as I know, had none.'

They both listened as the blackbird sang on. Above the relentless dull thunder of the traffic on Hammersmith Bridge and, in the distance, on the Great West Road. Also above the whining of the aircraft that, every minute or so, edged overhead as they followed their flightpath towards Heathrow Airport.

'For me,' he added, 'with apologies to Shelley and Keats, their song's as magical as the song of any skylark or nightingale.'

'It's beautiful,' she agreed. 'And even the noise of the cars and the planes can't drown it.'

'Before an early-spring dawn, when it's still quite dark, it's even better. Minute after minute of pure sound. No cars or jets or trains – or, for a time, no other birds – to challenge it.'

'But you're wrong about blackbirds not appearing in verse. Just ask any of the children in my class.'

From the depths of her memory, she dragged to the surface a childhood hymn.

'Tell me!' he told her.

She started, rather hesitantly, to sing.

'Morning has broken
Like the first morning...'

The cars and aircraft were forgotten, just as the children on their bicycles, the school crew and the barking dog had been forgotten a little earlier. He added his voice to hers. They stood by the river. They looked up into the branches. They sang together, neither self-conscious nor embarrassed, as the birdsong poured from the treetop.

'...Blackbird has spoken
Like the first bird.'

He clattered noisily down the stone stairs from his chambers. His heart beat almost in time with each step. He dashed down the last six or so steps and into New Court.

Here one of the cherry trees was in full and spectacular pink blossom. Here, too, the magnolias, surrounded on the ground by a scattering of fallen petals, now had only their last few flowers. And here, suddenly and for just a moment, he found he was blinded by the mid-April sunshine.

'Stephen!'

When his eyes had at last adjusted themselves to the bright sunlight, he caught sight of Joanna standing on the pavement by some iron railings. Her long pale-blue dress, short-sleeved and reaching almost to her ankles, was in great contrast with his own formal clothes, and with the uniformly dark suits and white shirts of the lawyers who were striding purposefully past her.

'Jo!'

His heart beat even faster than it had done on the stairs. He went up to her and, without saying a word, put his briefcase on the pavement and put his arms round her. He kissed her as passionately as she kissed him in return.

'Should you be doing this so close to where you work?' she asked in a feigned show of surprise.

'We agreed back on the towpath we'd crossed a frontier together. I'm not going to go back to the other side. Even if I'm appearing in court and cross-examining a key witness.'

'So what shall we do? I'm still on holiday. I don't have to get a bus back to Shepherd's Bush until much later. And I don't intend to go anywhere near school again this week.'

'I'm working on two or three cases. I'm not, though, meeting any clients until tomorrow morning. And I'm not in court until next week.'

She would have been happy to have done anything, as long as it was with him. So, as he was on his home territory, she handed the decision to him.

'You choose.'

'To steal those lines you delivered outside your school, I already have. We'll sit out on the grass in the gardens over there. Lincoln's Inn can often be a pretty gloomy place. Yet on a glorious spring day like this it's at its very best.'

'Shall we get ourselves something to eat and drink before we go and sit down?' she asked.

'Just to repeat myself, and because I wasn't sure how much time you'd have, I already have.'

He patted his briefcase as they walked along the paving stones together. Above them were some old gas lamps. To their right was a wisteria that had worked its way up the face of one of the buildings and had reached the second-floor windows. Its cascades of flowers bounced and swayed in the breeze. To their left were tulips, yellow, red, purple, orange. To their left, too, were bluebells and irises and narcissi on the far side of the grass.

'I've got a bottle of white Bordeaux I brought back with me from France last year. It came out of the fridge in chambers a couple of minutes ago. I've got some smoked-salmon sandwiches I bought in a delicatessen I know on the way here this morning. And I've got some tiramisu I saw there and simply couldn't resist.'

'Perfect!' she exclaimed. She was, though, thinking as much of the prospect of being with him as of the food and drink he had brought with him.

They walked over a few petals of cherry blossom scattered across the pavement. By a camellia covered with red flowers. Under a mulberry tree still as leafless as in midwinter. Onto the newly-mown lawn. The green of the grass was bright where the sun poured across it, dark where it was in the shadows.

They sat down under one of the huge plane trees. Some of last year's fruit was still hanging in clusters. Its new leaves were still small and often only partly open. The bark of its great trunk was rough, and with the texture of dried mud.

To one side of them was the Georgian simplicity, even austerity, of Stone Buildings. Framed by columns and Corinthian capitals, it was an exercise in classical symmetry. In front of them was the Victorian extravaganza of the Lincoln's Inn library. Its walls were of red brick. Between and above its windows were coats of arms and gargoyles carved in honey-brown stone.

He unpacked the wine and the sandwiches and the tiramisu. He laid out the plates and the glasses on the grass. He opened the bottle and filled their glasses. They had their first sips of the wine and their first bites of the sandwiches.

'Do you remember those leaves you pointed out to me on the river?' he asked. 'One minute separated, then beside each other, then together.'

'Very clearly.'

'I've been thinking about them a lot. And I'm not sure you've got it right. I'm not at all sure it's like that.'

She started, unsure what he was going to say. 'Why not?'

He poured some more wine with one hand. He

stretched out his other hand until it held hers.

'I agree it's more currents and winds and storms that determine what happens to them than what the leaves do themselves,' he told her. 'Though I'd add rain and tides and passing boats and more besides.'

'So you're as pessimistic about our ability to decide our own fate as I am.'

'No. I'm much more of a pessimist than you are.' He was, for a moment, silent. 'For me we're not so much two leaves floating down a river. We're two islands in a vast ocean.'

She looked at him in dismay. She wondered anxiously what he was trying to tell her, and how to reply.

'But, except in fairy stories, islands don't move any closer to each other.'

'I've got to agree, Jo. Except, or so I'm led to believe, through the movements of tectonic plates over centuries and millennia.'

'That's terrible!' she exclaimed.

She tried to think as quickly as she could how to counter his argument.

'Terrible, perhaps,' he agreed. 'But also, perhaps, true. And in one way not so terrible. The islands may not get any closer to each other. But nor do they move further apart. Except perhaps over hundreds or thousands of years.'

'And how much do these islands know about each other?'

'At the least they know absolutely nothing. At the most they know a minute, a microscopic amount. Nothing more.'

She suddenly - and unexpectedly - remembered words she had never thought of for years.

'So you say this in spite of what Donne wrote. In lines I once tried to learn by heart in the sixth form. And in lines this bookworm you're sitting beside is about to regurgitate.'

'So what did he write?' he asked.

'No man is an island, entire of itself. Every man is a piece of the continent, a part of the main.'

'Yes. In spite of that.' He searched his memory for a few seconds. 'Do you remember *The Rime of the Ancient Mariner*?'

'I read it once from beginning to end. Everything. Sadly, I remember almost none of it.'

'Alone, alone, all, all alone,' he recited from memory. *'Alone on a wide, wide sea.'*

She looked at him uncertainly. She was even more unsure than she had been a few minutes before about the reason he had mentioned the leaves on the river.

'Is this a cue for me to walk off into the sunset?' she asked quietly.

'Not at all,' he replied with a smile. 'If anything it's a cue for you to reveal a minute amount more of the person you are. And, in any case, the spring equinox was weeks ago. It won't be sunset for hours!'

'Will you?' she asked.

'Will I what?'

'You're in bed with a woman, aren't you?'

'I am.' He looked down at her body that lay beside his, as if searching for confirmation. 'No doubt about it. No doubt at all.'

'You're a fully-grown adult, aren't you?'

'I suppose I am,' he admitted, and a moment later added: 'Physically and mentally if not emotionally.'

'So,' she asked with mock frustration and annoyance, 'can't you reply to a perfectly simple question?'

'Which is?'

'Will you...' She hesitated as she looked away from his body and into his eyes. 'Will you make love to me? Here? Now?'

It was late afternoon on the following Sunday. They had met at Kensal Green, the nearest tube station to his flat, and had walked back to it for a few hundred yards along a succession of anonymous streets.

In these first moments in bed together, he had been stroking her hair. This lay scattered in disarray, brown on white, over the pillow of his bed.

For a second or so Elizabeth Siddal, model of Millais, Holman Hunt and Rossetti, icon of the Pre-Raphaelites, flashed unexpectedly into his mind. Partly because of the rich colour of the hair he was stroking. Partly because it was so dense, with twists and turns along its whole length.

He had been looking with a combination of delight and disbelief at her body he had, as yet, hardly touched. A body that lay stretched carelessly across his sheets. He thought for a moment of Velázquez' *Venus*, lying voluptuously on her couch. She was, however, not looking at herself in a mirror held by an attendant cupid. She was looking directly and enquiringly at him.

In her face he was sure he could see desire – and even, or so he hoped, desire for him. He looked, too, into her eyes. Irises green as he remembered them from their first meeting. Pupils larger and darker than he had ever seen them.

'Can you,' he asked, 'reply to a question that's just as simple?'

'Which is?'

'Will you?'

She seemed more than a little puzzled by his question. For a moment her face displayed more uncertainty than desire.

'Will I what?' she asked.

'Will you make love to me?'

She looked at him with a degree of surprise, even astonishment, he had not expected. It was as if he had asked a question she did not understand. A question outside the framework of her thinking. A question that was, in some way or other, an improper one for him to ask her.

'For God's sake! Why on earth do you ask me that?' she demanded.

'Because I need to know it's what you want. It's just as much your decision as it's mine. You've got to be as much a consenting adult as I am,' he told her. 'We are, after all, in this together.'

She began to smile. Her surprise was at least partly replaced by delight at his answer.

'And,' he went on, 'there's not much in it for you if you just lie back and think of England.'

She laughed, now wholly reassured. 'No man has ever put it like that before. At least not to me.'

'There's always a first time, Jo.'

They put their arms round each other. Held each other tightly. Felt the strong and rapid beating of each other's hearts.

'Like this,' she whispered, 'is the first time for us.'

CHAPTER TWO

'*Busy old fool...*' she whispered, suddenly remembering a sonnet she had last read – and at that time with much less interest than she had now – in the sixth form at school.

'*...Unruly sun,*' he added with a smile and without a moment's hesitation – and as much to her surprise as when he had quoted Benedick by the Thames at Hammersmith.

Since they had woken up, the shadows cast by the setting sun had crawled at the speed of a sloth around his small room. First they had moved across the blouse and skirt she would be wearing for school the next day, and across his pullover and jeans. All these lay scattered and abandoned like battlefield casualties on the floor.

Next they had moved across the double bed where they lay together on the blue sheets, their arms holding each other in a loose embrace. On the far wall they had reached a set of faded Mucha posters. These he had bought in those heady months after he had left school and before he had begun to study law.

Joanna and Stephen watched the shadows slide up the posters, until they reached the ceiling, until the room was filled with a soft evening light.

'But Donne's lovers were the early-morning victims of the rising sun,' he explained in a whisper as she tightened her embrace. 'And unless I'm even more disoriented than I feel, this has been the first sunset we've seen together.'

'Will you put those astronomical observations of yours to bed. And preferably not in this one?' she asked as she kissed him, first gently, then fiercely. 'And will you make love to me again?'

'And can I ask you again what I asked you I don't know how many hours ago? Will you make love to me?'

He felt her body begin to burrow eagerly and hurriedly under his. Then, as soon as it was under him, he felt it begin to wriggle. He felt her hands on his lower back, pressing against him, pulling him tightly against her. He felt, too, her legs around him, clamping his legs firmly between her thighs.

'We may overindulge ourselves by reciting poetry to each other,' she told him as she began to laugh. 'But if we do, our chances of making love even once more before sunrise are too close to zero for comfort.'

'Make love just once more before sunrise?' he asked her as he, too, began to laugh. 'If that's all we do, it's more our desires and our abilities than our chances that are close to zero.'

'It's only week or so since you and I met in front of *Venus and Mars*. That was only a few weeks after I'd finished with the boyfriend I'd been living with for the best – or was it the worst? – part of six months. He and I had both become more and more dissatisfied with each other. Though for completely different reasons.

'He complained more and more often that I didn't want him enough. I complained, I suppose more more often as well, that he wanted me I'm going to be a bit less evasive and a bi wanted me time after time after time.'

The room was now, apart from the weak orange glow of the street lamps outside the window, in darkness. They were still in bed. Each was propped up on pillows. Each was holding a large glass of armagnac.

He had asked her once again to tell him much more about herself – and not just the headlines. She had agreed, with less reluctance than he had expected. This was, though, on condition he would do the same. He had asked her whether she wanted to work forwards in what she would tell him – from past to present – or backwards – from now to then.

She chose to begin in time present. He agreed to do this as well. They also agreed to do what they had so comprehensively failed to do since they had first met. They agreed they would interrupt each other as little as they could. Or, if possible, not at all.

They agreed, too, to avoid as much as they could the ping-pong matches they had played with lines from plays and poems. But they admitted to each other they might use too many quotations by far, and only hoped these would not be too irrelevant or too annoying.

'One morning he'd already scored his first goal. I was already desperately late for school. I said *no* to his demands for a repeat performance. I offered to come back in the very early evening. I even offered to come back in the dinner break at midday.

'But both midday and the early evening were already on his agenda. He wanted me again that morning, that minute. And – however often and however firmly I said it to him – *no* was no answer.

'When I'd finished with my protests and, in spite of these, when he'd finished with me, I dashed off to school.

I was scorched with anger. I was now totally sure I couldn't carry on with him.

'He'd exhausted my body as it had never been exhausted before. At the same time, he'd left my mind completely untouched. At midday I stayed in my classroom. That evening I spent with another teacher who was also a good friend. That night I stayed in her flat.'

She paused. He saw in her face, and above all in her eyes, the anger she had felt.

'So how had you met him?' he asked as he stroked her hair.

His face, as she saw it, registered a great deal of sympathy for her predicament. What she did not see was his resentment that this man, whose prowess he was sure he could never equal, had preceded him.

'We'd met at a party in the aftermath of an affair I'd had that I can only describe as bizarre. But you may have other words for it when, one day or other, I get round to telling you about it. He was, in our first weeks together, reassuringly normal. A return to solid ground after a journey through marshland.

'He was, as they say, demanding. That, though, is more than an understatement. He wanted me every morning, every evening, every night. He wanted me every time he could escape from his car salesroom in the middle of the day. Weekends were nothing less than sex marathons. For these the weekdays leading up to them were little more than a gentle preparation.

'He exhausted me: yes. But in those first weeks, I was more flattered than exhausted. I was happy to be wanted. Though I realised they were excessive, I enjoyed his attentions. And, if I'm pushed to admit it, I enjoyed everything he did to me.

'As well as all that, there was somewhere inside me in those first weeks a voice that told me I was even enjoying being bruised and sore as I'd never been before. And, I think, as I've never been since. It told me I was even welcoming – at least some of the time – the pain he inflicted on me.'

On her face he now saw more embarrassment than anger. Especially after she had admitted how much she had enjoyed, in those early weeks, what her boyfriend had done to her. Especially when she began a blush she could do nothing to control.

'From what you say,' he observed, 'it's blindingly obvious he never got tired of you. But when did you begin to get tired of him?'

As she began to answer his question, she still saw his sympathy. She still, too, failed to see his resentment that her detailed account of her boyfriend's prowess had, if anything, strengthened.

'Week by week, the balance between exhaustion and flattery slowly changed. And so did my thoughts and feelings about him. It was never because I feared the unknown. In the demands he made on me, there was nothing I couldn't predict.

'It was never because I feared he was becoming bored with me. If anything, his demands grew by the week. It was as if he was trying to achieve and exceed ever more demanding showroom sales targets. As if he was trying to push his productivity to new limits. A sort of sexual Stakhanovite.

'With every success he notched up, with every new peak he scaled, my exhaustion reached new troughs. I hardly had the energy to walk to school. To teach lessons in the morning let alone in the afternoon. To stay awake when I was in staff meetings or on dinner duty or marking books.

'Though I so much wanted to get on with more of the poems I'd been reading when he and I had first met, I read not a single line while we were together. I never went near a theatre. The only films I ever saw were the Westerns he dragged me along to between evening couplings.

'I'd also become more and more aware that his interest in what I was thinking and feeling, in what I wanted to say or do, was minute. It wouldn't even have registered on the Richter scale. I wouldn't even have discovered it under an electron microscope.

'His affection for me, if ever there was any, was limited to a few hurried moments of kisses and caresses. His brief overture before the curtain rose on an epic of Wagnerian proportions.

'His vocabulary included a wealth of monosyllabic Anglo-Saxon words. Some of these were – in spite of the words I'd got to know at school and college – completely new to me. Sadly for me, the word *love* was never one of them.'

He saw her look down, shake her head, sigh. He recognised her sadness. But what he did not recognise was her relief that she had managed to tell him this chapter of her story. Nor did he recognise her foreboding at the prospect of telling him about some of its earlier chapters.

'What did you do to put an end to it all after you'd spent that night in your friend's flat?' he asked, as he topped up her glass with more of his armagnac. This was also as he found himself feeling more than content that she had, in this if in nothing else, found his predecessor wanting.

'I told him, and as strongly as I could, I never wanted to see him again. And to my complete surprise, off he went. But in the weeks after he moved out, he called on me more times than I care to remember. Telling me he wanted me more than ever. Never taking *no* for an answer. Leaving soon after he arrived. Going, you might say, almost as soon as he came.'

The first, even the second, time they had made love had been rushed, narrow, superficial. A display more of adolescent enthusiasm than of adult experience. Splashing about, so she had felt, on the surface of a calm sea. Not diving down together into its mysterious depths. Dancing, so he had felt, along the fringes of a forest. Not cutting a path together towards its unknown heart.

It had been the undergraduate sex he remembered with a mixture of amusement and embarrassment from his early twenties. On the banks of the River Cam in a brief and fumbling encounter after a noisy Saturday night dance in Easter term. In his college rooms in Michaelmas term between a late-morning lecture on torts and an early-afternoon game of rugby.

It had been the sixth-form sex she remembered – perhaps with less amusement and more embarrassment – from her late teens. In a narrow window of opportunity on one of the quieter stretches of the River Cherwell between the last lesson of the afternoon and the first homework of the evening. In an even narrower – though more comfortable – window in her bedroom between her mother's inevitable exit to play bingo and her father's predictable entrance at the end of his shift.

This time there was no urgency, no impatience, no imperative to perform. They kneeled together on the bed.

Their knees were touching. Their bodies were only a little apart as they faced each other.

He looked at her body more attentively and with more delight than he had looked at the body of any other woman. At her breasts, their flesh so amazingly pale and smooth. At her hips, hardly broader when she was kneeling down, thighs resting on calves, than they were when she was standing.

He looked, too, at her belly, as flat when she leaned forward in front of him as it was when she was lying on her back. At a body floating uncertainly and deliciously between teenager and woman. Almost, or so he thought, as much schoolgirl as schoolmistress.

When she looked at him what she saw was no Mars, no Achilles, no Samson. Nor was he a model for sports clothes or swimwear. Nor an advertisement for a fitness centre. But, all the same, what she saw was a firm body with powerful muscles on his arms and legs, with broad shoulders and chest, with a tight stomach.

He listened carefully to her as she talked. A voice at times no louder than a whisper. A voice he felt embraced and caressed him. She, at the same time, listened to him. A deep voice that wrapped itself around her. A voice, so it seemed to her, that offered her protection from the hostilities of the world outside.

She touched his hands with the tips of her fingers. She slid them slowly up his arms, over his shoulders, across his chest, down his stomach. He responded by brushing his hands lightly over her neck, her shoulders, her breasts, her belly.

She leaned forward. With her head on his chest, she stroked his feet, his legs, his buttocks. He, in turn, rested his head on her breasts. He moved his hands up from her toes to her calves, and from her bottom round her hips.

He moved up in the bed so that he could bury his face in her hair, and smelled its sweetness. She bent down, smelled the skin of his chest and his stomach.

His mouth tasted her forehead, her cheeks, her neck, her lips. Her tongue licked his skin, flickered over his body as she crouched in front of him, her hair falling across his thighs.

Their bodies were now touching. Their tongues were now, and more and more searchingly, exploring each other's mouths. He pressed his chest against her breasts, hard flesh against soft. She pressed her belly against his, soft flesh against hard. With their arms round each other, holding each other in a close embrace, they fell across the bed.

They had become, so he thought, two wild swans swimming together on a lake in the opening moments of their early-spring courtship. They had become two avocets dancing together in shallow estuary water, a ballet of black and white at the start of their delicate mating ritual.

Or were they, as she thought, like those two leaves floating down the river? One minute travelling separately, then moving closer? The next minute beside each other, then together? Or were they even two humans, thrown together by chance, but for whom the earth was about to move?

'Everything I've told you since we first met has been the truth and nothing but the truth. But, as I'm sure you've realised, Jo, I haven't told you the whole truth.

'Partly it's because, as I've explained to you, I've very much wanted to be with you in the present. Not diverted by what's happened to me in the past. Partly it's because I've never told anyone more than a few unrevealing headlines. Not my parents, not my brother, not my sister, not my friends.

'And there's another reason. I spend so much of my working life communicating facts. But I'm on foreign soil when it comes to talking about feelings. To be perfectly honest, I think I often deliberately avoid doing this.

'Why, or so I ask myself, should anyone else have to have the burden of sharing my feelings? And why should I have to reveal to anyone else on earth those most private parts of me?'

They had woken up just a few minutes before, and discovered it was well past midnight. Now each sat facing the other, both their hands holding the cups of hot chocolate he had made for them.

'So, Stephen,' she asked as she looked directly at him, 'what private parts are you going to reveal to me now?'

He looked at her, at the posters on the walls, at the ceiling. He forced a momentary smile to flicker across his face.

'I left my wife just a few months ago. Not with some dramatic exit stage left or right. Some grand flourish. Some cathartic climax. More unobtrusively. Tail between legs.

'Where I'd go, how I'd manage to live, I had no idea. For a week or so I slept – or, to be more accurate, I underslept – on a succession of spare beds and sofas. I appeared each day in chambers. Even when I was in court, though, my mind was miles away.

'There was, I suppose, an element of elation in how I felt. No longer did I leave for work in the mornings, as I'd done so often when she and I were together, to a barrage of shouts and screams. No longer did they echo with me for much if not all of the day. No longer did I go back home in the evenings to anything from lengthy accusations to silences that echoed with me for much of the night. From these at least I felt I was freed.'

He stopped. Though she did not suspect it, he was unsure whether he could tell her more without a lump filling his throat. Without tears filling his eyes. Without his wife's voice filling his memory.

'I think I can understand you must have felt some sort of elation,' she told him. 'But what other feelings did you have in those first days after you left her?'

She was beginning to understand, at least in this chapter of his story, there would be nothing lightweight or amusing as there had been in hers. He looked down, screwed up his face, seemed deep in thought.

'To be perfectly honest, I was much less elated than apprehensive. Less about where I'd live. How I'd cope with the practicalities of being on my own again. How I'd deal with everyone we'd ever labelled as our friends. How I'd face my parents who thought we were living in peace and harmony. More about what she'd do. And when. And how.

'It was this, in those first days, that most worried me. Each morning on unaccustomed journeys from here and there. Each day in chambers and in court. Each evening at awkward suppers with my one-night hosts. Each night as I tried, so often without success, to find an open door into sleep and oblivion.'

He stopped again, fighting to keep the turmoil of his emotions in check.

'Did she make any attempt to contact you?' she asked.

She was now seeing his distress, but was also trying to help him to tell her more about what had happened to him. 'Or was there a deafening silence?'

'For the first week after I left her there was total silence. Then, among the letters I picked up in the morning in chambers, there was one with handwriting I knew only too well. Her letter was no more than a few lines long. But it was more than enough to invade everything I did – or tried to do – that day.

'I had, she wrote, failed her in every possible way. I'd ruined her life which had been so full of promise. I'd abandoned her, and for no earthly reason. And what I'd done to her was in spite of everything she'd done for me.'

He shut his eyes, tried to swallow. He did whatever he could to hold back the tears he knew were close. She was now aware of his struggle to control his feelings. But she still hoped he would be able to tell her more.

'And was that all?'

'In that letter: yes. But a couple of days later came a second one. Page after page in that carefully-crafted writing I'd read once upon a time with such pleasure. This time there was no pleasure – though no great surprise – in reading how useless, hopeless, incompetent and inadequate I was.

'Yet what I remember most were her final sentences. That I'd live to regret what I'd done to her. That she'd do everything she could to make my regrets so huge they'd come to dominate my life.'

She saw he was even closer to tears than he had been a few moments before. She edged across the bed until his head rested on her shoulder.

'As well as those letters,' she asked, 'did she ever try to phone you?'

He snorted as he remembered the call she had made to him one morning just after he had arrived in chambers.

'How did you guess? And what she said on the phone was very much what she'd written. But she said it with a hurricane force that far exceeded all the storms of our years together.

'Whether I'd been useless, hopeless, incompetent and inadequate – and more besides – in the five years we'd been married I don't know. But I was most certainly all of these – and more besides – in my ability to survive that call of hers. By the time she put the phone down any peace and calm I had left had deserted me.'

Joanna put down her cup. She began to stroke his hair as she would have done to a child who was in distress.

'Then, unless I'm misjudging her, she came to see you.'

He responded with a bitter and hollow laugh that soon became a long, deep sigh.

'She did, as I suppose I knew she would. Sooner rather than later. Not for better but for worse. I remember I'd been trying to master some particularly difficult sections of the Partnership Act. I was, I'm afraid, being less than successful.

'I heard the quick tapping of shoes. First on the stone steps of the stairs. Then on the wooden floor of the corridor outside my room in chambers. I saw my door swing open.

'She stood in the doorway. Her eyes were narrowed. Her irises were drained of colour. The muscles on her face were tight. Her hands were clenched in front of her like the hands of a barefist boxer. I waited for the outburst. But she just stood there minute after minute. Looking at me with a fixed gaze. Saying nothing but at the same time saying everything.

'At last she moved. She stepped backwards into the corridor. She turned and disappeared. After what seemed like ages, the sound of her shoes on the stairs faded. Eventually there was silence.'

'How did you cope with all that?' she asked. From his fractured voice, she knew his tears might be only moments away. 'Was it as badly as you thought you'd coped with her phone calls?'

'I closed my eyes. Each movement, each look of hers repeated itself time and again in my mind. It was as if I'd looked too long at the sun. Then, with my eyes tight shut, as if I'd seen its image in a kaleidoscope of changing colours. Yellow turning to green turning to azure. All in a sea of orange.

'I looked down at the pages of the Partnership Act I'd been reading. I was able, and with little difficulty, to focus on the words themselves. But what they meant and how they were relevant to the case I'd been working on were completely beyond me. I'd never felt more useless and inadequate. I'd never agreed more with how she'd described me in her letter.'

She looked at him and saw a single tear trickle slowly down his cheek.

'Was this her only visit?' she asked quietly, as she saw more tears begin to trickle over his face and down onto his neck.

'If only it had been! If only. Her next visit was as unannounced as it was inevitable. This time there wasn't a second of silence between the time she burst into my room and the time she slammed the door behind her as she left. It was a repeat of those barrages of shouts and screams that had been with me on so many mornings as

I'd walked away from our flat. But this was worse. Far worse.'

'I know it's horrible and hard for you to tell me this. And please just stop if you want to,' she whispered as she kissed him on his forehead. 'But can you help me to understand why?'

With great effort, and to his great surprise, he succeeded at last to control his tears. With his voice now firmer and less broken, he tried to answer her question.

'It wasn't worse because of the accusations and threats themselves. It wasn't worse because they alternated with a flood of demands and questions about how I'd provide for her. It wasn't worse because she gave me no chance even to begin to answer her.

'It was worse because I'd left her at least in part to escape her outbursts. Then I discovered with this visit of hers the awful truth. That leaving her gave me no escape at all.

'Our flat had, as I saw it, been a war zone. Where attacks were on the cards at any time of day or night. Where I had, at least to some extent, anaesthetised myself and protected myself against them.

'My room in chambers was a refuge where I could enjoy peace and quiet. Where I didn't have any need to set up defences or to protect myself. It, rather than our flat, had become what I thought of as my home. But after these two visits, all that had changed. The walls of my refuge were breached. The peace I'd found in chambers was shattered.'

'Didn't you have any other refuge?' she asked, still stroking his hair and kissing his forehead even after his tears had stopped.

'By this time I did. I'd found myself somewhere to live.

Not a penthouse flat in Mayfair. Nor a bed in a Lambeth refuge for the homeless. Rather this little place in Kensal Rise.

'The estate agent who was letting it described it as a self-contained studio flat. Benefiting from this. Boasting that. But I recognised it at once for what it was. A place that could contain only myself. A toy-sized bedsit that benefited from very little and could boast even less.

'When I was alone here in those first evenings and weekends, I began to think about the life I'd have ahead of me. I was, after all, only thirty. I felt the years of my marriage had been in so many ways wasted years. I felt I had a lot to do to make up for lost time.

'I began to go to the mudflats along the Thames Estuary to look at birds, and to Kew Gardens to look at trees and flowers. I began to go to the theatre and the opera. I began to go to museums and galleries.

'I felt on my first visits like a stranger revisiting old friends after years in a far-off country. And there, once upon a time, and not so long ago, I met an angel called Jo and the rest you know as well as I do...'

'Not a sign of the sun this morning,' he announced. 'Busy or otherwise.'

They worked their ways methodically through a grapefruit and a pot of coffee at the breakfast table. This, small as it was, filled an entire corner of his cramped bedsit. It left little room for the cupboard on which, she noticed, was a group photo of freshmen from his college: rows of self-conscious young men at the start of their Cambridge years.

'But more than enough sex to make up for that,' she replied with a small smile as she looked up from her second cup of coffee.

'And as good a preparation as any for a day in court,' he observed with a deep chuckle.

He checked that the bag into which he had stuffed his wig and gown, and the case into which he had stuffed his brief, were by the front door where he had put them the night before.

'And,' she responded, smiling again, 'a better preparation than most for a day of teaching a class of twenty five or so boys and girls.'

They sat perched on two stools with the table between them. She glanced every few minutes at his alarm clock she had taken from his bedside and put in front of her on the table.

'I'll have to go very soon,' she announced after a second or third glance. 'Especially as I can't remember much about how I got here. I've got no more idea of how to get back from here to Shepherd's Bush than I have of how to get to the North Pole. But before I go, I've got a question for you.'

'What is it?'

She hesitated. 'Why were you so thoughtful and so gentle last night? Why did you think so much about what my needs were? About how I was feeling?'

His face registered more than a little surprise. 'Good heavens, Jo! I can't believe you're asking me this. I'm not sure I was particularly thoughtful or gentle. But I can't imagine behaving in any other way. With you or, to be quite honest, with anyone else.'

She, in response, and more than happy with what he had just said, held his hand tightly.

'And before we leave, Jo, I've got a question for you. A question I've been asking myself.'

She looked once more at the clock. 'We're in overtime. So be as quick as you can.'

He leaned over the table and kissed her forehead. 'Why did you let me do whatever I wanted to? So much more than I ever imagined or expected you would?'

Her face showed as much surprise at his question as his face had shown at hers.

'It's just as you said about yourself. I'm not aware I did. Like you, though, I can't imagine behaving in any other way.'

She stood and picked up her rucksack. It was crammed with her notes for the day's lessons she had never read, and with her nightclothes she had never worn.

'As well as that,' she added with a frown, 'in my experience it's what's expected of me. It's not that I want to be submissive. But...' She hesitated once again, and put the rucksack on her shoulder. '... it's that I've learned from experience I don't have the lead role.'

As she reached the door of his flat, she picked up an envelope that was lying on the carpet. She handed it to him. She watched his face freeze in dismay as he looked at the writing.

'From her?'

He looked away, into the far distance. It was as he had looked in the Nell Gwynne when he focussed on nothing. He nodded slowly and sighed. He put the envelope, unopened, into his briefcase.

'Yes. After weeks of silence. It's from her.'

CHAPTER THREE

'I can't believe it!' Stephen told her as he squeezed her hand. 'It's only a couple of weeks since we first met.'

'And what I can't believe,' replied Joanna, as she squeezed his hand in return, 'is that we've done so much together since then.'

'It hasn't been what I'd call a fairytale romance. It hasn't been played out with soft music in the background.'

'But nor,' she retorted, 'has it been a high-speed coupling in a one-night cheap hotel.'

They had decided to spend their first full day together by walking along the Grand Union Canal. And they had, by chance, selected one of those rare days in late April that were kind rather than cruel, that promised sunshine rather than showers.

The starting point she had proposed was just north of King's Cross, from which they had walked up the Caledonian Road, largely free of traffic at that time of morning, until they had reached the canal. The goal he had chosen was Little Venice on the edge of Maida Vale – and not too far from his flat.

Now they were standing together, holding hands. It was where the towpath ended at the brick and stone entrance to the tunnel that took the Grand Union Canal under Pentonville and the Angel towards Islington.

'Do you know how the barges got through that tunnel before there were tugs to pull them?' she asked, sensing that their exchange had reached its natural conclusion.

'No idea. No idea at all. You tell me.'

'The men lay on their backs on the barge and pushed with their feet against the tunnel walls. Even when the barge was fully loaded, they edged it forward until their horse took over again at the other end.'

'How do you know about this?' he asked, showing her he was full of admiration for her expertise.

'I did a little project on canals when I was at school. And when I was at King's, for some reason or other I can't remember, some of my fellow students and I went on a trip along the canal from Little Venice past London Zoo. That's the sum total of my experience. At least my experience of canals!'

'But it's much more than I know. That could be written on one side of one of those leaves that are floating past, and with room to spare.'

They walked slowly away from the tunnel. His arm was now round her shoulder, resting on the denim jacket she was wearing above her denim jeans. Her arm was now round his waist, under his green corduroy jacket, and holding the belt of his navy blue trousers.

They walked past old boats, a few with smoke rising lethargically from their chimneys, which were littered along the water's edge on the other side of the canal. Past one old wooden hull, now much more a wreck than a working barge. Past old walls of burned brick that separated the canal from the buildings beyond.

Some of these buildings they saw as being shiningly – even shockingly – new, and belonging to anywhere except a canal side. Others were in what seemed to them terminal decline. Plants were growing out of empty glassless windows, even out of gaps in roof slates or tiles.

'Look over there!' she demanded as a new panorama came into view.

They looked together at the enormous expanse of glass arching over King's Cross Station and glittering in the sunlight. At the huge redbrick extravagance, exuberance, excess of the old Midland Grand Hotel by St Pancras Station. At the gasholder between it and them: an obsolete iron skeleton. They walked on to St Pancras lock. Stood on the grey cobblestones beside it. Looked at the massive gates at each end. Leaned against the great wooden beams that opened them.

'What can you hear?' he asked before they left the lock gates.

'Water slapping quietly against the bricks on the walls of the lock. Streams of water bursting noisily through the lock gates. Two ducks quacking as they're waddling along the towpath.'

'Traffic?'

'In the background, yes. But far away. And, thank the Lord, not a car, not a lorry, not a bus in sight.'

Soon after St Pancras lock they saw above them the Constitution pub. This he had a vague memory he had visited once on a late-night journey back to north London. They walked under the road bridge. A little later they reached Camden Street bridge. Under this, where the canal bent sharply, they looked at the deep gouges in the iron bar fixed upright to the bridge's brickwork.

'You're the expert,' he told her, as he slid his fingers down the bar and along the deepest of the gouges. 'How did that happen?'

'A hundred years or more of ropes rubbing against metal as the horses pulled the barges along. Just that.'

Later still they reached the three Camden locks. More water pouring in a constant cascade between the gates of the Hampstead Road lock. More cobblestones beside the locks. Both of these they had, over the past hour, come to know.

What was, however, unexpected for them both was the narrow metal footbridge. It was a delicate arch painted black and white, with the reflection of the ripples playing across its underside. And, to their delight, as they discovered when they walked over it and back again, it crossed the canal not directly from one side to the other, but on a diagonal.

What was also unexpected was their return to the world of cafés and shops that crowded around Camden Lock, and to the hundreds of people who filled them. This they found more than a little difficult to adjust to after the solitude of their walk along the towpath from the tunnel. But here they decided to stop for a coffee. They sat down at a table under the warm late-morning sun, looking across the flagstones of the West Yard.

'What does your wife say in that letter of hers?' she asked softly, her hand holding his.

He had told her, when they had met that morning, he had not touched it since she had handed it to him at his flat two days earlier. This was, he admitted reluctantly, out of cowardice. Now he took it from his jacket pocket and tore open the envelope. He looked at the first couple of sentences and sighed. Then, slowly and sadly, he looked up at her.

'She starts by setting the scene. Creating the suspense. Raising my anxiety levels as she knows only too well how to do.'

He held the letter at arm's length, as if trying to distance himself from it. In a deadpan voice, though with his emotions hardly hidden, he began to read it to her.

'This is just one of the letters I shall be writing during the course of the next several days. I shall also be writing to your parents, to some of the people you call your friends and, last but not least, to some of your colleagues.'

He stopped. His hands were trembling. The muscles of his face were taut.

'And next?'

He sighed even more deeply than when he had opened the letter. In his eyes she thought she saw, as she had seen during their first night together, the beginning of tears.

'It's a summary of what she's told me time after time. About how I've let her down. But this time, or so it seems, I'm not the only one to be given the summary.'

'Can you read me some more?'

He looked back down at the letter, still at arm's length. His voice seemed to her in danger of breaking, but he read on.

'I shall be telling them what it has been like to have a husband like you. I shall be explaining to them that you have done nothing to help me to find a job, nothing to help me to keep up with my friends, nothing to get me out of this awful flat where you used to abandon me each day and have now abandoned me completely. I shall let them know how, more than anything, you have destroyed my self-confidence and humiliated me beyond belief.'

He looked up from the letter. His eyes met hers. In his she thought she saw a deep sadness. In hers he saw, or so he thought, a deepening anger.

'Why so sad?'

'Because what she writes is, I suppose, not as far as I'd wish from the truth.'

He looked away into some far distance beyond the canal. It was just as he had done in the Nell Gwynne on the day they had first met.

'And you?' he asked. 'Why so angry?'

'For Christ's sake, Stephen, it's only too obvious!' she exclaimed. 'What she's concerned about is, purely and simply, herself. For you, at least as I see it, she seems to have not the slightest concern.'

Just for a moment a smile flickered across his face. Almost imperceptibly, he chuckled. 'If that's what you think, what she goes on to write won't do too much to change your mind.'

'So what does she write?'

He glanced at the next paragraph. It seemed to her, as she looked at his face, he was beginning to overcome his initial horror, to make himself less sensitive to what she had written.

'*I shall be telling them what you have said about them. I shall explain to your parents how you have criticised them for the way they brought you up, for their narrow and old-fashioned view of the world, for having done so little with their lives. I shall tell your friends how false a friend you are, saying one thing to them face-to-face and the opposite behind their backs.*'

He stopped again. His face was now hardening. It was not yet defiant. But it was no longer devastated.

'What you think about all of that is your business,' she told him as calmly as she could. 'But if I were you I'd lose whatever cool I still had. I'm sure we're all vindictive from time to time. Even when we don't intend to be. But she's making vindictiveness into an art form. Taking it to an extreme I've never known before. Never in my whole life.'

'If you think that's the case, just wait for what comes next.'

He read on. He was now more the barrister reading evidence in court than the victim of a character assassination.

'*I shall, too, give them an insight into what you have done that relates to them. I am sure your parents will be interested to know that the money they saved to help you at Cambridge was spent on a succession of short-term mistresses and one-night encounters.*'

He paused for a moment. He shook his head, continued.

'*I am sure your colleagues, who may up to now have seen you as God's gift to advocacy, honest and upright in the best traditions of the Bar, will be more than a little surprised to discover that you have often gone to court in the morning grossly unprepared, and that, by the afternoon, you have on more than a few occasions been more than a little under the influence of drink.*'

'If I were in your shoes,' she exclaimed with a depth of passion that greatly surprised him, 'I'd be exploding with anger. When I'd calmed down, it wouldn't take long for me to decide she didn't like me one little bit. And wouldn't want to have anything more to do with me.'

'Then you're in for a surprise when you hear her finale before the curtain falls.'

She watched him look back down at the letter. As if he already knew its contents, he read the last sentences in a monotone.

'I have far better things to do with my life than to write these letters to your parents, your siblings, your friends and colleagues. I am sure you have far better things to do than to explain away to them what you have done. If you want to avoid this, all you have to do is to put a stop to this idiocy of abandoning me, come back to your home, and start to fulfil your obligations to me.'

'So I'm wrong about her not wanting you back. Why she wants you back, though, after everything she's written about you, is a mystery to me. As much of a mystery as sub-atomic particles or linguistic philosophy.

'But from what you've just read me I'm sure I'm right about her being concerned about herself rather than about you. And on top of trying to blacken your character, I now see she's perfectly capable of trying a bit of blackmail on you as well.'

He smiled, stood up, walked over to the canal side just beyond the West Yard. He struck a match he had found in a box on the table where they were drinking their coffee. Holding it in one hand, he set fire to the letter he was holding in the other.

They both watched as the breeze that blew along the canal helped the flame to lick its way up the page and across the neat handwriting. As the flame reached his finger and thumb, he dropped the letter into the water. They watched as the ashes floated away and as they begin to sink into the depths of Camden Lock.

They drank the last drops of their coffee. They stood up slowly. After a last look at the metal footbridge and the lock, they walked on. Over a stone footbridge alongside a warehouse. By a row of narrowboats moored beside the towpath. Opposite willows whose branches hung down until they almost touched the brown-green water. Past a succession of Regency houses for which the description *desirable residences* would have been a grotesque understatement. Through Cumberland Basin where the canal broadened.

Before they realised it, they had reached London Zoo. On their left were the canal-side enclosures. Here all they could see was a small pack of wild dogs and a small group of warthogs. On their right was the Snowdon Aviary. Peacocks were walking on the ground. Egrets and ibis were perching motionless, seeming to be more the products of a taxidermist's artistry than living birds that could fly.

For some minutes they said nothing to each other. The letter he had read to her at Camden Lock still echoed with them both. But she was also thinking how hugely she enjoyed being with him, and was asking herself why. And he, until he stopped and turned to her, had been wondering more and more urgently how to explain to her how he felt about her.

'I want to tell you, Jo, and quite simply, how wonderful for me the last days and weeks have been. Wonderful? The more I think about the word, the less well it describes everything that's happened and what I've felt about it. But I can't think of a better word, at least not right now.

'I know what I'm going to say will sound way over-the-top. I'm sure it's going to sound more like a letter I've carefully composed than something that's off-the-cuff. But, for what it's worth, here goes!'

As they stood and faced each other, he began by telling her about the early-morning train journey to Reading he had made the day before for a couple of hours in court.

'I had all my papers in front of me. Page after page of witness statements, documents, notes of meetings. But time after time the words on the page became a blur. The noise of the train and the voices of the people in the carriage faded into the far distance.

'You slipped quietly into my mind. A totally uninvited but totally welcome guest. I found myself remembering, and with such enormous pleasure, each time we've been together.'

He took both her hands in his as he told her what he remembered about their first meeting in the National Gallery.

'I couldn't stop myself whispering my enchantment at how Botticelli had painted Venus' face. You couldn't stop yourself whispering your reply. We couldn't hold back our laughter at what we'd said. I looked at you and felt, suddenly and unexpectedly and inexplicably, elated.

'Being elated was something I'd experienced so often at school, at university, in my first years at the bar. But I hadn't experienced it for such a long time. For too long. Far too long.'

He pulled her towards him. With their bodies just touching, he reminded her of their first drink together in the Nell Gwynne later that first morning.

'That's when I began to taste your sense of humour. Dry as a chilled glass of Tio Pepe. Sharp as the juice of a freshly-pressed lime. Until, of course, you asked me that knockout question. Was I, you asked, single or married or separated or divorced? This, as I know you realised, blew me like a pile of dry leaves in a violent autumn storm. From delight back to despair.'

He put both of his arms around her waist, and asked her to think back to their walk along the towpath at

Hammersmith.

'That's when we became so very aware, in spite of the noises off, of the magic of that birdsong. We stopped playing Beatrice and Benedick and started to exchange something more important than half-clever repartees. We first kissed each other and, for those few precious moments, the world around us retreated and disappeared.

'I've got to tell you how full I was of pleasure and happiness. Words that get used so much and yet explain so little. Just for a little while I forgot about the baggage of the last months and years that I've been carrying around with me, secured by straps and padlocks. Baggage I've been trying as hard as I could not to open.'

He pulled her closer to him, until they were in a close embrace. He told her how he had felt in the gardens of Lincoln's Inn.

'The wine and the salmon tasted exquisite. Not because one was vintage and the other was river-caught or oak-smoked or whatever. But because I was eating them with you. The shadows of the leaves danced across your face. You'll laugh your head off when I tell you this. But, in my imagination, I danced across the lawns with you in my arms.

'We talked about leaves on the river and islands in an ocean. And, just for a moment, we saw the world from very different angles. You were fearing we could never know more than a tiny fragment about each other. I was happy we could know that fragment rather than nothing.

'When we were together on that lawn, the words pleasure and happiness couldn't begin to describe how I felt. Ecstasy was the only word I could think of that was remotely adequate.

'That was the day when I wanted to take off the straps

and padlocks and tell you about my last months and years. But the day was too perfect to destroy by opening my baggage, even just a little and just for a moment. Or at least that was the excuse I used to myself.

'It was an excuse I kept on using until I began to tell you my story on our first night together. At best I used this excuse because of what I felt about you. And because I was worried how you'd react. At worst it was an act of cowardice, and one of so many.'

Before he began to kiss her, he whispered his memories of their first night together.

'That was when I saw you, as they say, in the flesh, in a way I'd imagined you so many times since we first met. When I stroked your hair and your body as I'd stroked them so often in my fantasies. When you asked me to make love to you and seemed so surprised when I asked you the same question.

'When we woke up through the night and held each other and came together, each time more gently and openly, until we fell asleep. Our embraces still unbroken. Our bodies still together.

'I'd been so very happy with you each time we'd met. But this was wholly different. I was more than ecstatic, if that's possible. And I was more than overwhelmed at my good fortune.'

He kissed her again, fell silent. He ended his monologue as abruptly as a midday skylark returning to earth. She tried desperately to hold on to what he had told her. She snatched at his sentences before they disappeared into the distance like falling blossom racing away in the breeze.

Now almost unaware of where they were, they walked on. On the far bank were more Georgian residences. These were grand beyond belief, more palaces than houses. On the side where they were walking were Edwardian flats, redbrick and respectable. These were behind private gardens that were carefully manicured, whose bluebells were in full flower but whose daffodils and narcissi had begun to fade.

They were soon walking past some willows, their hanging branches cut back so that canal traffic could pass under them. They then reached what seemed to both of them a chaos of canal boats. Some were double-moored along the canal side. Others were moored across part of the canal's width.

She had been thinking hard how to reply to what he had told her. As they walked past the narrowboats, she broke the silence.

'What I'm going to say will, more than likely, sound even more over-the-top than what you've told me. And I'm afraid it may be even longer. In spite of all of that, Stephen, and as you put it, here goes!'

As well as thinking while he had been talking, she had thought hundreds of times over the past days about what she wanted to tell him. In spite of this, she was more hesitant by far when she began than she had expected. She had little idea of what she would say. She had no idea at all of what she would have told him by the time she finished.

'You've told me you felt elated when we first met. I've got to admit, even before I saw you, I was more than a little elated myself. How could I have been anything else when I was looking at one of the greatest paintings I've ever had the good fortune to see?

'When we began to talk we were only playing tennis

with words. Hitting them across the net in a short and unremarkable rally. It was then, though, that I started to be elated in a very different way.

'It wasn't any surprise to me I was sharing my thoughts and feelings with you. I've shared them often enough since I was a child. With my sister as we walked to school through the local park. With my friends at King's as we drank more than we should have in a nearby pub. And sometimes, after our drinks, with one of these friends in bed.

'But with someone who was, in every sense of the words, a complete stranger? This was something I can't remember I've done before. And with a man who, even if he wasn't in the same league as Mars, wouldn't have looked totally out of place on Mount Olympus at a gathering of minor gods.'

She was still struggling to decide what to tell him about how she felt. But she found that, by beginning as he had done with their first meeting, it was easier for her to talk about her feelings as well as about his.

'You've talked about being blown from delight to despair at the end of our second rally that morning. Your Benedick versus my Beatrice in that alleyway pub.

'I understood your delight only too easily, because I was feeling the same. I'd been looking forward to the delight of seeing those paintings I go to look at far too seldom. I found another, and quite different, delight with each volley and backhand and smash. However amateurish our strokes may have been.

'I also, I think, understood your despair. Not because I had any idea that morning of what it was about. But because there are moments – in the middle of a lesson that's going well, in the depths of the night when I'm happily dreaming – when a subterranean stream of despair erupts into my mind.

'I don't know whether that despair of mine comes as often or as rarely as yours does. Whether it ends as quickly or as slowly as yours. Whether it has the same intensity as yours. But despair itself I know only too well. Just as I know that sudden transition from delight to despair. And this, for better or for worse, whether we like it or not, you and I both share.'

By telling him about the emotions she felt they shared, she had begun to be less and less hesitant, more and more confident.

'You've said you felt full of pleasure and happiness by the Thames that day we'd met outside my school. I can't do any better than echo what you told me. One minute we were playing our usual game of verbal tennis. The next we were under the spell of that blackbird. And between them we kissed.

'For me there's always a special excitement in a first kiss. Is it a beginning or an end? Will it take me on a voyage of discovery into unknown territory I'd only visited in my imagination or not even imagined at all? Or, after a few well-trodden sidestreets, will it take me into an all too familiar cul-de-sac?

'And for me it wasn't only that the world around us had retreated and disappeared when we kissed. Even if it was only in a small way, it was that the earth had moved.'

She was, by now, revealing her feelings much more easily than when she had begun. This was, she found, made even easier because these feelings were becoming more and more powerful.

'You've talked about our picnic together. And about

imagining you were dancing with me across the lawns. Believe it or not, in my imagination I was dancing as well. You were treating me as an individual with a mind. Not simply as a woman with a body. When we disagreed, you didn't insist I was wrong. You seemed to accept that I might be right. Just as much as you might be.

'But why most of all was I dancing? It wasn't only because we'd been looking at a painting together. Because we'd been listening together to birdsong. Because we'd come together with a kiss. It was because we were talking about things that were really important.

'We weren't being original. Far from it. We were, though, exploring each other's ideas in ways I've so often wanted to do. So often, though, I haven't been able to do this. Or else I've been hopelessly unsuccessful when I've tried.

'I'm sure we're all seeing, hearing, touching, tasting, smelling every waking minute. And perhaps, when we're asleep, in every dream. But I'm just as sure these experiences so often race past us. We seldom reflect on them. All too seldom do we try to talk about them to someone else.'

With these memories of their picnic together, she had begun to reveal even more of her emotions – and of their growing depth.

'What you've told me about our night together was, if you think about it in the cold light of day, more than a little excessive. But if I were to think about it, and if I were to try to tell you how I felt, I'd probably say the same. And much less well!

'As you realised that night and the morning after, I was so very surprised when you asked me if I'd make love to you. I told you no man had ever asked me that before. I told you I couldn't imagine doing anything except letting you do whatever you wanted to with me.

'And it's this, as much as these pleasures of the flesh, that excited me and that I'll never forget. It helped me to understand I'd never met a man like you before. It helped me to see you had qualities that attracted me to you in ways I'd never, in ten years of adolescent and adult life, been attracted to any man.'

By now she had lost many if not most of her uncertainties. She had been talking with a passion that had delighted him and that had, at the same time, been a great surprise to her.

'From that very first time we met I've loved your sense of humour. I've loved listening to you talking. About birdsong one minute. About philosophy the next. You've shown me a depth and range of thinking I've enjoyed so very much.

'I've loved the uncertainties that surround you. Your modesty about yourself. Your concern to keep some things very private. I've loved, above all, your gentleness, your thoughtfulness, your understanding, your sensitivity towards me. Even when you know so little about me. And from the first time we kissed to our first night together and beyond.

'Just to bring this back down to earth, I've loved looking at you and touching you. I may have fallen in love with your mind. But, even for a man as old as thirty, you haven't got a bad body either!'

Now, when she talked about him and how she responded to him, she found she had none of the hesitancy she had when she began.

'What you told me during our first night together

about leaving your wife filled me with dismay. Some people can, I suppose, be unaffected by shouts and screams, by accusations and silences.

'They're able to take it in their stride. Treat it light-heartedly. But you, from what little I know of you, are at the other end of the spectrum. Devastated by silence. Destroyed by a whisper.

'I was just as dismayed by what you told me about what happened after you left her. Threats like the ones she made aren't easy for anyone to live with. But for you, I'm sure they've been almost impossible.

'More than anything I was dismayed by the awful discovery you made. That, by leaving her, you hadn't escaped her outbursts. That your refuge at work where your defences were down was no refuge at all.'

Even when she spoke about his wife, which was where she knew his emotions were at their most raw, she was now able, and without any difficulty, to tell him what she felt. All her uncertainties about responding to what he had said had evaporated.

'You may be asking yourself why I've gone on so long – for far too long! – about what you've told me. Perhaps it's been to avoid talking any more about myself. But however much I've been trying to avoid it, and however difficult it's going to be, I'm going to have to reveal more of my own past. Tear off more of the outer leaves. Feed you more fragments of the truth. But please, Stephen, please not today!'

Silent again, they walked on through a short tunnel, dark and cool and lined with bricks. They then discovered that the tunnel in front of them had no towpath. They were forced to walk across the Edgware Road, crowded with traffic, and along footpaths, crowded with people, until they were able to rejoin the canal.

They passed more – though smaller – Georgian houses, more canal boats double-moored. They passed by Junction House with its brick walls and slate roof and, just after it, under another metal road bridge.

To their left now was an extension of the canal leading down to Paddington Basin. In front of them the canal broadened. Here, complete with island and willows, geese and ducks, was their goal of Little Venice.

'And now?' he asked once they had reached their goal.

'On a day like this it would be madness to be anywhere but out of doors.'

'I absolutely agree.'

'As I hoped you would.'

'So what do you suggest, Jo?'

'To be mad and...' She turned to him. She kissed him and whispered: '... to go to your flat and spend the rest of the day together in bed!'

CHAPTER FOUR

They stood together on Magdalen Bridge, leaning against the stone parapet. Joanna was wearing a short white dress covered with pink flowers that Stephen had told her was a mini-dress in all but name. He had chosen to wear his navy blue blazer and cavalry twill slacks and, with an impish sense of humour, a Cambridge University tie.

Just a few yards upstream was an island, overwhelmed by trees, that briefly divided the River Cherwell. Below them was the water on which an endless succession of white petals were floating slowly downstream. At the water's edge was a row of newly-varnished punts lined up neatly along a slipway.

Above these, and the object of their scrutiny, was Magdalen College's medieval bell tower, built of yellow stone. Its wall that faced them was bathed in mid-morning sunlight. Its bell, strong and clear even above the noise of the traffic, had struck ten just as they had arrived.

'I can't believe it, Jo! It couldn't be more beautiful.'

'Much as I'd like not to, Stephen, I've got to agree with you. Just for once, you're absolutely right!'

They had decided, after their walk along the Grand Union Canal a week earlier, to spend the first day of May – a Saturday – out of London. They had thought time after time about where to go. Somewhere along the south coast: Hastings, Littlehampton, even Brighton? Somewhere along the Thames: Marlow or Cookham or Henley? A cathedral city: Salisbury or Winchester, Chichester or Canterbury? But, in spite of their debates, their exhaustive examination of pros and cons, they had reached no conclusion by the last day of April.

'Let's go to Oxford for May morning!' she suggested suddenly as they were drinking a cup of hot chocolate together the evening before. 'We won't be able to get there at six o'clock to listen to the choir singing at the top of Magdalen tower. We could, though, catch an early train from Paddington and be there by the middle of the morning.'

He agreed, without a moment's hesitation and with a mixture of enthusiasm and delight. For, as he told her, his only days in Oxford had been when he had taken an entrance exam in his last year at school.

His memories – of the streets he had walked along, of the colleges he had seen, even of Exeter College where he had stayed – were hazy in the extreme. He had, however, a painfully clear memory of the letter that had arrived from the college a week or so later. It told him, briefly but clearly, he had failed to win a place.

'It's also where I was born,' she explained as they were finishing their hot chocolates. 'And where I grew up. As well as that, though I'm not thinking of visiting them today, it's where both of my parents still live.'

It had been her suggestion, too, to begin their visit on Magdalen Bridge. Here hundreds of people would, she told him, have gathered that morning to listen to the choir. Yet, by the time they reached it, these had all disappeared to have breakfast or, more than likely, to go back to bed.

'Magdalen's the closest link I've got – or I'm ever likely to have – to the university,' she told him.

'Can you explain?' he asked, puzzled at what she had just said.

'My father was there.'

'That's a close enough link, isn't it?'

'But he wasn't one of the dons. Or even one of the undergraduates.'

'So what was he?'

'He worked in the porters' lodge. From the day he was demobbed at the end of the war until the day he retired a few years ago. A loyal and devoted servant of the college, my dad was. But town and not gown. Without any of the aspirations of Jude the Obscure to become an undergraduate and study Latin and Greek. As much an outsider to the university as I am.'

They walked under the succession of gargoyles – some fierce, others grotesque – along the front of the college. They continued past the dimly lit porters' lodge, crossed the High and turned into Merton Street. This was a street she knew so well, but he knew not at all.

Here they abandoned the pavement and carried on up a road that was surfaced with round brown stones laid in total disarray. Soon they reached Merton College: more yellow stone, more gargoyles and, above the entrance, unexpected carvings of a camel, a monkey and a unicorn.

'Whenever I come along here,' she said as they passed the college, 'I feel I'm travelling back in time. Back into the distant past.'

'That's exactly how I feel,' he agreed. 'This is all so timeless, unchanging. All that changes, I guess, are the people like us who pass by. It may sound pretty stupid to say this to you. But in so many ways I prefer travelling back into time past than having to live in time present.'

After passing Merton's bell tower, squat rather than elegant, they turned left through a high iron gateway and strolled along a narrow path into Christ Church Meadow. Here the cricket pitch was an uninterrupted expanse of green. Here, too, the wild stretches towards the Thames were covered with buttercups and dandelions.

They sat down on a wooden bench. The short spire of Christ Church Cathedral was on their left. Magdalen tower in the distance was on their right.

'If we'd sat here a hundred years ago, we'd have seen just what we're seeing now,' she whispered, and gave him his first Oxford kiss.

'Even a few hundred years before that,' he replied, 'it mightn't have been much different.'

They turned to face each other. With the glories of Oxford if not forgotten then at least pushed into the depths of their consciousness, they kissed again.

For some minutes they said nothing. Each felt the pleasure of lips against lips, tongue against tongue. After their mouths had moved apart, and again in a whisper, she broke the silence.

'You told me yesterday evening you'd had another letter from your wife. I'll ask you the same question I asked about her last letter when we were having coffee at Camden Lock. What does it say?'

He put his hand into the inside pocket of his blazer. He got hold of an envelope he had, with a huge effort of will, opened as soon as it had arrived. He took out the letter. In the same monotone she had last heard at Camden Lock, he began to read.

'I have, as I said I would in my last letter, written to your parents, your brother and sister, as well as to a selection of your friends and colleagues. You will, no doubt, be hearing from at least some of these, though others may be too disgusted at what you have done to put pen to paper.'

'So she's a woman of her word,' she said with a hint of anger in her voice. 'She's done exactly what she threatened to do. But is that all she's got on her agenda? Doesn't she have any other rabbits to pull out of her hat?'

He smiled. Not the full smile she saw whenever he greeted her, whenever they embraced. This was a smile with sadness as one component and, perhaps, with bitterness as another.

'No such luck. What she says is that the letters she's written are just one of her attempts to make me see what she calls sense.'

'What then – apart from those letters she's sent to all and sundry – is she threatening you with now?'

He looked at the letter he had put down beside him on the bench. Though with some difficulty, he read on.

'I know when you left home, you took some of your clothes and a few of your books, records and photographs. I know, too, when you calculated I would be sure to be out, you came back and took some more.

'In spite of what you carried away, most of your possessions are still here. You took none of your recordings of Beethoven symphonies or Mozart concertos or Verdi operas. You left behind hundreds of your Victorian photographs that you told me you began to collect when you were in the sixth form, as well as your entire collection of first editions, including Dickens and Tennyson, that you often told me were your pride and joy.'

'So what's she done with everything? Sold them off to

the highest bidder? Thrown them into the dustbin? Put them out for the refuse collectors?'

'So far, so she says, she's done nothing.'

He picked up the letter again. Holding it open on his knees, he read her the next paragraphs with as little emotion as he could manage.

'*At present, everything is exactly as you left it. Your clothes are in your wardrobe, your books and records are on the shelves, your photographs are up on the walls and in the drawers of your desk.*

'*At the same time, you cannot expect me to be responsible for looking after your possessions for ever. They are, too, taking up space that I could well use for my own purposes. In addition, as I am sure you will appreciate, it is emotionally no easy matter for me to know that they are here and that you are not.*'

'Then I'll reword my question. What does she say she's going to do with everything? Were the guesses I made a moment ago totally hopeless? Or, just possibly, weren't they too wide of the mark?'

'Far from hopeless,' he replied with a grimace. 'And far too close to the mark for comfort. Though at least dustbins themselves don't seem to figure in her plans.'

'So tell me the worst.'

He looked at the page on his knees again. He struggled, though with little success, to suppress his despair.

'*I plan at the end of next week to pack everything of yours into cardboard boxes. I shall then dispose of them by selling whatever I can, by giving to the local charity shops whatever they will accept, and by taking the rest to the nearest rubbish dump.*'

'My God! That's awful!' she exclaimed. 'I've thought of committing some fairly evil acts against some of the men

I've known. But I've never threatened any of them like that. And certainly I've never done anything like that.'

'But you're not the injured party,' he explained to her. 'You're not the abandoned wife. Wronged by her husband. Left to fend for herself.'

'If she's capable of getting rid of everything of yours as she says she will, is she capable of something even worse? My intuition may be wide of the mark. But it tells me she is.'

'You're not just close to the mark. You've hit the nail on the head.'

He glanced down, flinched. With an effort she could all too easily see as painful and distressing, he read on.

'I am also aware, as you must be, that you left behind all the passbooks of the building societies in which we have joint savings accounts. Although it was you who deposited all the money that is now in them, it is I who have the passbooks, and my signature is just as acceptable as yours.'

'So what's she planning to do with that money of yours?'

'Not mine,' he explained. 'Hers and mine. And her plans are as clear as could be.'

Without looking down at what his wife had written, he recited from memory the next sentences.

'Beginning this week, I shall be withdrawing the money that is in these joint accounts. I shall be doing precisely the same with the money that is in our joint bank account.'

'I couldn't be more innocent about money. And I'm certainly no lawyer. But is she really within her rights to take out all the money you've put in? To do this without asking you? And without your say-so?'

'You might say she's not being wholly reasonable. You

might even say she's behaving pretty badly. And I might agree with every word you say. But, without the shadow of a doubt, she's absolutely within her rights. And there's nothing, nothing at all, I can do to stop her. Apart, that is, from getting on to the bank and the building societies. And giving them chapter and verse about why I'm contacting them.'

'Is there really nothing you can do?'

'There's one thing I can do. It's something she comes up with at the very end of her letter. It's what everything she's written has been leading up to.'

'Which is what?'

'She writes she's determined to do everything she says she'll do. But then she throws me a lifeline – or, looking at it from another perspective, a poisoned chalice.'

Very slowly, very deliberately, very quietly, he read the last sentence.

'*Nothing, however, will give me greater pleasure than to leave the money you have put into our joint accounts untouched and to leave your possessions exactly where they are, so that you can enjoy them to the full as soon as you return to what is, after all, your home – and to your wife.*'

She felt her heart beat faster, her throat tighten. Would all that he had gone through be for nothing? Would he give in to her threats and go back to her? Would this trip together out of London be both their first and their last? Would he be just one more link in a chain of her brief encounters? Would she be back exactly where she had been a few weeks before?

'So how do you see it?' she asked nervously, hesitantly. 'Lifeline… or poisoned chalice?'

He stood up and walked away from her along a broad gravel path between the cricket pitch and the meadow.

When he reached the Cherwell he half turned on the steep grassy slope. She saw him tear up the letter and, piece by piece, drop it into the water.

He watched the pieces as they floated away downstream. He came slowly back, his hands behind his back, his head bowed. He sat down, turned to her. In little more than a whisper, he explained why he had destroyed it.

'I can see her letter for what it is. In moments of deep gloom or self-delusion or paranoia I may feel I'm the victim of this or that. But...' His voice became stronger, harder. '... I've no intention whatsoever of being the victim of her blackmail.'

As the bells struck eleven, they walked back from Christ Church Meadow into Merton Street. Past Corpus Christi with its memories for her, fond but brief, of Charles. Past the stone columns and capitals of the back entrance to Christ Church with its memories, even fonder but, alas, briefer, of James. Past Oriel with its memories of a disastrous evening with Paul.

Across the road when they reached the High was their first glimpse of the Radcliffe Camera. This was partly hidden behind the Church of St Mary the Virgin.

'I'm not sure how to describe this city of yours,' he admitted to her as they walked on. 'Breathtaking? Spectacular? Superb? What would you say?'

'I wouldn't say anything. Partly because I don't think I could find words that would do anything like justice to it. Partly because I think it's better just to look and listen and feel.'

They sat down in the sun on the paving stones, their backs against the wall of the Old Bodleian Library. In front of them, and surrounded by iron railings, was the circular Radcliffe Camera.

On one side of them was Brasenose College, its castle façade broken only by a single wooden gate. It was, he thought, though he was not certain, a college he remembered. On the other side of them was All Souls. Of this college, most of which was hidden behind its protective stone wall, he had no memories at all.

In the distance they heard a recording of a chamber orchestra playing Baroque music. Neither of them recognised what it was. Both agreed, however, that it was the perfect music for where they were. He put his arm round her shoulders and held her against him. Again, and at length, they kissed.

'Can you tell me more about your life before we met?' he asked Joanna. 'Can you take me along at least a few more of the streets and alleys of your past?'

She looked around her – at All Souls and the Radcliffe Camera and Brasenose. She knew very well he was an understanding and sympathetic listener. She still, however, needed to decide what to tell him... and how to tell it.

'On our first night together, Stephen, I told you about my last boyfriend. I told you as well I'd had before that an affair I could only describe as bizarre. It had begun, so you might say, quite normally. I used to go over to his flat. At the end of the evening, I used to come back home.

'One evening, about a month after I'd met him, I found he'd invited his best friend, together with his girlfriend, to join us. And, as I soon discovered, he hadn't invited them just for supper.'

'For what, then?' he asked, wholly uncertain what she would answer.

'After supper, and as we always did, he and I went into his bedroom. As we were getting undressed, they came in and sat down on two chairs by the window. They watched us as if we were performers in some Soho strip club. And as if they were fully paid-up members.

'He didn't ask them to leave us alone. Invite them to watch television in the room next door. Suggest they go into his other bedroom and follow our example. Instead, my boyfriend simply put his arms under my thighs and round my back and carried me over to the bed.

'We launched into a sex show that wouldn't have been out of place in late-night backstreet Bangkok. They just sat together holding hands. Our display reached its end – and for him though not for me its climax. They congratulated us with a round of applause. They then stayed on to watch us get dressed.

'I'm not exactly the most modest of people. But that evening I was, as you can imagine, embarrassed and humiliated beyond belief. Up to then I'd enjoyed being with him. What I enjoyed, though, was being a consenting adult in private. Not a participant in a public performance.'

'Good God!' he exclaimed. He looked at her, half in disbelief, half in admiration. 'I'm not sure I'd have been able to cope with all that as well as you did. I think I'd have walked out – that habit of mine again – as soon as the two of them walked in.'

'I'm not sure I had too much of a choice,' she admitted. 'It was abundantly clear he wanted me. It was just as clear he wanted them to watch us. And he was big enough and strong enough to make sure he got what he wanted.'

'I can't think of anything more dreadful,' he told her as he tried – and largely failed – to imagine what had gone on. 'Especially as the two of them, the onlookers, were total strangers to you. And, from what you say, what he did to you was for their benefit – and no doubt for his own. It wasn't, as far as I can see, for yours.'

'It could have been much worse, you know. I was almost expecting they'd stop being spectators and become part of the action. And I might have been with a man I didn't know or didn't like. Not a man I was – certainly up to that evening – crazy about.'

'And before him?' he asked quietly.

She blushed as she began to recollect what she was sure he would see as yet more evidence of her dissolute past.

'Before him, I'd been with a man who certainly didn't view sex as a spectator sport. It was, as I discovered after just a few dates with him, little more than an afterthought.

'Sex was, for him, the mint chocolate after the gourmet dinner. The encore after the symphony. When the sex came, it was just that. An encore, short and sharp and not much more.'

'Sometimes I think I only understand some of what you tell me,' he complained. 'This time I'm sure I don't understand you at all.'

'For him, the focus of his sexual world, the source of his delight, was flagellation. What he wanted above all, what excited him most, what he devoted his energies to whenever we met, was to beat me.

'His one preoccupation, his overriding passion, was my bare bottom. And, I suppose, the bottoms of all the women who came – and, in another sense, failed to come – before me.'

He was surprised and shocked by what she had

revealed. But she signalled to him to let her finish what she had to tell him.

'I had to stand upright like a soldier at ease on parade. With my hands held not behind me but in front. I had to bend over like a gymnast until my fingers touched my toes.

'I had to kneel on the carpet like a Muslim at Friday prayers. I had to lie flat on my front, with my arms and legs stretched out. Like a parachutist in freefall.

'Only after he'd beaten me, only after he'd seen the red marks on my behind, was his interest in any other part of my body aroused. One day, after the thrashing and before the sex, I realised the truth.

'It was only because he'd beaten me, only because he'd seen what his beating had done to my bottom, that he wanted my body for sex. And, as I grasped a bit later, it was only because of the violence he'd done to me he was able to have sex at all.'

Stephen had become even more shocked and surprised as her story had progressed. Again, however, she signalled to him to be silent.

'Though I was sometimes sore for days afterwards, I was, I suppose, able to take his beatings in my stride. They were part of life's rich tapestry. Or so I persuaded myself at the time. They were part of my journey of discovery. Between my last years of adolescence and my first years of adulthood.

'There was, on the other hand, an imbalance I found increasingly unsatisfying. It wasn't so much that I wanted fewer of the gourmet dinners. But I needed more, many more, of the mint chocolates.'

He looked at her, partly in amazement, partly in disbelief. For she had opened a window on a world for which Sedbergh, Cambridge and Lincoln's Inn had completely and utterly failed to prepare him.

'I'm sure I couldn't have managed it as well as you did. I think I'd have abandoned the gourmet dinner even if I hadn't eaten a mouthful. And even if there were box after box of mint chocolates on offer.'

She shook her head, and rested it on his shoulder.

'But for me, it was something I was prepared to experience. It wasn't exactly a normal experience. It wasn't exactly on the straight and narrow. That I grant you. But, unlike some things I can think of, it wasn't an experience I wouldn't or couldn't countenance. Then or, to be perfectly honest, now.'

'There's so much I dream of doing with you,' he replied. 'But I'm afraid my imagination is much more limited than I'd ever thought. And my dreams must be pathetically middle-of-the-road.'

'Why so?' she asked, as she tried unsuccessfully to suppress first a smile then a laugh.

'Because for better or for worse, beating your bottom – bare or otherwise – has never flashed across my mind. Not even for a split second.'

They walked from the pavement in front of the Radcliffe Camera into the Bodleian Library's Jacobean quadrangle. They went on past Christopher Wren's Sheldonian Theatre. They stopped for a moment to look up the Broad, of which he had the vaguest of memories from that long-ago visit.

'Again, Jo, and though it's not too characteristic of a barrister, I'm lost for words. I can't thank you enough for today. It's been, like so many ideas you've had, nothing short of brilliant.'

'If we have to trade compliments, I can only say in reply that you are – as you've been every time we've seen each other – a brilliant companion.'

Arm-in-arm they turned round. As bells from every direction competed with each other to strike twelve o'clock, they walked under Hertford College's copy of Venice's Bridge of Sighs. Soon, after two sharp turns, they reached the entrance to New College.

With more twists and turns they continued down the narrow lane, hemmed in by limestone walls on each side. After five or ten minutes they reached the High. They found they were close to where they had begun their visit on Magdalen Bridge.

An hour or so later they sat down by the side of the Cherwell. They were not on the bank itself, which was carpeted with daisies and celandines. They were, instead, on the seat of a punt they had hired at the slipway under Magdalen Bridge. This they had tied rather perilously to an overhanging branch.

Above and around them were huge trees that must have been part of the landscape of Victorian, perhaps even of Georgian, Oxford. Some had roots that stretched into the water. Most were now in full leaf. Across the river he identified for her the brief hollow call of a pheasant and the repetitive call of a chiffchaff.

In the direction from which he had punted them was Magdalen's tower, now hidden by trees. To the north, which for him was uncharted territory, were the University Parks.

He told her how he was reminded of Millais' painting of Ophelia. Floating on her back with open arms and flowers in one hand. Gazing upwards and singing before she died. She told him how she was reminded of

Tennyson's Lady of Shalott, robed in snowy white, carried downstream on a boat towards her doom.

As the Cherwell slid past, she forgot the agreement they had made to try to avoid quoting lines of plays and poems. She recited, with his encouragement and applause, two of those she had learned at school.

'Thro' the noises of the night
She floated down to Camelot.'

They had eaten their late lunch of rolls with Parma ham and Roquefort cheese, followed by strawberry cheesecake, all of which she had bought the evening before. They were still drinking the bottle of white Burgundy he had taken out of his fridge minutes before he had left his flat.

'I've opened more pages of my past than I'd intended to,' she admitted, more than a little wearily. 'Though perhaps I should have torn some of them up. Or at least cut out the episodes I'd least like you to remember and least like to remember myself. Now it's your turn.'

'So what do you want me to tell you about?'

'You've told me more than enough about how your marriage collapsed. And about why you walked out. You've told me next to nothing about your marriage before it went wrong. Was there ever heaven before hell? A golden age before the decline and fall?'

She saw a smile flicker for a moment across his face. She watched his eyes look up into the trees.

'So much of those first months after our wedding couldn't have been better. I was beginning to get my first cases. I was enjoying, even revelling in, the work I did.

'I was over the moon when I made my first momentary – though far from momentous – appearances in court. I had, or so I felt, found my true vocation. And that in spite of the wigs and gowns and formalities of the court.'

'And what about your wife?'

'Erica and I did so much together that was a joy. We went to concerts at the Roundhouse and the Albert Hall. We walked along the Ridgway in Berkshire. Along the South Downs in Sussex. Along the Norfolk coast at Cley. We went to every possible exhibition in town. We could have found the Tate and the V&A blindfold.

'We went out to eat together as often as we could possibly afford to. Tortellini and marscapone one night. Moussaka and baklava another. Moules frites and crème brûlée on a third. We talked late into the night about everything under the sun. We picked up where we'd left off at breakfast.'

'So was it all walking and eating and talking?' she asked mischievously. 'With concerts and exhibitions thrown in as well?'

'I've got to admit we took every advantage of living – and sleeping – together. No more the brief afternoon adventures in my rooms in college, with footsteps thundering up and down the staircase.

'No more those equally brief excursions into carnal knowledge in the echoing Islington flat she rented with two of her friends in the months after we'd left Cambridge. No more for us Lady Chatterley's snatched moments in Mellors' gamekeeper's cottage.

'We were, instead, able to be together whenever we wanted to. As soon as I returned from work. Before we went to sleep. After we'd woken up. All the barriers of time and place, all the inhibitions of times past, had disappeared at a stroke.

'We were at long last, and as we'd never been before, able to enjoy ourselves – and each other – whenever and however it took our fancy. I felt – and I'm sure Erica felt the same – for better or for worse, till death us do part, free and fulfilled.'

She poured another glass of wine for each of them. She put the empty bottle down on the floor of the punt.

'The way you talk about it makes it sound nothing short of a marriage made in heaven. Nobody could be less qualified than I am to pass judgment. Never married. Never even engaged. But I can't believe it could have been better. Wasn't there any advance warning, though? Any hint of what was going to happen?'

'In those first months of wedded bliss there was, as far as I was aware, only one. It was after I'd given a drink to a client who'd visited me in chambers late one afternoon.

'She was more than a little nervous about her appearance in court the next morning. Even though it was a cut-and-dried case in which her husband had abandoned her and her two children. Even though he'd failed to pay a penny of maintenance since the day he'd disappeared.

'I took her round to the Seven Stars. After we'd drunk a bottle of Rioja together, I set off home. Erica was angry I'd got back later than she'd expected. Furious I'd gone out drinking without her. Uncontrollably hysterical because I'd been with another woman.

'I watched, with something not far short of horror, as her hands clenched and unclenched. As the colour drained from her cheeks. As her whole face contorted as if she was in terrible pain. It was only the second time I'd seen this metamorphosis, Dr Jekyll becoming Mr Hyde.

'It was also, as I've told you perhaps too often, the prelude to how she behaved throughout the rest of our time together. Dark clouds that grew suddenly and unexpectedly in a blue sky. That exploded with bursts of thunder and flashes of lightning. Until that morning when I walked out.'

He stopped. In one long and excessive gulp, he emptied the last of the wine from his glass.

'You said what you felt when it happened wasn't far short of horror. But what did you feel afterwards? After that dark cloud had disappeared over the horizon?'

'I was disturbed and disoriented. Not totally devastated. But not far short of that. And that's how it had been the first time it had happened.'

'When was that?' she asked, seeing how agitated he was becoming, yet also wanting him to tell her more. 'Obviously before you were married. But was it even before you'd got engaged?'

'It was when we'd been engaged just a few months. We were setting off from Cambridge to go to London by train. I'd seen an ex-girlfriend at the far end of the platform. I walked up to her. Kissed her on her cheek. Introduced Erica to her as my fiancée.

'All, or so you might think, perfectly normal. But Erica's face spoke volumes, and she said hardly a word. She turned round and strode off, leaving both my ex-girlfriend and me acutely embarrassed. On the train, as we travelled to Liverpool Street, she alternated between total silence and outbursts of anger.

'When I tried to ask her about it, to discuss it with her, her response was more silence and more anger. I realised I was to blame for the way she'd reacted. I was the cause of her anger. I should have known how she'd react to meeting a girl I'd once – or, to be precise, much more than once – had in the same bed Erica and I were then sharing.

'I should never have kissed the girl. Never have introduced her to Erica. And if I'd had no alternative to introducing them, I should never have admitted she'd once been my girlfriend. I should have been streetwise enough to know that honesty, even with one's beloved fiancée, isn't always the best policy.'

He stopped, looked at her. He shook his head sadly.

'In my naivety or stupidity, I never for a moment thought, never imagined, there could be any other explanation than this for the way she'd behaved.'

'In other words you blamed yourself.'

'Exactly!'

He looked down into the water at the side of the punt. He saw among the ripples not only the reflection of the leaves and branches above him but also the reflection of his face. It was the sad face Joanna had seen in the Nell Gwynne when they had had their first drink together. When she had asked him if he was single or married or separated or divorced.

'I've got a question I hope doesn't sound too cruel,' she told him as she stroked his arm. 'And I hope it isn't too painful for you to answer.'

'Please ask it,' he urged her. 'And even if it's painful I'll do my best to answer it.'

'Why, after what had happened at the station, did you carry on with the engagement? Why did you marry her, when you must have at least suspected it might be for worse and not for better?'

'I had to put this one-and-only episode during our engagement into some sort of perspective. I had to balance it against so much that was nothing short of delight. So much I can only describe as idyllic. Just as the time had been before we'd got engaged.

'In those early days, she told me time after time how much she loved me. How much she wanted to marry me. How much she wanted to be with me for ever. She couldn't have been more affectionate or loving or caring.

'In those early days as well, we'd explored each other's bodies as passionately as we'd explored each other's minds. Compared with your expeditions to the outer fringes of eroticism, it was very much middle-ground sex.

'It was, at most, a succession of brief encounters whenever the opportunity arose. The only beatings she suffered were gentle and affectionate taps on her rump. Our only excess was a second coupling on an occasional Sunday afternoon in my college rooms.

'But it was, for all its limitations, hugely enjoyable. And, from time to time, it was highly amusing. There were moments when we both lost control. When we rolled around wildly on the bed. It wasn't because we were experiencing any orgasmic ecstasies. Far from it. We were, to put it quite simply, like children playing party games. We were laughing till we cried.'

'I do wish I'd been the one who was with you. Even if all we'd had were brief encounters. Even if your only attacks on me had been taps on my rump.'

'It's just what I'd have liked as well. Though...' Here, in spite of how he had felt a few moments before, he began to chuckle. '... at that time you'd have been seriously under age!'

CHAPTER FIVE

Joanna and Stephen strode briskly together out of the Sun Inn, with its whitewashed stone walls and small windows framed by black-painted stone. As she had predicted rain if not worse, she had brought with her an anorak, a pair of waterproof trousers, and some Wellington boots. These, in spite of the blue and almost cloudless sky, she had insisted on wearing.

Believing he knew much more than she did about good and bad weather in the Dales, he had predicted a fine day. He had put on an ancient tweed jacket, some corduroy trousers that had seen better days, and a pair of well-worn walking boots.

They turned to their left along the narrow cobblestone street. They turned left again and headed away from the village towards the hills. Soon they reached the footpath of loose stones by the side of Flinter Gill, and began the steep climb.

They walked up past primroses and violets and anemones on the damp bank of the beck. Past holly and hawthorn bushes. Under sycamores and larches and occasional pines. All these grew up the hillside, following faithfully the beck's descent towards the valley.

'See that pile of stones over there?' he asked. 'That

used to be a lime kiln. And that's where a few of my pals and I used to sit and talk and tell each other stories. Still in short trousers we were then. And see those stone barns on our right, scattered across the fields? They're the places we often used to run to when we were playing hide and seek.'

This weekend at the western edge of the Yorkshire Dales had been his idea. For their first day together out of London, she had chosen the place where she had been born, where she had grown up. For their first weekend together two weeks later, he had done the same.

He had, so he had told her, been born in a tiny dales village called Dent. It was where his father had taught at the village primary school until, a few years before his retirement, he had moved east across the Pennines to Richmond.

After six or so years at his father's school, he had won a scholarship to the public school in the nearest town, Sedbergh. Here he had studied until he won another scholarship, to read law at Selwyn College, Cambridge.

They had arrived in Dent late on the evening before. This was after a slow-speed and tiring motorway journey on the Friday evening – passing Birmingham at twilight and Manchester after nightfall – in a car he had borrowed from a friend. They had had dinner – a huge plate of gammon steak and mashed potatoes, and more than enough draught bitter to satisfy even a hardened beer enthusiast – at the Sun Inn.

This was the pub in the middle of the village he had walked past thousands of times in his boyhood. Yet it was a pub which, until this evening, he had never entered, and in which he had certainly never spent the night.

The sun was rising high above the hilltops to their left

in the mid-May sky. After about half an hour of steady and unhurried climbing, the path by the beck ended. They had reached a broad track. Some of it was grassy, some stony. It was, too, framed by walls from which, so she thought, moss hung down like fleeces hanging off sheep before shearing.

Some of the walls on the other side of the dale climbed up, ramrod straight, until they disappeared over the horizon. These walls beside the track, however, were creeping along the hillside between open moorland on one side and fields enclosed by yet more walls on the other.

Here he stopped. He sat down on a large flat rock, and invited her to do the same. He unzipped his rucksack, took out a thermos flask he had asked the landlord to fill before they had left the inn, and poured out a cup of coffee. They passed it to each other. At the same time they looked across the fields towards the River Dee that snaked down the dale between a succession of flat meadows.

'Let's walk this way,' he suggested as he pointed to the east. 'It's a walk I know so well I could do it in the thickest of fogs. Or in the heaviest of snowstorms. But it's one I never tire of doing again and again.'

'In Oxford you followed me,' she replied with a broad grin. 'Here I'm as happy as could be that the shoe's on the other foot. But before you take me any further on, can you take me back again into your past? Even further than you did when we were sitting in our punt on the Cherwell a fortnight ago. Back to your student days before you met your wife. Back, perhaps, to those schoolboy days of yours in Sedbergh.'

Whenever he had told her about his years with his wife he had found it difficult to think clearly and to talk coherently. And this was true even when he had told her about his good years. He had found it just as difficult to keep his emotions under any sort of control. To avoid the lump in his throat, the tears in his eyes that he so much wanted to hide from her.

He had found it impossible to tell his story of those years as comedy, which she seemed to do so easily when she told him about the men she had known. But the few years before he had met his wife belonged, or so he felt, to a totally different world.

He was more than happy to tell her this chapter of his story, and to tell it as comedy – except where it belonged to the theatre of the absurd. He was equally happy to laugh at his escapades and, most of all, to laugh at himself.

'I'd had fewer than a handful of girlfriends in my first year at Cambridge. The last was the girl Erica and I had met so disastrously at the station there. I'd first met her when I tripped and fell over her. At a lecture on one of the more forgettable facets of criminal law.

'Before her there was a girl in her final term at one of Cambridge's secretarial colleges. This was a place which, among us freshmen, was reputed to admit girls whose skills and aptitudes weren't only secretarial.

'The first was a girl I'd sat next to in a liberal club meeting. A girl whom, in a moment of over-confidence that was at best wafer-thin, I'd invited for a drink.'

She bent her head to one side, looked at him at the same time quizzically and with amusement.

'So, even early on at Cambridge, you had three bites at the cherry.'

'Absolutely not. And more's the pity. With the first

of them I soon found I was a total failure. Her liberal principles extended far and deep in the fields of politics and economics. She argued passionately and effortlessly for sexual liberation. But how she actually behaved was, as I very soon discovered, totally at odds with everything she said.

'True, my attempts to kiss her were tolerated and, or so I felt, welcomed. But my attempts to slide my hand inside her blouse were repulsed before I'd advanced more than a few millimetres. My attempts to stroke her thighs, even when they were fully protected by her tights or her skirt or both, were stopped in their tracks the moment they started.'

'So you only had two bites at the cherry.'

'Wrong again. With the second, as I'd be the first to admit, I wasn't in the least concerned about her secretarial abilities. I explored her body from her waist upwards as often and for as long as I could. And this, I have to tell you, was more than a little pleasurable. Certainly for me.

'Yet as soon as I tried to put even the tips of my fingers inside her panties, I was dismissed with a sharp slap on my wrists. Once I was repulsed with an equally sharp knee in my groin. It was, I could only conclude, a response she'd learned in one of her lectures on how to deal with the unwelcome advances of her future bosses.'

'So when did you hit the jackpot?' She laughed as she imagined how frustrated he must have felt. 'After all the energy you'd devoted to these women, you must have had some reward. You must have had some return on your investment of all that time and effort.'

'With the third, after I'd put in so much effort with her predecessors and got so little in return, I hit what you so inelegantly call the jackpot.'

'So tell all!' she demanded.

'It was at around teatime on a wet winter afternoon. After I'd blundered through the preliminaries. Knowing neither what to do, nor how, nor when. With an amateurism she must have found comic in the extreme. In a performance noteworthy only for its brevity. It was then she surrendered her body to me and I surrendered my virginity to her.

'It was, so she told me, a surrender she'd already accepted from a battalion or more of virgin soldiers. That was during her last terms at school, and in her first terms at university.

'But however grand the scale of her conquests had been, and however small a part I played in them, I'd made my first conquest. I'd become at last a fully-grown man. And, or so I thought at the time, I'd become an adult in every sense of the word.'

She could hardly suppress her laughter, and patted him affectionately on his back.

'Did she put you on an intensive training course? Or did she quickmarch on to her next new recruit?'

'She gave me as intensive a training course as I've ever had in my life. She was as eager for sex as I was. She jumped into bed with me whenever the opportunity arose. Even when there was no bed – as when we found ourselves by the Cam one summer's night after a dance – she was as eager as could be.

'She was like Boccaccio's Alibech with her Rustico, who was exhausted by her demands. Almost inevitably, she insisted on a repeat performance before I'd even begun to recover from the first. I was still needing – to use that expression you used in Oxford – to stand at ease.

But she was ordering me to stand to attention once again.

'There were, though, no expeditions beyond the middle ground. We studied together the graphic pictures of less orthodox positions I'd discovered in an explicitly illustrated *Karma Sutra*. Yet we coupled in ways no Victorian except the most prudish could have objected to. Even on the banks of the Cam, we conformed fully and faithfully to the missionary tradition.'

'Were you always just a twosome?' she teased him.

'I've got to admit there was just one time on just one evening when we weren't totally a twosome. How can I put it? We had what I can only call a sudden explosion of overwhelming mutual desire. It was at a party. We started to make love on our host's bed.

'He and his girlfriend, who no doubt had exactly the same intention, discovered us at the height of our passion. To their and to our intense embarrassment. But apart from this one public exhibition – as unintended as it was unfulfilled – our sex was strictly in private.'

'And wasn't there ever a single slap as the trimmings?'

'If flogging is what you mean by the trimmings, that was never part of the training programme. We never once mentioned it. Not once. I'm just as sure we never even thought about it.

'If we had, I'm as sure as can be she'd have run a mile if not a marathon to avoid it. Just, to be perfectly honest, as I'd have done. And in as close to world-record time as someone as unfit as I was could have run!'

She listened with a combination of fascination and amusement to his account of his quest for knowledge and experience in his university years. Yet, at the same time, she wondered if this was where his quest had begun.

'And before Cambridge? Were you really as innocent, as untouched by human hand, as you're suggesting?'

'When I was in the sixth form, my friends and I talked almost as incessantly about sex as we did about soccer. There couldn't have been a single day when we didn't ask each other questions. Though to most of these questions – even the simplest and most obvious – we hadn't the slightest idea of the answers.

'To some of our questions we found the answers in our local library's manuals. Well-thumbed if not well-understood by generations of inquisitive teenagers.

'To other questions we found less dry-as-dust answers in the deliciously arousing photos in girlie magazines. These we clubbed together to buy from our local newsagent's much visited – and no doubt highly profitable – top shelf.

'Some of us read to each other – before and after school – the most explicit bits of *Lady Chatterley's Lover*. And for comic relief we recited to each other, and to any other boys in our class who cared to listen, all the bits of *The Ballad of Eskimo Nell* we could remember.'

'But hadn't you learned anything from your masters? Or, for that matter, from your parents?'

'From our masters, even our biology master: not a word. From our parents: hardly a word more. We exchanged details of whatever our fathers – or, for two of us, our mothers – had told us about the so-called facts of life.

'We suspected, though, that these revealed only our parents' narrow sexual pasts. We reckoned they had nothing to do with what we saw as our own broad sexual futures. And, of course, we boasted to each other about our exploits. But, as you know very well from what I've told you, our boasts were based on our inventions and not our experiences.

'On my last day I walked out of school, through the gates and, or so I thought, into the adult world. I had a head crammed with facts, ideas, opinions. My body had, as you can imagine, experienced all the usual novelties and surprises of puberty. It had, though, no experience with any member of the opposite sex. Or, for that matter, with any member of my own.'

After they had finished some of the coffee in the flask they stood up. Their bodies were just a little stiff after their rest on the rock. They began to walk, hand-in-hand, up the dale along the track.

'We're going towards High Moss and Deepdale,' he told her. 'But if we're going to be back at the Sun Inn for lunch, we won't get quite as far as either of them.'

A few minutes later he stopped, grasped her arm. He pointed towards the moorland up on their right.

'Do you hear that curlew up there?'

'I can hear it loud and clear. But I can't see a thing.'

'You'll see some of them before long. Especially if there's one close by when we walk past and it raises the alarm.'

After a few hundred yards he stopped again. He pointed down at the fields in the distance by the river.

'Did you hear those alarm calls down there?'

'I heard something. But what it was I've got no idea.'

'They're oystercatchers. More often than not they're in the meadows by the river. And, no doubt, we'll see more of them when we get there.'

Above them, a skylark burst into song, and sang on without a moment's break as it flew ever higher. In the shallow pools scattered along the track, hundreds of tiny tadpoles wriggled through the water. Across the track, narrow becks raced down from the moors. They then sneaked through the grass, bounced over stones, bounded on into the fields.

'When I was a lad I came up here as often as I could. Sometimes with my mother and father. Sometimes with pals from school. But mostly by myself. When, like countless others before me, *I wandered lonely as a cloud that floats on high o'er vales and hills.*

'It was then, when I was on my own, I realised something hugely important. Listening to the wind as it whistled through the walls. Looking across the dale at the jigsaw puzzle of walls and fields. In the height of summer wading between tussocks of long grass. In the depths of winter wading through deep drifts of snow.

'It was that this natural world excited me, delighted me, more than I could ever tell you. It was that this might not have been heaven itself. But, without a doubt, heaven was very close by.'

She turned to him, put her arms round his neck. With the skylark still singing overhead, she kissed him on each cheek and then on his mouth. With her arms still round his neck, he bent down, put his arms round her thighs, lifted her up.

He carried her a little way along the track. Over some stepping stones across a beck. Onto a smooth slope of short grass by the edge of the water. Here he put her down. Then, as soon as he had taken off his rucksack, he lay down beside her.

'This is the spot I came to so often in my teens. On those days like today, few and far between, when there was hardly a cloud in sight. On those days that seemed to follow each other for weeks on end, when clouds crawled or skated across the sky from the west. Or when they hung, thick and heavy, above the dale and hardly shifted from dawn to dusk.'

They lay beside each other on their backs. Looking up at the handful of clouds that drifted lethargically across the mid-morning sun. Listening to the skylark that climbed up and up until they could hardly see it. Feeling the splashes on their faces from a small waterfall where the beck reached the track. For some minutes, until he spoke, lying in silence.

'Turn to me, Jo.'

'If you turn to me, Stephen, you'll see I've turned already.'

They held each other, kissed again. As it had been those weeks before by Hammersmith Bridge, now it was above Dent. For a few moments, perhaps minutes, they saw no clouds, heard no skylark, felt no splashes. For each of them, all that existed was the other. Both felt, as he had done when he was a boy, they were close to what they understood by heaven.

After a time – how long it was neither of them knew – he sat up. He took the flask from his rucksack, poured another cup of coffee.

'It's your turn now,' he told her. 'Take me back to your first years of teaching. And, before that, to your last years of being taught when you were at King's.

'Take me back to what I'm sure were less tame and inhibited years than mine were. To what I suspect, from what you've already told me, were golden years. When you sowed many if not most of your wild oats. When you let your hair down as far as it would go if not further. And I promise you I'll interrupt you with my questions as little as you interrupted me with yours.'

She knew she needed to talk more – much more – about her past. She knew he was the first man she had known in whom she could fully confide. Before she could begin to tell him more, however, she scratched her head, stroked her chin, rolled her eyes, licked her lips, furrowed her brows. Then, when she had exhausted her repertoire of facial expressions, she launched into her answer.

'These were years when – for better or for worse – my knowledge and understanding of children grew by the day. And when my knowledge and understanding of men grew by the night.

'At long last I'd escaped from what I'd felt more and more in my mid teens was the prison I lived in at home. I was – or at least that's what I thought at the time – now free to enjoy myself to the full.

'After the day's lectures were over, and later after I'd taught the last lesson of the day at school, that's exactly what I did. I showed a passion and enthusiasm I can hardly credit myself with when I look back at those years. I devoted myself hook, line and sinker to my poetry – the pleasures of the mind. I devoted myself even more to what you might call the pleasures of the flesh.

'One of the most obvious features of that night life of mine was the number of men I got to know – which I now find more than a little embarrassing. I didn't have the battalions of them your first conquest at Cambridge said she'd had. But there were certainly a platoon. And fully up to strength at that.

'I'd gone out with only a few Oxford undergraduates while I was still at home. I was no Zuleika Dobson, and didn't have to move on to Cambridge as Max Beerbohm's heroine did after she'd run out of men in Oxford. And, at

King's, I definitely didn't have a different man every night of the week as some of my friends used to boast they had.

'But there were, just as definitely, some weeks when I had more than one. And there were some months when I had more than that. In the evenings I tried to read as much poetry as I could, and became more and more interested in early English poems. But – much as I'm reluctant to admit it these days – my staple evening diet, often running to three courses and sometimes to more, was sex.

'A lot of what I wanted to do at the time was to have a good time. To live for the moment. To do this as much as I could. Certainly not just now and then.'

'But,' he interjected, 'were you simply in the business of volume?'

'I can't deny I went in for volume. But I went in for variety as well. I never read through the pages of the *Karma Sutra* as you did. Though I'm sure in those years I tried out most if not all of its permutations. Even the most uncomfortable. I also think I could have contributed at least a few addenda to any update.

'As a by-product of this I managed – though not intentionally – to expand my Latin vocabulary. I discovered at first hand the meaning of *fellatio* and *cunnilingus*. The words I used to describe them in those uninhibited days were, though, both Anglo-Saxon.

'I also discovered at first hand the meaning of *flagellation*. One or two of my boyfriends persuaded me to tie them up and beat them. But after I'd obliged, I suspect my hands and arms hurt more and for longer than any parts of them.

'More of them told me – even once or twice on our very first date – they wanted to beat me. Perhaps I attracted men who had that hidden desire. Perhaps they'd heard on the grapevine from their friends I was able and willing. Whatever the reason, this became from time to time part of my repertoire. Most recently with the boyfriend I told you about when you and I were in Oxford.

'I didn't always enjoy their efforts, especially when they lost some of their control and hurt me more than they – or I for that matter – expected. Often, though, they followed the stage directions of their performance to the letter. As well as that, these efforts were no more than an episode in their foreplay. Pain before pleasure.'

He listened with at least as much fascination to her account of her university years as she had listened to his. But he also wondered if she could have left school in a state of innocence as profound as his own.

'Did all this begin when you were at King's?' he asked her. 'Or had you already had some early adventures at school into that world you seem to have explored so thoroughly after you'd left?'

She smiled and then laughed at his questions. She tried to decide how to word her answers.

'My first adventures, if that's the right word, were when I was in the sixth form. I'd already been at the receiving end of those hurried kisses behind the bike sheds. Those slaps and tickles on the stairs up to the science labs. Those amateurish gropes in morning assembly during prayers. But in the sixth form I wanted passion, romance, love. And, if there wasn't any alternative, sex.

'I remember – as I suppose we all do – the first time. An early evening, with the sun almost below the horizon. The first of the autumn leaves already falling. By the banks of the Cherwell. Not all that far from where you and I picnicked on our day in Oxford. I'd like to be able to say that the earth moved. But for whatever reason all that moved – and even then so inexpertly – were our bodies.

'Perhaps it was because, just as you told me about yourself, neither of us knew sufficiently well what to do. And that in spite of the lessons devoted to sex education he and I'd had at our comprehensive school. Perhaps it was because it had rained the day before and my back and my bottom were wet as well as cold. Perhaps it was because an Alsatian raced up to us at exactly the wrong moment and tried to join in.

'What I remember most clearly about my first boyfriend, though, wasn't that poorly acted scene of open-air theatre. It was a few weeks later, after he'd found one of those schoolboy love letters I'd had from another classmate.

'He pinned me down on my desk so I was lying on my stomach like a seal stranded on a rock at low tide. Pulled my panties down. Thrashed me. Then tried to apologise for what he'd just done. With a mixture of enthusiasm and incompetence, though it's only the incompetence I remember, he did his best to make amends.'

'So was this the very beginning for you? Or was there something that happened even earlier you haven't told me about. Or even hinted at?'

For a minute or more she was silent. She looked away from him, embarrassed and beginning to blush. She had been able to make a joke of what had been close to a decade of couplings, to make fun of herself, to tell stories at her own expense.

She may have done this, she thought, because it was the easiest way for her to talk to him about her past –

even if she was not being totally honest, either with him or with herself. Or she may have done it because she did indeed look back at her past not as a series of small-scale tragedies but as a comedy of errors. And, perhaps, she saw them as comedy rather than as errors. Where the real truth lay she was far from sure.

But the very beginning was something she was wholly and hopelessly incapable of telling as comedy. It was the same as she knew she would be when she came to talk about one other fragment of her past.

She knew she would find it as difficult to tell him about these – and about the profound effect they had had on her – as he had found it to tell her about his life with his wife. She began to search for words to tell him what she had told nobody before.

'My sexual sunrise, if that's what I should call it, was almost a year earlier. Mary – one of the girls in my class who lived only a few doors away – came round after school one day. We were going to listen to Rod Stewart's *Baby Jane* I'd just bought with the pocket money I'd been carefully hoarding for weeks.

'We were on my bedroom carpet. Lying on our backs. Slapping our thighs to the beat of our very favourite singer. Suddenly she rolled round onto her side. She embraced me and started kissing me. I've got no idea why. But I found myself embracing and kissing her as passionately as she was kissing me.

'Without saying a single word to each other, we took off all our clothes. When a whole class of us dashed through the showers as fast as we could after netball, we all saw each other naked. But apart from this, she was the first girl I'd seen naked since my body had tumbled out of childhood and into adolescence.

'We were on the one hand extremely self-conscious. On the other hand we were extremely curious. And, after we'd had a thoroughly good look at each other, Mary began to touch me. I began, again with no idea why, to touch her.

'Softly, gently, yet with more and more excitement, we stroked each other's bodies. She touched me, so she told me, as she'd touched nobody else. I touched her as I'd touched only myself before. We were, I suppose, doing in fact what Fanny Hill and Phoebe Ayres had done in fiction.

'I felt myself floating, and wanting to float further. Into a new and wonderful world with more delight than I'd ever experienced, ever even dreamed about. And a world I've visited since only a handful of times at most.'

He held her arm so gently she could hardly feel his touch. He began to talk so quietly she could hardly hear him.

'You've experienced something that's completely unknown to me. Something I've never thought I'd ever experience. But how did you both feel about what had happened to you? About what you'd done together?'

'We talked about what had happened after we'd got dressed. We agreed that for both of us – though without knowing why – the earth had moved. We also agreed we'd walked through one of the doorways into adulthood. A doorway which, until that afternoon, we'd been totally unaware of.'

She fell silent. Looked down at the grass where she was sitting. Tried to decide how to complete her chronicle of what had happened.

'A little later, I thought about that afternoon. And about those extraordinary and unforgettable afternoons and evenings with Mary that followed it. I became more and more worried and disconcerted.

'I knew what we'd done together had made me feel so completely marvellous. But had this astonishing pleasure she'd given me, and the pleasure she told me I'd given her, been somehow wrong, bad, sinful, evil? And was I, because of this, sinful and evil myself?

'After nights when I was never fully asleep and days when I was never fully awake, I came up with the answer to my questions. I decided I'd done something awful, terrible, wicked, depraved. I remembered lessons I'd had on religion years before. I decided I must never commit that sin again.

'Very occasionally these days I start thinking about that past of mine. It's then I think about what I did when I was in my late teens and early twenties. And I think this is one of the explanations of my willingness, even my desire, to be at the receiving end of violence. Wanting to be chastised, chastened, castigated, punished. Feeling an overwhelming need to atone for my sin.'

CHAPTER SIX

'One day I'd like to ask you to tell me more about everything you and Mary did together. And about how it affected you. But now we need to start getting back to the Sun Inn before closing time so we can have something for lunch. Let's begin to head down towards the river.'

Joanna and Stephen began to walk steadily along a downhill track. They crossed one field after another until they reached the riverside. On their way they watched the lambs, some still very small, dashing here and there across the grass. They listened to their bursts of high-pitched and insistent bleating. On the bank they watched the brown water race past them where the river was narrow, move along at slow speed where it deepened.

'This walk couldn't have been better,' she told him as they stood side by side at the water's edge.

'Especially when we're not surrounded by blocks of flats and towers of offices. When there's no monotony of concrete and glass. When there's no symmetry of horizontals and verticals. Of flat surfaces and straight lines. And,' he added as he held her hand in a firm grip, 'especially now, when we're walking along together. But that's another story.'

He squeezed her hand, stopped. He raised his head

and looked upwards.

'Whenever I'm here I love to look at the sky. At the clouds sliding across it from one horizon to the other. When I'm walking in so much of London – even in Lincoln's Inn – I can see so little of it. And that makes seeing all the sky here so precious.'

'For a bone-dry barrister,' she observed with a quiet smile, 'you're quite a poet.'

'I could say the same about you.'

'Except I'm no barrister.'

'But,' he retorted, remembering their earlier Benedick and Beatrice exchanges, 'even a schoolmistress can be a poet on a good day.'

'And is it a good day?'

'For me? Most certainly it is. But, as I said a moment ago, that's another story.'

They stopped again and turned to each other. Once again, they held each other and kissed.

'It was over there, where the river's not quite so shallow, that my pals and I used to come and try to swim after school. Whenever it was warm enough. And often when it wasn't.

'We used to dogpaddle upstream with every ounce of energy we had. But we found when we were dog-tired we'd done no more than end up where we'd begun. We used to tickle trout as well. Though – except one day when we bagged a fish that must have been on its last legs – we never did more than catch the odd stickleback.'

With their lunch at the Sun Inn forgotten, she sat down on the grass, her head resting against his legs. First she looked at the sloping hillsides in the distance. Then at the flat fields by the river. Finally at the river itself.

'I'd love to have been able to watch you.'

'You could have watched everything we did. Yet you'd have understood next to nothing of what we said.'

'But I can understand you perfectly.'

'Now: yes. But then, unless I'm badly misjudging how I spoke, you'd have understood me very much less than perfectly.'

She grabbed hold of his hands, and pulled him down onto the grass beside her. She lay back, the whole length of her body stretched out on the ground. She looked up at the clouds that were scattered across the sky, and whose shapes and sizes changed from moment to moment.

'So what's the difference between now and then?' she asked in all innocence.

'Now *but* rhymes with how you say *cut*, *gut*. And, for good measure, *slut*.'

'And then?'

'Then it rhymed with the way you say *foot*, *put*. And even *soot*.'

She repeated the words several times. First in an uncertain whisper. Then, as her confidence grew, more loudly.

'Even for somebody like me who feels she's in a foreign country up here, that's not too difficult.'

'Nor is *glass* that I now say as you say *pass* and *grass*. And, if you'll forgive me, *arse*.'

'Then?'

'Then it rhymed with the way you say *mass* and *lass*. And, when it's a fish and not a singer, *bass*.'

She echoed what he had just said. Next, to her surprise as well as to his, she found herself shouting the words across the river at the top of her voice.

'That's not too difficult either,' she told him. 'Especially for someone who spent at least a little of her misguided youth studying Anglo-Saxon. And who dipped her toe, if not much more, into medieval English.'

'So I'd guess you'd have no problem with one of the words that oversexed ex-boyfriend of yours must have used to you on every conceivable occasion. Now I say it – though not in polite company like yours – the way you say *luck* or *suck* or *muck*. Then – even though I hadn't the slightest idea what it meant – I said it the way you say *book* or *cook* or *look*.'

'And what about another of his favourites?' she asked him. 'I rhyme it with *punt* and *runt*. And always have done since I learned what it meant from the girl I sat next to at the back of the class in my last year at primary school.'

'Then I rhymed it with *Dachshund*. At least the way Germans say the word.'

Though she had no idea why, she abandoned all modesty and self-restraint. Sounding like a steam engine on an extreme incline, she yelled out in her best imitation of a Yorkshire dialect the words her ex-boyfriend had used so often.

'But what was it that happened to you?' she asked him. 'When we've been talking to each other today, you've sounded much more like a London lawyer than a Yorkshire yokel. And you've sounded just the same every time we've been together since we first met.'

'Here with my schoolmates I used – if you'll forgive the imagery! – a longboat full of words I'd inherited from my Norse ancestors. But year after year, slowly and surely, how I used to speak was squeezed out of me. Partly at home by my parents. Partly at school in Sedbergh by the masters. But mostly at Cambridge by almost everybody

I met.

'I'd thought of myself as a Yorkshire lad and proud of it. Yet by the time I first walked through Lincoln's Inn dressed up in my wig and gown, and without understanding this until it was too late, I'd lost what was at very heart of being one.

'And as well as losing the way I spoke back here in the dales, I was talking in sentences as full of good grammar and clever words as they were empty of any deep meaning. Sad to say, except when I'm up here, I never find any of it again.'

He looked away from her towards the river, then towards the path they had been following.

'It's along this path I used to come and walk. At night when the moon was bright enough. In the evenings between homework and supper. On those winter days when the snow was too deep to walk up to the moors.'

'With your friends?' she asked as she tried to imagine him as a boy. 'Or on your own?'

'Almost always on my own.'

'But you had friends. You've told me you had.'

'Of course I had. And there was a lot I used to do with them. I showed you where we used to get together when we were walking past the ruins of the lime kiln. I've just shown you where we used to go swimming after school in the summer.'

'Anything else?'

'As well as that we used to go up onto the moors and – to my eternal shame – collect all the birds' eggs we could find. We hunted for rabbits in the pastures and threw stones at them. If by some mischance we ever caught one, we carried it back down to the village. Our hope was that one of our parents could break its neck and put it out of its misery.

'And when the time for pig-killing came in the autumn, we used to beg for the bladder. We blew it up, then kicked it around between us until it burst.'

'So where did you go on your own?'

'It wasn't only along this path we're on now. It was also along the track on the fells where we were a couple of hours ago. Over the moors towards Crag Hill. Downstream past Gawthrop. But it wasn't only when I was walking that I was on my own.'

'When else?' she asked.

'At school I'd often stay in the classroom. Even when the playground was a perfect sunshine paradise. Even when it was a perfect snowball battleground. At home I'd often go upstairs to my room as soon as I'd had supper. Rather than sit with the rest of the family and watch television or listen to the radio. Rather than go a couple of doors along the street to see one of my pals.'

'What was it you could do on your own that you couldn't do with your friends or your family?'

'I could do what we've been doing some of today. Which, as I discovered to my dismay, didn't seem to interest them. Watch lambs and listen to oystercatchers in the pastures. Smell heather and listen to curlews on the moors.

'On my own I could climb over a five-barred gate or a dry-stone wall and cross an invisible frontier. Into a natural world where everything I saw was so much brighter, where everything I heard was so much clearer than it was the rest of the time.'

'And when you weren't alone?'

'With other boys – even the ones I enjoyed being with

– no colour was ever as bright. No sound was ever as clear. No smell was ever as strong. But it wasn't only that.'

'So what else was it?'

'When I was with my pals, I found what they were talking about did little or nothing to answer the questions that interested me most. Questions that kept me awake whenever I woke up in the middle of the night.

'If I wanted to think something through, to get a better understanding of something, the best way to do it was to be by myself. I'm not the first by any means to believe that *He travels the fastest who travels alone.*'

She had been listening carefully to what he was revealing of himself. Now she put her hand on his head and stroked his hair. She tried to show him without words that she understood at least a little of his revelations.

'I came to realise the awful truth of what I was telling you about in Lincoln's Inn when I quoted *The Rime of the Ancient Mariner* to you. But one day, when we both dig down even deeper into our histories, I'll give you another explanation for being a schoolboy loner. Semi-detached if not more so from the world around me.

'It'll be uncomfortable for me to give you this explanation. But it may be a little closer to the truth. Unless, of course, the real truth is that I'm suffering from a touch of autism!'

They stood up. Looking to the outside world like two teenagers who had just met, they held hands. They turned to face each other. A couple of oystercatchers called as they flew low over the field behind them. Three curlews called as they flew high overhead. They smiled at each other, leaned towards each other, and kissed.

'It's wonderful to be here with you,' he told her. 'And I

could very happily stay here all day. Very soon, though, we'll have to head back.'

'Before we do, can I ask you a question?'

'What is it, Jo?'

She hesitated. She feared her question might destroy at a stroke the delights of the morning.

'Have you had another letter? I knew before we walked along the Grand Union Canal you'd had one, because I picked it up by your front door. I knew before our day in Oxford you'd had another, because that's what you'd told me. This time I've got no idea at all. Though my guess, for what it's worth, is that you have.'

'You're right,' he sighed, pressing his lips together and grinding his front teeth. 'It came a couple of days ago. This time as well, just like with the first of her letters, I've been too much of a coward. I've got it here in my rucksack. But I haven't even taken it out of its envelope, let alone read it.'

'I know it must be hard for you to do. But can you read it to me? Even if you haven't already read it yourself?'

'I'd hoped to drive back to London from here with no more idea of what's in it than I had when we drove up. I'd hoped by walking with you this weekend I'd have been able to forget it. But I haven't been able to forget. And I've got to read it sometime. So maybe now is as good a time as any.'

He sat down, unzipped his rucksack yet again. He took out the envelope, tore it open. She heard his breathing quicken, become shallower. He felt his heart beat faster, felt it thump against his ribs. With his legs apart and the letter lying on the grass between them, he began to read it to her.

'At the end of my last letter, I told you that nothing would

give me greater pleasure than to leave your money and your possessions intact so that you could enjoy them as soon as you came back home to me.

'*As you have not come back, and as you have not even had the courtesy to reply to my letter, I have begun to do precisely what I said I would do. I have already withdrawn some of the money that was in our savings accounts and our bank account. Next week I shall be withdrawing all that remains.*

'*I have already packed all your clothes, books, records and photographs into boxes. Next week some of these will go to second-hand and charity shops in the high street. Whatever they will not take will go to the refuse tip.*'

'So, Stephen, once again she's doing just what she said she'd do.'

'Yes,' he agreed. 'But she goes on to say this isn't why she's written the letter.'

'So why in Heaven's name has she?'

His face contorted in pain as he skimmed the next paragraphs. It lost none of that pain when he began to read them to her.

'*The purpose of this letter is not to give you an account of what I have done and what I will be doing with your money and your possessions. It is to give you some understanding of how your actions have damaged and humiliated me, and how I see my responses up to now to these actions of yours.*

'*Even in those early days when we were newly engaged you distressed me by your misbehaviour. You had the effrontery to introduce me to an ex-mistress of yours. Your thoughtlessness and lack of consideration towards me – in kissing her and in talking to her rather than to me – I still find amazing. Yet my only reaction was mild annoyance.*'

'When you told me about that,' she observed, 'it sounded to me much more than mild annoyance.'

'But she and I may have seen what happened quite differently. She may have seen how she reacted as mild annoyance. I saw it as something very much stronger.'

'How does she go on?'

He looked down at the letter again, and began to read what followed.

'At our wedding, as I am sure you remember, you made the most solemn and sacred of vows. The vicar asked you whether you would comfort me, honour and keep me in sickness and in health and, forsaking all others, keep yourself unto me, so long as we both shall live. Your answer was an unequivocal and enthusiastic yes.

'You vowed to have me from that day forward, for better for worse, for richer for poorer, in sickness and in health, to love and to cherish, till death us do part. Before God, our parents, our relatives and friends, you declared with words I remember each day, that with this ring I thee wed, with my body I thee worship, and with all my earthly goods I thee endow.

'Yet in spite of those wedding vows, you soon repeated your earlier misbehaviour. One instance was when you took some woman out for the evening and plied her with drink, totally forgetting that I was here on my own and waiting for you to return. Again, my only reaction was annoyance.

'The more I think about my responses to these actions of yours, the more I understand how disproportionate they were. By expressing annoyance and nothing more, I under-reacted to what I now recognise was an absurd extent. I should have done far more to make you understand how I felt, and to correct the errors of your ways.'

'For God's sake! I've never met your wife. And I suppose I'm never likely to. On top of that I'm no psychologist.

Nor even much of a judge of character. But she doesn't seem to me to have any sense of the real world. At least of the world as I know it.'

'If that's what you think, just wait for what's to come.'

He bent his head down until it touched his knees. He turned the page, went on.

'*Just as disproportionate were my reactions to your subsequent betrayals of your marriage vows. On one occasion you returned home after midnight and were hardly capable of stringing two words together, except to justify yourself with the excuse that you had been drinking with old friends. On another occasion you went alone to a black-tie dinner, and only afterwards did I discover that it was a dinner which the wives of all your colleagues had attended.*

'*There was, after each of these events, a retribution of sorts. You may, as a consequence of your actions, have had a small scratch or a temporary bruise. It is now abundantly clear to me that you deserved far more: a penalty fully commensurate with the offence.*'

'The more you're reading to me, the more I'm convinced she's living in a world I don't begin to understand. And that she's in real need of some sort of help. But what can she mean by *a penalty fully commensurate with the offence*?'

'Let me read you the last couple of paragraphs. They'll give you some idea.'

He looked back down at the end of the letter and gave her his wife's answer.

'*Your behaviour in the past was, however, as nothing in comparison with the way you are damaging me in the present. What you have done by abandoning me is so monstrous, so totally unjustified and unjustifiable, that it demands a suitable response.*

'*This time it will in no way be disproportionate. Have no*

doubt about it, as and when I so decide, I will ensure that the punishment will fit the crime. It will, too, be a punishment that you will never, never forget.'

Even after he had reached the end, he went on looking down at the pages on the grass between his legs. He stared at them until the words became blurred, until they floated in total disarray in front of him. She stared at him, watched the colour drain from his face. He looked, more than she had ever seen him, deeply dejected.

'You've read me two of your wife's letters before. Each of those had threats that were bad enough. But the sorts of threats she's making in this letter sound so much worse. Even though she doesn't spell them out.

'I can't believe any woman in her right mind would dream of making them. Let alone put them down on paper. And as for doing what she threatens to do, whatever it may be, that's way beyond anything I can understand.'

Without saying a word, he picked up the letter and stood up. He walked forward to the edge of the river. He stood on two stones a foot or so from the bank. As he had done in Christ Church Meadow a fortnight before, he tore the pages into shreds.

He threw them into the peat-stained water. He watched them as they were carried away downstream. Some bounced as they scurried between rocks. Some revolved slowly in calm water. None sank. Only when the last shred had floated off did he turn and walk back.

'I've got my Achilles' heels,' he admitted to her. 'Perhaps more and bigger than most of us have. But – at least up to now – giving in to threats, from her or from anybody else, hasn't been one of them.'

He leaned over to her. He kissed her on her forehead as

he had done so often since they had first met. Holding hands again, they walked slowly along the path.

They passed under the trees that lined the river and shaded them from the early-afternoon sun. They left behind the lambs that were still dancing noisily about, and the ewes that were still feeding without a sound. Soon they reached the little stone bridge on the road from Dent up across the Pennines to Hawes.

'We're nearly back,' he told her. 'You can see the church up there. The Sun Inn's just on the other side of the street.'

They stood for a few minutes on the bridge, watching a couple of trout swimming lazily in the water below them. They then turned back towards the village. They passed the first of the stone houses, walked back onto the cobblestones. In front of the inn, just before they crossed the street, she grasped him by the arm, stopped him.

'Wait a minute,' she whispered. 'There's something I've got to tell you. I should have told you before. But I didn't or couldn't.'

He looked at her, his face suddenly wreathed in worries.

'What is it? Tell me now.'

'In those rollercoaster years of mine, I kept a lot of my emotions backstage. But over the last weeks, days, hours, they've pushed themselves centre stage. Whether I like it or not, whether you like it or not, and hollow and corny as it's going to sound to you, I think I'm falling in love.' She blushed. But, for once, she was completely unconcerned. 'And just in case you haven't worked it out, it's with you.'

A small and uncertain smile flickered onto his face, and grew steadily broader.

'Up to now, I've said as little about love as you have,'

he replied. 'But for me it's not that I think. It's that I know. And it's not that I'm falling in love here and now.

'I don't know when or where it happened. In Oxford. Along the Grand Union Canal. In Lincoln's Inn. By Hammersmith Bridge. Even, perhaps, in the Nell Gwynne the day we first met. But I fell in love with you weeks ago.'

They stood on the cobblestones in the middle of the street. She was now smiling as broadly as he was. They held each other tightly and kissed once again.

'So, dearest Jo, *cry havoc!*'

'So, dearest Stephen, *let slip the dogs of war!*'

CHAPTER SEVEN

'Stephen!' whispered Joanna as she began to open her eyes and, with growing surprise and pleasure, as she began to look around her. 'Are you awake?'

She wriggled towards him across the bed. She put one arm round his waist. She kissed him on the back of his neck.

'You won't ever believe what I can see!'

He rose sluggishly, reluctantly, from the depths of his sleep towards consciousness. He rolled slowly from his side onto his back. He pushed himself up the bed until his elbows were on his pillow. He cracked open his unwilling eyes and began to focus on the room around him.

'What is it?' he asked her in a hoarse voice. 'And what won't I ever believe?'

He looked first at her. At her face, some of it lit up by the sun. At her hair that covered much of her pillow. He then looked across the bedroom. At the whitewashed walls and the sloping ceiling, supported by wooden beams that were crudely cut. At the little square window almost opposite their bed.

'If I really have to wake up, Jo, I've got to say this is a wonderful way to do it. And what a way to start the first day of our first holiday together! From what I can see of it, it's a brilliant morning outside. This is a bedroom where I could happily spend day after day. And perhaps, for all I know, that's exactly what I'll do. Above all, I've got you in bed beside me.'

They lay together on their backs, their bodies just touching. They looked with delight at the shadows of leaves playing on the wall to their left, created by the sunlight that flooded in through the window.

They looked, too, at the leaves themselves that almost reached the window. Some of these that were untouched by the sun were dark green. Others were a lighter green where the sunlight hit them.

'I'm not sure I can find the right word for all this,' she told him. 'But the word *perfect* can't be far wrong.'

They had arrived the night before after a full and exhausting day's journey. By early-morning train down to Dover and by ferry across to Calais. By train to Paris and by metro across the city from the Gare du Nord to the Gare de Lyon. Here they had caught their southbound train with minutes to spare.

For several afternoon hours they had raced silently and smoothly through the French countryside towards the Auvergne. For a couple of evening hours they were in buses and then a taxi once they had abandoned the urban bustle of Clermont Ferrand for the rural calm of the Cantal.

At last they had reached the village of Giroux. Here one of the barristers in his chambers owned a house which he had invited them to use for the week of her half term.

That evening they had been so exhausted they had done next to nothing. They had unlocked the door with an enormous old key. With the help of a torch they had walked across some creaking floorboards and climbed the narrow wooden stairs. As hastily as they could, they had made the double bed with sheets and blankets and pillows they had found in a wooden chest.

At last they had clambered into bed. They had embraced and kissed for no more than a few moments. Then, straight away, they had fallen asleep. Even the midnight calls of an owl in the tree outside their window had failed to wake them. They had, too, slept through the clamour of bells of a small herd of cows a villager had driven past the house well before dawn.

'Gorgeous as they are,' he whispered in her ear, 'there's much more to see than this room and the view through the window we've got from our bed. Let's go downstairs and find out if you still think it's so perfect here.'

'But before we go down,' she countered, 'before we go and greet the morning, can we, just for a little while, greet each other?'

From lying on their backs, they turned to face each other. They held each other tightly. Their lips and tongues and, for the first time since they had left London the morning before, their bodies met.

'Now I'm ready to go down,' she declared with great certainty. 'Now I'm ready for whatever the day may bring.'

They found two dressing gowns hung up behind the bedroom door. One behind the other, they walked downstairs. On the bottom steps they stopped, astonished by the room in front of them. They had hardly noticed it when they had crossed it by torchlight the night before. Yet now much of it was filled with sunlight. Even what was in the shadows was bright.

'Incredible, Jo! This is beyond anything I'd imagined when I was in chambers and hearing about the place before we set off. All I can do is repeat what you said upstairs. It's perfect.'

In front of them was a huge fireplace cut into the wall. Inside the fireplace were two benches, one on each side of a low stone platform. On this the grey ashes from the last fire that had been lit still lay.

On the opposite side of the room was the door they had come in through the night before. On each side of it were small, square windows. Through these they could see some of the little garden they had stumbled across after they had left the taxi and come through the gate.

Just to their left and, like the fireplace, built into the wall, was a roughly-carved stone sink. Above them were massive wooden beams that had been blackened by smoke and time.

'I can't think of a better place for this first week of ours together,' she told him after she had looked around the room. And, to herself, she whispered: 'With you, it's a place where I think I could spend a lifetime.'

They walked outside. Turned round under the huge lime tree that dominated the garden. Looked at the house they had seen the night before only in darkness.

They looked at the slate roof that sloped steeply and was covered with lichen and moss. They looked at the grey walls, at the stone slabs that framed the door. They looked, too, at the stone-walled barn, joined to the house on its left and with massive double doors, their wood rough and weatherworn and unpainted.

'You couldn't be more right,' he replied as they walked around the garden together. 'I hope we'll have the time of our lives here. A week, I'm sure, we'll both always remember.'

At breakfast they sat beside each other at one end of the long wooden table that filled the middle of the room. She was wearing a green T-shirt, a pair of purple woollen leggings, and her trainers. He was wearing his college sweater, an old pair of tracksuit trousers, and an equally old pair of trainers.

As they had gone to bed with no supper, they had no difficulty in eating half a dozen croissants. These they had bought at a village bakery on the way from Clermont Ferrand. Nor did they have any difficulty in drinking cup after cup of coffee. This they had found in a cupboard built into the stone wall.

They decided after breakfast to cycle to the small town of Salers a few miles closer than Giroux to the mountains of the Massif Central. Partly to explore what the guide books they had read in London had described as one of the jewels of medieval Cantal. Partly to have their first French lunch together. Partly to buy enough food and drink to last them for the next two or three days.

'It may be nothing remotely like what we've read about. All the restaurants and shops may be shut. There may be more neon signs than we've got in Piccadilly Circus or Oxford Street. But,' he chuckled as he put on his rucksack, 'we'll still get some healthy exercise.'

He locked the door, put the key under a stone by the doorstep. Together they walked over to the barn. They opened the double doors and wheeled out the bicycles his colleague had told him they would find against the far wall. Then, without a moment's thought to check the height of their saddles, the state of their tyres, or the efficiency of their brakes, they set off.

First they cycled slowly uphill along the narrow lane that cut through the village. On their left were tall hedges and stone walls. On their right were farmhouses scattered at random beside the lane. Some were roofed with slates, others with tiles. All were stone-built and looked as solid as castles. In front of one was a yard paved with cobblestones. To one side of it, and dwarfing it with its bulk, was an enormous barn.

'For Christ's sake!' she gasped as she struggled up the lane, swaying from one side to the other in bottom gear. 'How much further do we have to go before it gets flat?'

'From what I remember about the last seconds of our journey here last night it's certainly not much further. Just as certainly, though, it's not quite yet.'

Soon they reached a crossroads. Here, at a run-down inn, they saw a signpost to Salers. They turned left onto a straighter, wider, and – to her great relief – rather flatter road. A few moments later she braked noisily, stopped abruptly on the grass verge. She shouted to him as he was pedalling strongly in front of her.

'We've got to stop. Here. Now. My heart feels it's about to burst. I'm gasping for breath. It's as if I've just finished running a mile or more. I've used up every bit of energy I ever had. But that's not why I'm stopping. Just come back here!'

He jumped off his bicycle. He laid it on the grass by the roadside. He ran back to where she was standing.

'I've always wondered what the Elysian fields I'd read about at school might be like,' she told him breathlessly. 'Now I think I know.'

She pointed at the small herds of cattle on each side of the road. Some of the cows stared at them, hardly moving. Others seemed completely unaware of them. All moved slowly towards them, dipping their heads from time to time before they began to graze.

'Look at the colour of them!' she demanded.

He had lived for more than half of his life in the farming country of the dales he had shown her on their first weekend together. He had, though, never seen coats of such a rich, deep chestnut.

'Now listen to them!'

As the cows moved, even a little, the brass bells that hung from leather straps round each of their necks rang across the fields. In some ways, she thought, the noise they made was wholly discordant.

But she then looked at the low hills patchworked with fields on one side of the road and, beyond the fields on the other side, a deep valley. With these, she decided, the clamour of the bells was perfectly in tune.

'Good God!' she exclaimed when they reached Salers after half an hour or so of cycling, and after more stops than they could remember to look down into the valley on their right. 'It's unbelievable!'

'Wonderful!' he replied after they had walked for a few minutes between the stone walls of houses and into the small town square.

'With those turrets and towers I can easily imagine I'm back in time half a millennium or more. Even further back than I felt most of the time I was guiding you round Oxford on May Day.'

'All that's reminding us we're in the twentieth century – and with the twenty-first only a few years away – are the shops we've been in and the people we've seen.'

He stopped in the middle of the square by the stone fountain. He put down his rucksack, full of the food and drink they had just bought for the next few days.

'How many bottles of that Auvergne red did we buy?'

she asked him.

'Four – though at the moment it feels like much more.'

'And cheese?'

'Some Bleu d'Auvergne. Some Saint Nectaire. And a large piece of young Cantal. All local. And, with the baguettes we got, enough to keep us alive and well for a couple of days. Or, depending on how far we are from starvation, for even more.'

'And meat?'

'Quite a few slices of Auvergne ham. Two breasts of magret de canard. Some lamb. And – though they looked more than a little suspicious to me – some home-made sausages.'

They looked at each other and – as they had done so often since they had first met – they burst out laughing.

'You're pretty hungry, aren't you?' he asked after he had studied her face.

'I could eat a horse and still be hungry.'

'I couldn't manage a whole horse – or even a pony – if I tried. And even if I wanted to. But I could do reasonable justice to a three or four course lunch.'

They walked out of the square. Down a short alleyway. Into a street that was longer and wider.

'There's a place we could eat in!' she declared.

'Shall we try it?'

'Why not?' she asked in reply. 'If it's a failure, blame it on me.'

'And if it's a success?'

'The success will all be yours.'

Two hours later they were still drinking their coffees and the last drops of a bottle of Bordeaux. They had, after some debate, decided to begin with a thick vegetable soup. They had gone on to a thick slice of jambon d'Auvergne.

For their main course they had a monumental plate of gigot d'agneau. And finally – in spite of her protestations that she was already full to the brim – they managed to eat some îles flottantes to the last mouthful.

'That's one of the best meals I've ever had,' Stephen admitted as he wiped his mouth with his napkin.

'And for me,' Joanna added with more than a hint of a smile, 'one of the reasons it was so good was because of the man who's sitting opposite me.'

They were slowed down as they cycled back by the weight of the food they had bought and by the meal they had just eaten. Yet by mid afternoon they were back in the village. The sun was still high in the sky. There were only occasional clouds that moved across from west to east.

They lay in the hammocks they had found in the barn and had tied between the lime and two smaller trees. They convinced themselves they were simply recovering from their exertions. But, in reality, they were more asleep than awake.

In spite of this, he urged her to listen to the dry calls of the crows in the nearby trees and the high-pitched crying of two buzzards floating above the valley. He urged her, too, to watch the dipping flight of the jays and the effortless flight of the kites as they soared overhead.

'We biked through one half of the village when we struggled up from here to the top end. And, on our way back, when we freewheeled back down. Would you,' he asked when she seemed a little more awake than asleep, 'like to walk down to the other end of the village before we open our first bottle?'

'For you,' she replied with as much conviction as she could manage, 'I'd walk much further than the end of the village. Even when my stomach's hopelessly bloated from our feast. When my legs are aching from all that pedalling. And when my bottom's as saddle-sore as it's ever been.'

She rolled uncertainly off her hammock, and helped him to roll off his. With their arms round each other's backs, they set off downhill. First they walked past a small barn next to their house. Next they passed a slate-roofed farmhouse up the hill on their right. On their left they came to a tall house with grey shutters. Finally, on the same side of the road, they stopped in front of a long farmhouse with a stone roof.

'I thought Dent was wonderful when you took me there,' she told him. 'But this, even though it's so much smaller, is more than wonderful.'

'I suppose I should be loyal to the village I was born in. But I'm afraid I can't disagree with you. This place is so calm and quiet. Beyond anything I'd thought possible.'

Soon they passed the last house in the village. They reached a short stone bridge over the stream that writhed along the valley floor. They watched the water as it rushed over some of the rocks. As it dashed against others. As it raced over a small waterfall. As it calmed when it reached the deeper water beyond.

'Why do I think this is so beautiful?' he asked her as they both leaned against the side of the bridge.

'What do you mean?'

'Is it because it's so beautiful in itself? Or is it so beautiful because I'm with you?'

She had no answer. Instead she turned to him, put her arms round him. Oblivious of any cars or lorries or tractors coming downhill towards them from either direction, she held him tightly against her body.

Soon after they had come back from their walk through the village, great grey clouds began to tumble across the sky. By early evening, the rain was torrential. They could see nothing of the hillside beyond the stream. Even the stream itself, as well as the fields that sloped down to it from the house, were indistinct, veiled by the downpour.

Just before the rain had begun, he had gathered some kindling and some small logs from a pile of wood he had found in the lower part of the barn. He had crumpled a few sheets of a French newspaper, put the kindling and then some of the thinnest logs on top of them, and set fire to them.

The rain beat incessantly against the windows. He squatted by the fire and used some bellows to strengthen the flames. She opened one of the bottles of red wine they had bought in Salers. She put his glass down in the recess in the wall on one side of the fire. She put her own down in the recess on the other side.

She sat, entranced as she had been the whole day. Watching the flames that were beginning to lick their way up the great blackened chimney. Listening to the crackling of the kindling and the hissing and spitting of the logs. Smelling, for the first time in her life, the burning wood of a cherry tree.

He was equally entranced. He leaned over her, kissed her. He sat down on the bench opposite her. They looked at each other's faces. Some parts were lit up by the flames. Other parts were in deep shadows. Still other parts moved into and out of the shadows as the flames lurched upwards.

'This morning when we woke up, I used the word *perfect*,' she whispered. 'I can't think of a day that's been more perfect. At least for me. Being here, being with you, beats anything I ever experienced when I was at school or at college. Or, for that matter, anything I've experienced since. I'm sure you'll laugh at me for saying this. And I know it'll sound so corny. But it's like a love story where the only tears are tears of joy.'

He looked at her through the flames. As he finished the last drops of his first glass of wine, he smiled.

'When we were talking on the hillside above Dent, Jo, you were telling me about those school and college days of yours. But is this evening a good time – or, perhaps, as we're so close to each other, a better time than any other – for you to dig even further back in your memory? To those years before what you called then your sexual sunrise. And,' he added, 'to tell me what you unearth.'

She stared into the flames. She was hypnotised by the way they moved until they were extinguished as they disappeared up the chimney. She thought back to the moment when that other difficult fragment of her past had flashed through her mind as they were sitting together on the edge of the moors above Dent. After a minute or more of silence, and with a grimace playing across her face, she looked up at him.

'It's something I've never talked about – not even once – to anyone else. It's something I've done everything I could to avoid thinking about. And it won't be at all easy for me to tell you. Even in Oxford, even in Dent, I couldn't have told you.

'But this evening, and after today, I'll try to tell it all. Just as it was. Or, at least, just as I remember it. I'll try to be honest with you about what, whenever it crawls into my mind, I think of as my deepest, darkest secret. Even deeper and darker than my afternoons and evenings with

Mary.'

He leaned across the front of the fire. He held her wrist lightly. 'You try your best to tell me. I'll try my best to understand.'

'I've told you my encounters with boys – and with their violence – began at my secondary school. But being smacked and hit began well before that. Perhaps, though I can't remember for sure, even before I started at my primary school.

'Sometimes when I got back from school, the first thing my mum did was to lay into me. My socks or shoes were splashed with mud. My pullover was splashed with bits of school dinner. Or, quite simply, I'd got back later than she'd expected.'

'So what did she do to you?' he asked.

'She smacked me on my arms, my back, my bottom. Wherever she could hit me as I dodged around the kitchen. When I ran upstairs to my bedroom to cuddle my teddy bear or bury my head in my pillow, she kept on shouting at me. Until, after what seemed little short of an eternity, she stopped.'

'How often did she do this to you?' he asked her.

'She wasn't violent every day. Or even every week. But, as I walked out of school, down to the crossroads, across the park, up the path to the front door of the house we'd lived in ever since I can remember, I always expected the worst. Every day I carried with me the fear she'd find out whatever I'd done wrong. As well as the expectation that, because of what I'd done, she'd hit me.

'When she wasn't violent, when she greeted me instead with a word or two, or a smile, or even a kiss – though this was a rare treat – I felt I was the luckiest of girls. What I remember, though, weren't those days when I escaped her anger. I remember much more those days when I didn't.'

'Did you have any idea then – or, for that matter, do you have any idea now – why she did this to you?'

'Until I was much older I never understood that her smacking me probably had nothing at all to do with the reasons she gave me for doing it. Though at the time her reasons seemed to me very real, I've come to see they were the flimsiest of excuses.

'I now understand each day of her life she was imprisoned – or, more to the point, each day she imprisoned herself – in a cast-iron routine. Washing on Mondays. Cleaning on Tuesdays. Ironing on Wednesdays. And so on till she cooked the inevitable roast on Sundays.

'As each day wore on, I'm sure she must have become more and more overwrought. By the time I got home, she must have been ready to explode. Whatever she decided I'd done wrong provided her with the release she needed. Then the ritual I expected each day began.

'But at the time, and for many years afterwards, I thought she smacked me simply for what I'd done wrong. Punishment for the crimes I'd committed. Retribution for my evil deeds.'

'Unless I've missed something,' he told her, 'I can't see this has anything to do with any deep, dark secret you've kept to yourself all these years. And tried your hardest to keep even from yourself.'

He looked searchingly into her eyes, until she felt a blush spreading out of control across both her cheeks.

'You're quite right,' she admitted.

'So,' he guessed, 'is it about what your father did to you?'

She hesitated. Then she replied, almost in a whisper: 'Yes. But only partly about what he did to me.'

She looked down at the flames again. Could she tell him, even now? Could she tell him everything, as she said she would try to do? It was now she wanted to be able to tell him clearly and fully what had happened. Yet she felt hopelessly confused. She was sure she would be completely useless when she tried to tell her story. After a minute or more, she looked up.

'When he got back home, my dad always changed from his dark suit into his old clothes. Corduroy trousers, tartan shirt, motheaten grey cardigan. As well as those, he changed from the black shoes he'd worn at work into his shabby carpet slippers.

'He'd then, as likely as not, tell me off for something he said I'd done wrong. My comics were lying around on the sitting room floor. My toys were scattered around in the hallway. My mum had told him I'd been making her mad.

'When he ordered me to bend over I knew exactly what to do. I kneeled down on the carpet beside one of the dining room chairs, with my tummy across the seat. I lifted up my skirt and held it by my waist. He, at the same time, took off one of his slippers. Always the left one, though I never knew why. Then he started to hit me.

'I can't say I looked forward to what he did to me. But he never hit me more than five or six times. And it was never really painful. Nor was I ever really afraid. Over the years it became, as with my mum's violence, almost a ritual, a performance.

'It was something I came to see as a normal part of my life. And, until I found out the truth from my friends, I believed for years it was as normal a part of their lives as it was of mine.'

'You've told me why you thought your mother hit you. Do you have any idea why your father hit you?'

'Why he felt he had to do it I never discovered. Was it because he was obsessed by the need for everything to be neat and tidy, spick and span? Was it a hangover from his wartime service in the army?

'Or did he – like my mum – have to find a release for his pent-up frustration after a day of kowtowing to students less than half his age and to foreign tourists demanding to visit the college? Or was it what his father had done to him when he was a boy? Was he simply continuing the cycle? Or – in spite of only ever touching me with his slipper – was this the outlet for some secret desire of his? I simply don't know.'

'You've just said you weren't afraid of being hit like that. So what did you feel about what he did to you?'

She swallowed hard. She felt the pain her memories caused her. At the same time she felt the pleasure, at long last, of sharing these memories and not keeping them to herself.

'My dad didn't, perhaps couldn't, show me affection. Stroke my hair. Put his arms round me. Cuddle me. Kiss me on my cheeks. But, at least when he was hitting me, I had the proof he was paying some attention to me. He was showing he knew what I'd been doing. Even if he didn't like it.

'And this may, just possibly, help to explain some of the ways I behaved when I grew up. Desperate for affection and, if not that, for attention. Ready to do almost anything to get them.'

'I can understand this may not be something you'd like to talk about to people you don't really know. Or even to people you don't know all that well. But,' he asked, 'is this really that deep, dark secret of yours?'

'That's what comes next. When I've worked up just a bit more courage.'

Yet again she looked down at the flames. Then she began to talk, so quietly he could hardly hear her, with her eyes still focussed on the fire.

'One day when I was eleven, in my last year at primary school and, I suppose, at the entrance gates to my adolescence, the ritual began as usual. I went down on my knees, bent across the chair. But I didn't just lift up my skirt up to my waist as I always did. I pulled down my panties which I'd never done before.

'My dad walked in from the kitchen, his left slipper in his hand. But instead of hitting me, and for the first time ever during any of the beatings he'd given me, he spoke to me. I was now, he said in a voice that seemed to me to be hiding a bundle of emotions, too old for this. He told me to get up and go upstairs. And he never hit me again.'

Stephen stood up. He walked round the fire to the bench she was sitting on. He bent over, put his arms around her. 'Why did you do it, Jo? Do you have any idea?'

'Why I did it I've never been able to decide. Maybe I did it without a thought in my head. Some sort of spontaneous act. Maybe I'd just wanted to see how he'd react to the sight of my bare bottom. An act of bravado. Maybe, just maybe, there was some quite different reason.

'Had I – perhaps unconsciously – actually wanted him to see my behind? Had I wanted him to touch me, hold me, embrace me? To do what he'd never done since the very first memories I've got of my childhood? Once again, I simply don't know.'

He sat down beside her. One hand was round her shoulder. The other was caressing her face. 'And the effect on you?' he asked in a voice now as quiet as hers. 'Was it something you soon pushed to the back of your mind? Or was it something that kept echoing in your memory? Something that flooded into your mind the moment you found yourself awake in the middle of the night?'

'Throughout my teenage years and beyond, I remembered what had happened that afternoon as clearly as I remembered that first afternoon with Mary. But why I'd done what I did is as much a mystery to me now as it was then.

'All I was sure of was that I'd been horribly, dreadfully sinful. And what I'd done was unnatural, abnormal. Of the seven deadly sins it wasn't gluttony or greed. It wasn't sloth or envy or pride or wrath. But was it, I always asked myself, the sin of lust?

'And this, like my times with Mary, may be another explanation for so much of what I did in later years. That I wanted to be beaten by my menfriends to atone for these sins. That I needed to be promiscuous to persuade myself I was, in spite of what I'd done, a natural and normal woman.'

CHAPTER EIGHT

On their second night in the Auvergne, Joanna and Stephen slept as deeply and for as long as they had on their first. Their sleep was, however, broken twice. Each time when they began to wake up, they found to their surprise and delight they were in a close embrace. And, without becoming fully awake, they made love.

Some hours after the crescendo of the dawn chorus, of which not even he had heard a single note, they awoke. The leaf shadows on their bedroom wall danced and quivered in the sunlight as they had done the morning before.

With a great effort of will, undermined several times by kisses and cuddles, they climbed slowly out of bed. Just as slowly, they clambered downstairs.

They carried their modest breakfast of a baguette with myrtle jam and a pot of coffee with cream into the garden. They sat together at a small wooden table. They looked up at an almost cloudless sky. They then looked downhill at the farmhouse below them and at the smoke that rose drowsily from its chimney.

'What shall we put on the menu du jour?' he asked after they had eaten the last crumb of the baguette and drunk the last dregs of the coffee they had brewed. 'Apart, that is, from our food and drink.'

'I can't get out of my mind that valley we looked down at yesterday as we were biking along to Salers. Whenever I shut my eyes, there it is in my memory. That river slowly worming its way along the valley floor. Those flat meadows nudging up against it. Those hillsides strewn with woods and pastures. And, beyond the valley, those mountains stretched out across so much of the far horizon.'

'So what's your idea? To bike along the same road we biked along yesterday? To look down at the valley again?'

She shook her head. Unable to restrain herself, she burst into an uncontrolled stream of giggles.

'I know what I said yesterday about my saddle-sore rear. And I can still feel it ache and groan and protest every time I move it. But I'd love to bike again. Though down in the valley this time, not above it as we did then. I'd so much like to feel we're inside it. Like the locals who live down there. Not like most tourists who, I guess, just observe it from outside as we did yesterday.'

They cleared their breakfasts away. They brewed and drank another pot of coffee. They then, in the same clothes they had worn the day before, cycled up through the village to the crossroads. Instead of turning left to Salers, however, they went straight on.

They cycled along a road that soon careered steeply down the hillside and into the valley. As they freewheeled down the road, it echoed with the screeches and howls of protest of their brakes until they reached St Martin Valmeroux.

Here they left their bicycles outside the sombre stone church. They strolled along the handful of streets. They passed the two bakeries and the grocer's store. They walked between the houses that kept them for much of the time in the shadows.

Although it was close to mid morning, the streets were almost empty. But at one corner they passed two women. Both were well into middle age and were dressed from head to foot in black. Both were talking loudly and gesticulating to each other.

At another corner they came across three men. Two of them were in blue overalls and berets. The third was in a pair of mud-stained trousers held up by a broad leather belt, and in a sweat-stained shirt, its sleeves rolled up and its front buttons undone. All three were shouting and laughing. It was as if they had already had their first cognac or their first aperitif – or, quite possibly, both.

'My French is pretty dreadful,' she admitted. 'Or so my teacher used to tell me after she'd given us dictation which, once she'd marked it, put me close to the bottom of the class. But I can usually understand one or two of the words that somebody says. And, though not too often, whole sentences. But when I was listening just now, to the men as well as the women, I understood absolutely nothing. Not a single word.'

'If you'd been with me when my colleague gave me my briefing, you'd have understood perfectly well why you've understood absolutely nothing. Either they're talking with an accent that's hugely different from the schoolgirl French you used to learn. Or – and believe me I'm not joking – they're not speaking French at all.'

She looked at him and frowned. She was sure he was telling her the truth. She was, however, more than a little perplexed by what he had just said.

'So if it's not French, then what is it?'

'It's Auvergnat,' he replied with a smile. 'One of those

languages they used to speak all over the middle and the south of France. But I won't bore you to tears or send you to sleep, as I fear I did when I was telling you about the way I used to talk back in Dent. I'll give you a lecture on it some other time. And not a word of dictation, I promise you!'

From St Martin they cycled up the Maronne valley towards the mountains. Past single farms standing solidly, almost monumentally, along the roadside. Past the tiny hamlet of Le Theil. Over the stone bridge that crossed the river. On to the hillside village of St Paul de Salers. Here they decided, after a late-morning hot chocolate in a bar they had found open, to turn back.

'I'm not as hungry as I was yesterday,' she shouted as they set off. 'I certainly couldn't eat a horse. And I couldn't eat anything like as much as we ate in Salers. But a snack before we tackle the climb back up from St Martin. That I reckon I could just about manage.'

'And so you shall,' he shouted back.

He raced across the stone bridge with more speed and less control than he would have wished. He feared he would crash into one of its sides if not into the river, but luckily – and by no more than a few inches – he avoided disaster.

In St Martin they found a small restaurant at the edge of the village on the main road towards the city of Aurillac to their south. She forgot her modest aspiration to eat just a snack. They both forgot the previous day's excesses in Salers.

They worked their way steadily through course after course. Generous helpings of pâté de foie gras. Two trout that were so big they could almost have been mistaken for salmon. A plate of half a dozen or so local cheeses. And, finally, two oversized helpings of crème caramel. All this with a bottle of Chablis the patronne had strongly recommended to them.

'After what we've just eaten I'm not sure I can bike at all,' she declared, patting her stomach.

'At least let's try,' he replied. He looked at his watch, and told her: 'If we don't bike some of the way, I doubt if we'll be back much before sunset.'

For a few hundred yards, and already in low gear, they succeeded. But then they left the main road and started to climb the hill where they had been forced to brake so heavily on their way down. Here they abandoned the struggle and admitted defeat. They got off their bicycles and began the climb on foot.

It was a long, slow walk on an afternoon that was becoming more and more hot and humid. Every few minutes they stopped. Partly this was to get back their breath and mop their brows. Partly it was to look down at St Martin, which they saw now as a collection of grey roofs. Partly, too, it was to look at the Maronne valley, a rich kaleidoscope of greens and browns.

At last they reached the plateau with its small herds of cattle that had delighted her so much the day before. Here they got back on their bicycles and started to pedal again. Finally, for the last few relaxing minutes, they freewheeled down through the village to their house.

'What now?' he asked her after they had put the bicycles back in the barn and he had unlocked the door. 'What's better for your sore bottom? Hammock or bed?'

'Hammock first, then bed. And,' she added with a provocative smile he now easily and fully understood, 'what my bottom will need more than anything when it gets to bed will be a lot of tender, loving care.'

By the time they came back downstairs an hour or so later it was almost evening. They were more exhausted yet more contented than when they had gone up.

'You biked quite a few miles this morning,' he told her. 'You gorged yourself at lunchtime. You performed in bed this afternoon like a gymnast in her final weeks of training for the next Olympics. After all that, you can't have an ounce of energy left.'

'Even after all that, I might have just an ounce left. And with your encouragement, that ounce could keep me going until we climb back into bed – or even...' She winked at him and turned her head away demurely. '... with the right sort of encouragement from you, a little longer.'

'Then what I'd like to do is to take you on a magical mystery tour. One that'll be as much a mystery to me as it'll be to you. But, unless I'm making a bad mistake, it's one that'll be as magical as anything we've done here over these last couple of days.'

They walked together through the garden gate. Up a lane on the other side of the road. Past a long stone barn with rounded roof slates. Here they left the lane and clambered across the rough grass that covered the hillside.

Already they could hear the bleating of a flock of sheep, as well as the ringing of cowbells. Some were pitched high, others low. Some resonated, others sounded hollow as if the bells were fractured.

Above them they could hear the deep croaking of two ravens as these flew strongly towards the setting sun. They heard, too, the virtuoso performance of a solitary skylark whose song never faltered as it climbed higher and higher into the sky.

Somewhere in the distance they could hear the short call of what he told her was a hoopoe, as well as the braying of a donkey. Each was as repetitive and monotonous as the other. But both, so they thought, were as much a part of their pleasure as the elaborate song of the skylark.

Soon they reached a large stone, covered with moss, in the middle of a field. Here they sat down. Around them was a carpet of daisies and dandelions, clover and ragwort, and tufts of long grass flattened by each gust of wind from the south west.

On the edge of the field, and all in flower, were blackberry bushes, rose bushes and hawthorns. Above these were the branches of trees. Some were in constant and even violent motion. Others hardly moved, even when the wind blew most fiercely.

All the flowers and bushes and trees they saw were very familiar to them from their childhood onwards. But what lay in the far distance was a landscape that took their breath away. It was a landscape the like of which they had never seen before their arrival in the Auvergne. For what they saw were the mountains of the Massif Central.

One of the mountains closest to them, that they later discovered in their guidebook was the Puy Violent, had the dramatic profile of a volcano. The others, all further away and with some partly hidden by thin bands of cloud, were less obviously dramatic. They were rounded rather than jagged, soft rather than sharp.

Much of the higher ground on the mountain slopes was, as far as they could see, treeless. The lower ground, however, was covered with woods and open pastures. Everything they could see as they sat on the stone with the sun slowly setting behind them was hugely impressive and deeply memorable.

They sat almost silent, marvelling at everything they saw around them as the shadows cast by the trees edged slowly across the grass. Then, as the first dark cloud crept towards them from the south west, the sun disappeared. On the mountains in the far distance, though, it shone as brightly as it had done when they had first sat down.

'Enough?' he asked.

'Of this?' she asked in reply. 'For me, I can never get enough. Never.'

'But enough for now? Enough for you before the weather breaks? Which I'm sure it's going to do by sunset if not before.'

'All right,' she agreed reluctantly. 'Enough for now.'

The skylark was still serenading them from above. The cattle bells were still ringing from all sides. He stood up, pulled her to her feet in front of him. As so often that day and the day before, they held each other and kissed.

The last fragments of daylight were fast disappearing. The rain was beating down on the slate roof as it had done the evening before, but perhaps even more furiously. They sat facing each other.

Beside each of them were the glasses of wine she had poured while he had gathered enough firewood in the barn to last them for the whole evening. Between them was the fire whose flames once again lit up some parts of their faces, and left other parts in shadows.

'Just like yesterday, it's been a day I'll never forget,' she readily conceded as she looked at him over the flames.

'For me it's been exactly the same. Today and yesterday. One perfect day after another. It's just what you said when we were last sitting by the fire. And it wasn't corny at all. It's been like a love story where the only tears have been tears of joy.'

They each remembered the stories of their pasts they had told each other since they had first met. These were stories that had ended in tears – and tears of anything but joy. Now they smiled at each other through the flames, delighting in their good fortune.

'Yesterday, Stephen, you asked me to dig back into those memories of mine of my schoolgirl years. It wasn't easy to tell you what I'd kept hidden for most of my life. But let me be more accurate and more honest. Telling you about it was one of the most difficult things I've ever tried to do.'

'I think I understood that, Jo. Not completely. But at least a little.'

Her face revealed an impish smile as she looked directly at him. 'But what about you?' she asked. 'Did you glide easily and effortlessly through those boyhood years of yours? Or do you have a box of memories with a lid that's firmly shut?'

He looked briefly down at the burning logs. His mind was in overdrive as he tried to decide both what to tell her and how to tell it. After a few moments, he looked at her again.

'Compared with what you told me last night, my boyhood years were pretty easy. Unlike you, I was never given a hiding in any regular or predictable way. Though for me one of the horrors of a hiding was never knowing when I'd be given it.'

'Can you tell me about it? What did happen to you at home?'

'From the outside, everything looked calm, peaceful, even idyllic. My father was, as I've told you, the headmaster of my primary school. From everything I heard about him, he was greatly respected both in Dent and beyond.

'My mother must have been one of the most popular women in the village. One of the stalwarts of the Women's Institute. As respected as my father was. When they walked with my brother, my sister and me from our house at the edge of Dent to the middle of the village, we all held hands. A happy family if ever there was one.'

'So what did this family life of yours look like from the inside? What did it look like to you?'

'Time after time when my father was out, I watched my mother as she suddenly, and for no reason I could fathom, lost control. I watched her beat her chest with her fists. Bang her head against the kitchen wall. Kick the nearest door.

'And there were so many times when my father was at home in the evening and my brother, my sister and I were upstairs in bed. Times when I couldn't avoid hearing him as he shouted at her, and listening to her screams as he hit her.'

Yet again he looked down. He was silent, deep inside his own private world. When he continued, his eyes were fixed not on her but on the flames.

'Almost always when this happened I hid under the blankets. Put my hands over my ears. But once, just once, I tiptoed down the stairs. Stood at the bottom by the banister. Watched him in the sitting room as he slapped her across her face with the back of his hands. Watched her as she tried, though without any success, to protect herself.'

'So your mum was being violent to herself. Your dad was being violent to her. But awful as that must have been for you, weren't you for most of the time just an onlooker?'

'My mother wasn't the only one to feel the rough edge of his tongue and the back of his hand. I remember so very clearly those times when he exploded in an uncontrollable rage. When he screamed at me. When I felt his hand hit my face. When I felt the poker, the broom handle, that walking stick of his, hit my legs or my backside or my shoulders.'

He looked up. His eyes searched her face uncertainly and anxiously as he tried to discover how she reacted to what he was telling her.

'Even though they were always unpredictable, I know I should have been able to come to terms with his rages and his violence. To have accepted them as one of the facts of life. To have taken what he did to me if not like a man then at least not like a cry-baby. But even after years of his hidings, even when I was in my mid teens, I was no less shattered by them than I'd been the very first time he'd hit me.'

She looked at him across the fire. She was as full of sympathy and understanding for what had happened to him as he had been the evening before for what had happened to her.

'You've talked before,' she told him, 'about how badly you react to violence. Was what your mum did to herself and what your dad did to her and to you how it all began?'

'This was, I suppose, one of the reasons why I hated violence so much. One of the reasons why I wanted to be on my own. To be independent of other people. But another reason was what happened one day at school. I remember it so very well, as if it were yesterday, this morning, just a few minutes ago. Yet when I tell you how I coped with it, I'm afraid you'll be as unimpressed with me as I've always been with myself.'

'Can you tell me about that as well?' she asked. 'Can you tell me what happened to you?'

The evening before, when she was telling him about her father's violence and how she had reacted to it, there was both the pain of the memories themselves and the pleasure of sharing them at last. This evening, with that same mixture of emotions, he began to give her his account of that day.

'It was when I was seven or eight. I was strolling around by myself at the far end of the playground by the back wall. I was, I suppose, in a bit of a daydream. I'd just finished having my school milk. I was, as likely as not, waiting for the end of break.

'Three boys from the year above me ran over to me. They grabbed hold of me, frogmarched me into a corner. One of them held my hands behind my back. Another held my knees together to stop me from kicking. The third lifted up my pullover. Undid my belt and my fly buttons. Pulled down my shorts and then my pants.'

'My God! So what did you do?'

'I stood there, helpless and horrified, as they pulled and twisted and pinched those microscopic genitals of mine. I watched as a gaggle of girls from my class skipped towards me. When they saw what was going on, they burst into giggles. Then into peals of laughter. I couldn't hide myself. I was humiliated beyond belief. As I'd never been before or since.'

He looked down again at the burning logs. And when he looked up, it seemed to her he was doing just what he had done in the Nell Gwynne the day they had first met. He was looking not at her but past her, into the far distance.

'All at once, as they were absorbed with what they were doing to me, I lost control of my bladder. My tormenters found their hands soaked, and their jacket sleeves covered with splashes. Instead of pulling and twisting and pinching me, they now punched me with their fists and hit me with their knees.

'Then the bell went for the end of break. As soon as it rang, they ran off with the girls to the classrooms. I'm afraid all I did was collapse in tears on the ground.'

'And is this what you remember so well? What you can't forget?'

'For those boys it was probably no more than a minute or two of horseplay. No doubt they'd completely forgotten it by the end of school that afternoon. If not much sooner. For the girls it was, I'm sure, no more than a moment of innocent amusement. Forgotten just as soon. For me, though, it was devastating. And it's as impossible to forget now as it was then.'

'And what do you think it did to you?' she asked as soon as he had finished telling his story.

He snorted. Whether this was because of what he had just told her, or because of the answer he was about to give her, she had no idea.

'I became so very cautious and wary. Of other boys at school. Of late-night drinkers in Cambridge. Of alcoholic tramps in Lincoln's Inn Fields. Whenever I've seen even the remotest possibility of being attacked, I've got away as fast as I could.

'And whenever, after what had happened in the playground, I saw I might be dragged into an attack on another boy, I got away just as quickly. Even though these attacks happened quite often. Even though they ended almost as soon as they began. Even though the only damage was to the victim's dignity. Even though he might have thoroughly deserved it. Whatever mischief I might get up to with other boys, I'd decided hurting somebody else would never be on my agenda.

'Everything you've told me about your schoolgirl days may, as you've said, help to explain some of the things you've done in later life. It's just the same with what happened to me back in Dent. It may help to explain a lot of what I've told you about. And, whether I like it or not, it's baggage I'm going to be carrying with me for the rest of my life.'

'After what I've told you,' she observed, 'and after what you've just told me, we're in a new place. We have, you might say, left each other's secrets with no place to hide.'

'For better or for worse,' he replied, 'we've stripped each other nearly bare. We pulled off the outer leaves of our lives weeks ago. Along the canal, in Oxford, in Dent we pulled off some more. Now, I guess, we've pulled off almost every leaf. As you've just said, we've reached somewhere quite new.'

Without saying another word, he left his seat. He picked up some cushions from the chairs that were scattered around the room. He laid them next to each other on the floor in front of the fire.

'Come here,' he whispered, beckoning her to join him.

She stood up. As if in a trance, she walked over to him. Slowly, almost methodically, he took off her clothes. He folded her T-shirt and leggings and underclothes, and put them together on the table. She stood in front of him, one side of her body in shadows, the other side lit up by the flames.

'Lie down,' he told her in the same quiet voice which

was, though, a voice that commanded rather than asked.

She kneeled on the cushions, stretched out, rolled over onto her back. He stood looking at her, enchanted by her body. He took off his own clothes and put them by hers. He lay down with her, felt the warmth of her body.

The flames flickered beside them. The smell of burning wood surrounded them. They held each other in as tight and eager an embrace as they had ever known in their weeks together.

'I feel now we're journeying into what's new territory for both of us,' she whispered in return. 'Somewhere you and I have never been before.'

'I'm moving closer to you than I've ever been. And I feel closer to you now than I've been to anyone.'

'Those two leaves floating down the river. They're not just bobbing along beside each other now. They're as firmly joined as could be.'

'The earth is moving for me now as it's never moved before in my life. And, perhaps, it's about to move even more.'

When they woke a little before midnight, they found they were still lying on the cushions he had put down in front of the fire some hours before. There were now no flames leaping up the chimney, no hissing of water trapped in branches, no sweet smell of burning wood.

Instead there was a red glow of embers under the blackened logs. There were thin and occasional coils of smoke climbing upwards. There was a gentle heat warming rather than scorching their skin.

Very slowly, still more asleep than awake, they stood up. Forgetting their clothes on the table, they walked across the room from the fireside to the door. As they walked into the garden, drops of water were still dripping off the roof and off the lime tree onto the grass. But the rain itself, so torrential when they had fallen asleep, had stopped.

The leaves of the lime were shivering in a breeze from the west. Bands of clouds moved relentlessly across the night sky. They were lit up clearly when they parted to reveal the moon. They were indistinct when they hid the moon behind them.

But Joanna and Stephen saw nothing of the leaves, the moon, the clouds. Nor did they hear the water drip down or feel the breeze caress their bodies. They heard only a nightingale that, as soon as they began to listen to it, filled their world with its overwhelmingly beautiful song.

They listened in silence. Whether it was for minutes or for much longer they had no idea. They were aware neither of time nor of place. Both of them sensed that this was one of the most magical, most memorable, moments of their lives. They sensed, too, that it was a moment neither of them would ever be able to forget.

As they stood there, just outside the door, the rain began again. First it fell lightly, then as heavily as it had fallen a few hours before. The roar of thunder echoed up and down the valley. Forked lightning tore the sky apart and lit up the clouds. The nightingale fell silent.

They were, however, as oblivious to what was now happening around them as they had been when they had first walked outside. They felt nothing of the rain that splashed against them and trickled down their bodies. They saw nothing of the lightning. They heard nothing of the thunder.

All they did was to listen to the nightingale, now singing in their memories as powerfully and magically as it had sung before the storm had silenced it. They were now in what both of them felt was a state of ecstasy. One that was greater than they had ever known.

'The earth is moving again,' he told her, 'even more than it did when we came together by the fire before we fell asleep.'

'Even though,' she replied, 'since we came out here I haven't even touched you. Nor have you touched me.'

'It's what you said yesterday. It's what I said again today. It's a love story whose only tears are tears of joy.'

They turned towards each other. They put their arms round each other's rain-wet bodies.

'*Nightly she sings in yond pomegranate tree,*' he whispered.

'*Believe me, love,*' she whispered in reply, '*it was the nightingale.*'

CHAPTER NINE

'So begins our third day together in paradise!' declared Stephen with mock solemnity.

'Another wonderful day I'm sure we'll always remember,' Joanna replied with heartfelt passion.

Still in the clothes they had worn on their first two days in the Auvergne, they were lying out on their hammocks in the garden, with the sun high in the sky to the south east. The night storm had passed. The dawn breeze had faded. Only a few small clouds, almost transparent and hardly moving, hung above them.

After they had slept by the fire the evening before, and after they had listened by the door to the nightingale, their sleep was even longer and heavier than it had been on their first two nights. In the morning, after they had woken up and after they had made love, they decided to have breakfast outside again.

One baguette was completely finished. Another was already started. Their first pot of coffee was almost empty. They agreed to lie out on the hammocks and do precisely nothing for the rest of the morning.

They agreed, too, that the only exception to this would be to make some more coffee and to eat a myrtle tart. They decided to postpone until the afternoon or even later the visit they had thought of making to some of the villages beyond Giroux.

He was daydreaming, his mind floating from one memory to another, about the delights of their last two days. She was recollecting the pleasures of their last two nights, until a quite different thought leaped without warning into her mind.

'When we went up to Oxford, you'd got with you a letter from your wife. A letter you'd already opened and read. When we were by Camden Lock and in Dentdale, you'd got with you letters of hers you hadn't even opened, let alone read.'

She looked directly at him, straight into his eyes, as he had so often looked into hers. 'What about this time?' she asked him. 'Have you had another letter? Did you leave it behind in London? Or is it somewhere here in Giroux?'

He looked up into the sky. He was at the same time smiling and sighing.

'Yes, I've had another letter,' he admitted. 'No, I didn't leave it in London. Yes, I've got it here in my rucksack. No, as I guess you've guessed, I haven't even opened it.'

He turned to her. He stretched out his hand from his hammock to hers, stroked her arm. 'You might think I didn't want to open it because I was a coward. Or because I didn't want it to damage these days of ours in paradise. Or both. Now, though, I'm well prepared for whatever she might throw at me. And the truth's quite different. These days with you here have been so wonderful I'd totally forgotten about it. At least until you reminded me just now.'

'So what, I wonder, does she say this time?'

He swung easily off his hammock. He strolled into the house as if he had not a care in the world. A minute or so later, he returned with an envelope.

'Here it is!' he announced, holding it up above his head and waving it. 'The latest and, no doubt, the greatest piece of her vindictiveness so far.'

He tore the envelope open so much more confidently than he had done at Camden Lock and in Dentdale. He was, she noticed, so much less nervous, less hesitant than he had been then. He manoeuvred himself back onto his hammock. Swinging slowly from side to side, he held the letter against his knees and began to read.

'*After much thought and much agonising, I now deeply regret everything I put into my earlier letters. I am, indeed, greatly ashamed I ever wrote them.*

'*I offer you my unreserved apologies for having made all the threats I did and, even more, for having carried out so many of them.*

'*I apologise, too, for my acts of violence against you over the years which, had you at any time come back to me, I would, I promise you, never have repeated.*

'*I fully recognise how grossly thoughtless and inconsiderate I have been. It is I who have failed you, and not in any way the reverse.*'

He stopped abruptly. 'What the hell!' he exclaimed. On his face she saw a surprise and puzzlement at least as great as her own.

'I don't understand,' she told him.

'Nor,' he replied, 'do I.'

Her surprise was that everything she had just heard was so unlike what he had read her in those earlier letters. He, too, was surprised that everything he had just read was wholly unlike what his wife had written to him before. His surprise was also that it was so very different from what she had said to him in those months, even years, before he had left her.

'What does she go on to say?'

He glanced at the next sentences. She saw a frown begin to grow deeper across his forehead. His heart was beating more quickly. He was now beginning to feel confused and bewildered as well as surprised and puzzled. He started to read her the next couple of paragraphs in a voice that was becoming quieter and quieter.

'*I have come to understand that you must be free to do whatever you wish, whenever you wish, and with whomsoever you wish. I have come to realise, perhaps belatedly, that your actions are now none of my concern.*

'*At the same time I have come to realise the corollary of this. It is that I must be equally free. It is, moreover, that my actions are now no concern of yours.*'

The expression on his face had changed dramatically since he had begun to read the letter to her. What she now saw was dismay and alarm.

'What in God's name does she mean?' she asked. 'Does she really accept you've got to be free? And to be with anybody you want to be?'

For her, this seemed to be something they should both welcome. But the frown on his brow she had first seen a few minutes before was becoming even deeper.

'You've focussed on the first part of what I've just read you,' he told her. 'I'm focussing on the second part. That what she does is none of my business.'

He looked at the letter again. In an even quieter voice, he read on.

'*I am, though you may not know it, overwhelmingly sad that the man whom I loved to distraction is no longer with me. I am, I think, saddest of all that I never had the good fortune to have his child.'*

He closed his eyes. Using his left hand, he pressed his thumb against one eyelid and his forefinger against the other. After he had opened them again, he blinked several times before he read on.

'The consequence of this extreme sadness is that I have, at last, come to see my future quite clearly. As my reason for living disappeared with your departure, I shall, one day before too long, depart myself.'

She saw his hands begin to shake as he put the letter down on his chest. She saw, too, some of the colour was starting to drain from his face. She watched one tear, then another, crawl across his cheeks and down his neck.

'I can't believe she's written this to me,' he told her in a voice that was cracking with emotion. He suddenly shuddered. His whole body shook. 'Because of what I've done to her, she's telling me she's going to kill herself.'

Until this moment, she had felt quite calm. Now her calm began to collapse. She felt a flood of uncertainties begin to engulf her. 'Could she really mean what she says?' she asked. 'Do you believe she could ever do that to herself?'

'How in Christ's name can I know?' he replied. 'How can I possibly know?'

He brushed the tears from his face with his knuckles. He picked up the letter from his chest. With his hands still trembling, he held it in front of him again.

'It will in no way be a dramatic exit and, just to reassure you, there will be no final letter blaming you for what I have done. This is, indeed, the very last letter I shall write you.'

He shook his head slowly from side to side in disbelief. He pressed the palm of one hand against his forehead as he struggled to continue.

'My exit will, on the contrary, be quiet and unobtrusive. There will, to misquote one of your favourite writers, be no bang and no whimper.'

In his face she saw a deep despair and dread as he looked into the far distance. It was the gaze she had come to know since she had first seen it in the Nell Gwynne. Then, though, it had been much less intense than it was now.

'No bang and no whimper,' he echoed in a voice that cracked even more than it had done a minute or so before, and that she could hardly hear.

She felt a great divide was beginning to open up between them. It was like a crevasse in an Alpine glacier, though growing so much faster than any crevasse. And it was, she sensed, growing with each moment that passed.

'Is that all?' she asked in a voice now as quiet as his.

Without looking at her he shook his head. Instead he concentrated on reading the neat handwriting to the bottom of the page.

'After the funeral I would urge you to do everything you can to forget the times, even the good times, we had together, and to do your best to forget that I ever existed.

'Above all I would urge you to enjoy your life and to live it to the full. I had hoped to have played some part in helping you to do this, but in this, as in so much else, I failed you.

'My only remaining hope is that you achieve in your professional and, far more importantly, in your private life, the success and fulfilment you so richly deserve.'

She watched his face with foreboding as more tears trickled across his cheeks. He was now more distraught than she had ever seen him. She felt her own tears filling her eyes.

Though he told her neither what he was thinking nor what he was feeling, she knew the letter had moved him profoundly. She also knew it had catapulted him, at a stroke, far away from her.

'What can I say?' she asked helplessly. 'What can I do?'

For several minutes, perhaps longer, he said nothing. His mind was a battleground of conflicting thoughts. Conflicting feelings churned around relentlessly inside him. In front of his eyes he saw a blackness filled with coloured points of light. These gyrated, vibrated, swung in and out of focus. He felt suddenly as if he was going to faint.

Through her tears, she watched him walk away, though so much more slowly than they had walked the afternoon before. He climbed up the lane towards the hillside pasture where they had sat together, so happily and with such delight, on that afternoon.

'I don't know what to think. Though I know I have to think,' he had told her as he set off. 'And I've got no idea what to do. No idea at all. Though I have to do something. All I know now is I need to be, I have to be, alone.'

It was just past midday when he walked round a corner of the lane and disappeared. Soon after that, and to be ready for his return, she put some ham and cheese on the garden table. She carried out the baguette they had begun at breakfast. She opened another bottle of wine and set it down with two glasses in the middle of the table.

Two hours later he had still not returned. She put the food and drink back in the house. She sat down on the grass in a corner of the garden. She tried to start reading a book of poems she had brought with her but had not had time even to open since their arrival. She found to her distress, though not to her surprise, she could not manage to concentrate even on the first poem, and put the book down.

She tried to look at the trees in the valley below her, their leaves swaying just a little. At the high clouds lazing across the sky. At the butterflies around her that danced from one flower to the next. But she found nothing to divert her from her growing anxiety and apprehension.

As the afternoon wore on, and as she looked down at her watch more and more often, so this anxiety and apprehension deepened. After everything his wife had written in her earlier letters, could she possibly mean that she and not he was at fault?

And could she possibly mean to do what she said she would do and end her life? She read and reread the letter he had left on his hammock. Even after she had done this, however, she had no answer to either question.

Would he be able to seize the freedom his wife seemed to be offering him? To begin a new life, perhaps a life with herself? Or would he be thinking only about the rest of what she had written? And, if that, what would he decide to do?

Again, hard as she tried to think clearly, and to think as he might be thinking, she found no answers that even remotely satisfied her. Instead she found more and more questions, doubts, uncertainties. These ricocheted incoherently and endlessly in her mind.

By four o'clock the shadows cast by the trees had begun to lengthen. Her anxiety and apprehension had grown so great that all clarity of thought had abandoned her. She had already stood time after time at the garden gate, looking up and down the road and up the lane where she had last seen him. She had already walked up the lane and back more times than she could remember.

She had heard footsteps. She had seen one man walking towards her down the road from the crossroads. She had noticed another man walking up the road from the bridge at the other end of the village. Neither, however, was Stephen. Both were villagers on their way home from the fields.

By six o'clock she was more alarmed than she had been at any time in her life. She had, for much of the afternoon, tried to comfort herself by recognising there was so much he had to think about. She also remembered, as he had told her so often, he very much valued being on his own.

She had, too, tried to convince herself he had lost his way among the hills and valleys around Giroux. That he had been trying to reach the nearest house he could find to ask where he was. That he would soon be back. But he had been gone for almost six hours. Her only certainty was that something, though what it was she did not know, was very wrong.

Almost without thinking, and in spite of wanting nothing to eat herself, she laid out on the table in the house the food and drink she had laid out hours earlier in the garden. She then sat dejectedly on the grass in a corner of the garden. Suddenly, shortly before eight o'clock, with the heat of the day gone and the light beginning to fade, he opened the gate.

Without a glance to his left or right, he walked past her into the house. She was shocked because he had walked past her without any word of greeting and without any recognition she was there. She was even more shocked because of the way he had been walking.

They had walked together along the Thames towpath at Hammersmith, along the towpath of the Grand Union Canal, in Oxford, in Dentdale, here in the Auvergne. Whenever they had done this, she had always found it difficult, and sometimes quite impossible, to match his pace. What she saw now was a walk that was hesitant and heavy. It was more the walk of someone old and exhausted than of a young man in his prime.

From the day they had first met at the National Gallery, too, she had always seen him walk upright. It was not as if he were on parade. But it was not far short of that. Now what she saw was a bent-back figure. It was as if he had passed his day in heavy labour in the fields. It was as if he were carrying the troubles of the world on his shoulders.

With her heart suddenly beating much faster, she stood up. She followed him into the house. She found him sitting at one side of the fireplace. In the half dark, and with the fire unlit, she could not see many of the details of his face. But what she could see shocked her even more than the way he had walked.

In the hours he had been gone, the skin of his face seemed to her to have crumpled, sagged, collapsed. She was sure the deep lines she saw on his brow had not been there when he had walked off. Nor had there been the lines that now cut deeply down each cheek.

But what shocked her most was the change in the colour of his face. It was now a pale grey that was almost white. And the skin below his eyes was now a dark grey that was almost black. His eyes themselves were dull and bloodshot. As they had done just before he had gone up the lane, they were staring emptily into the far distance.

She was, she thought, looking at the face of a man not of thirty but, perhaps, of almost twice that age. He looked more like an inmate of Auschwitz or Dachau than a barrister of Lincoln's Inn.

'Are you all right, Stephen?' she asked as she stood in front of the fireplace.

She knew he was not. But she did not know what else that was more thoughtful, less banal, she could say or ask. He turned his head slowly, almost painfully. For a few moments, he looked in her direction. He did not, though, look at her, not into her eyes.

'Please tell me,' she pleaded. 'Please.'

He turned away. He turned his empty gaze back towards the far distance. He looked at what she could never see.

'What have you been thinking?' she asked.

Without answering her questions and without appearing to see she was sitting opposite him in the fireplace, he looked down into the ashes and cinders. These were all that remained of the fire that had warmed them as they had slept beside it the night before. Now they were cold and dead.

'What have you made up your mind to do?' she pleaded in a voice that at once betrayed her turmoil. 'And how can I help you – which is what I want to do more than anything in the world?'

For the first time since he had come back, he looked directly at her across the ashes and cinders. 'You can help me most, Jo, by trying to understand. To understand what I've been thinking and feeling. To understand what I've made up my mind to do.'

'I'll do my best,' she replied as her heart sank to new depths of distress. 'I'll try to understand.'

He held his hands together tightly on his knees. He looked down at them so that she could see little of his face apart from his forehead. He cleared his throat.

'I'd expected that letter to be like all the others. Accusations. Threats. Anger. Hostility.' He cleared his throat again. 'I'd never expected a letter like that. Never, as they say, in a month of Sundays.'

His voice broke. It was only with a great effort of will he was able to carry on. 'I could cope with whatever she might say about me. With whatever she threatened to do to me. After all these years that's water off a duck's back. But with what she's threatened to do to herself? That I can't begin to cope with.'

She had tried to stay silent, to listen. She could not, though, hold back the question she had been asking herself so often that afternoon as she had waited for him to return.

'How honest do you think she's being with you? Is she really being serious when she makes those threats about what she'll do to herself? Or is she deceiving you? Playing some sort of game with you? Trying a last throw of the dice to get you to go back to her?'

'That I don't know. Though the threats she made to write to my parents and my brother and sister she carried out to the letter. And the threats she made to destroy my clothes and books and photos? Unless I'm very much mistaken, they've been carried out as well.'

'But surely what she's threatening now is something completely different.'

'Of course it is. I don't know, though, if she's serious or not. I can't be sure.' He breathed deeply, once, twice, three times. 'And because I don't know, because I can't be sure, because I've got enough humanity or common decency or whatever you like to call it in me, I can't take the risk. If I were to be wrong, if she were to end her life one way or another, I could never begin to live with myself. Not for a second.'

He was still looking down at his hands which were clenched tightly. She was still looking at his face. She was trying to understand him through the language of his eyes and his mouth, as well as through what he was saying to her.

'So what is it you've decided to do?'

He clenched his hands even more tightly. He screwed up his face in what she could only interpret as a demonstration of the pain he was suffering. When at last he spoke, it was in a strangled voice she could hardly hear. She could understand him only with great difficulty.

'I have to go back to her. And sooner rather than later. There's nothing else for it. It's the only thing I can do.'

It was the answer she had feared most of all. It was also the answer she had admitted to herself more and more throughout the afternoon and evening that he might give her. She closed her eyes. She felt her head throb out of control as the blood raced through it. After a silence of minutes that felt to her as if they were hours, she forced herself to put her final question.

'What about us?' she asked. In spite of her best efforts, she added the question she had most wanted to avoid asking: 'And what about me?'

'My heart's heavier, far heavier, than it's ever been in this pathetic life of mine. I'm more reluctant to do what I'm going to do than you can ever imagine. But I'm going to have to give you up, Jo. I'm going to have to go against all my better instincts, against my better judgment. I'm going to have to abandon you.'

Again, though only for a short time, he looked directly

at her. His eyes filled with tears as they had done when he had read the letter to her that morning.

'Even though it's the very last thing in the world I want to do. Even though I'll be losing the woman I've loved and valued more than anyone else in the world. The woman I've felt closer to than anyone I've ever known.'

He reached over to her across the ashes and cinders. He held her hand almost fiercely. 'With you,' he continued, 'the earth has done much more than move. With you, I've discovered no man is an island. I've come to realise we aren't always by ourselves. But I know what I have to do. Whether I like it or not, whether I want it or not, I can do no other.'

Her tears were now as plentiful as his, if not more so. And when she spoke she, too, was strangling her words. 'Without you,' she asked him, 'what can I do? I love you so much. Just as you loved me. I feel so close to you. Just as you felt close to me. I can't begin to imagine what it'll be like to be on my own again. To be without you.'

Her voice, though not the flow of her tears, dried up. Although his afternoon had been spent in deep thought about what he should do, he now tried his best to think of her predicament rather than his own.

'I can't give you an answer that's any better than hopeless. In those weeks we were together, from morning to night, I thought of you and forgot almost everybody and everything else. Every day I was living for the moment I'd see you next.

'Every time I saw you I was in a state of delight. Sometimes I was in a state of what I can only describe as ecstasy. But to be absolutely and brutally honest with you, I can't, I mustn't, think of you now.'

He closed his eyes, perhaps, she thought, in an

admission of total defeat. He turned his mask face away from her.

'If it weren't such a total obscenity, I'd echo to you what my wife wrote to me in that letter. That you should do everything you can to forget the times, even the good times, we had together. That you should do your best to forget I ever existed.'

She gasped in absolute horror at what he had just said. She cupped her hands and pressed them as hard as she could against her cheeks. Although she had had nothing to eat or drink since breakfast, she was suddenly and violently sick.

He stood up. He stepped awkwardly away from the fireplace. Without going over to her to comfort her, without looking at her, without a word more, he shuffled across the room.

He passed the untouched supper on the table and reached the foot of the stairs. She heard each step creak as he trod heavily on it. She heard the creak of the floorboards in the bedroom above her. Then silence.

For some time – how long it was she had no idea – she sat shivering in front of the dead fire. She did not feel the sick that had soaked through her dress and was now sticking to her breasts. Nor did she feel the tears that kept slithering down her face.

At last she, too, stood up. She walked across the room, climbed the stairs. She crawled into the other side of the bed from the side where he lay. She turned away from him to face the wall.

She wanted to close her mind, end her nightmare in sleep. But for some absurd reason she could not begin to understand, she found herself remembering *Ragnarok*, the Norse myth of the Doom of the Gods, that she had last read at college.

'*The sun grows black,*' she whispered to herself in the darkness. '*The earth sinks into the sea. The bright stars vanish from the heavens.*'

As she finished, the awful truth began to sledgehammer itself into her head. Her days of heaven were over. All she had to look forward to was an eternity of hell.

They reached the Gare du Nord the next day after a long and difficult journey. It had taken a succession of early-morning phone calls for him to find a local taxi in St Martin or Salers to take them back to Clermont Ferrand.

They had missed by a whisker the fast train they had hoped to catch. They had reached Paris at the height of the rush hour. Their metro journey across Paris to the Gare du Nord had been an ordeal for which they were hopelessly unprepared.

They had said little to each other during their hurried and unwanted breakfast, their brushing and dusting of the house, their taxi journey to the station, their hours in the train. Both had been imprisoned in their own thoughts of the empty future that stretched ahead of them to the horizon and beyond.

All he had said of substance was he would need to do whatever he could to prepare himself for his return to his wife. He would stay on in Paris for at most a couple of days. All she had said was she would have to be back at school the next Monday at the end of her half-term holiday. Apart from these brief, bald statements of their intentions, there had been silence broken only by a few awkward and embarrassing platitudes.

At the Gare du Nord, they were surrounded by the bustle of passengers and porters. The train for Calais was already beside them on the platform. They stood facing each other. They knew neither what to say nor how to say it. He held out his hand. She held it in hers.

She looked at him. His face was grey and empty. It was no different from the one she had seen the evening before when he had come back to the house.

He returned her gaze. He saw a face that seemed to him to have been shipwrecked and shattered by a storm. It was no different from the one he had seen whenever he had looked away from the train window on the way to Paris and glanced guiltily towards her. Both of them looked – and felt – incalculably sad.

There were a few minutes still to go before the train was scheduled to depart. He carried her luggage on board. He found her a seat next to a window. He put her bags down on the seat, and walked back to the carriage door. She followed him passively, automatically.

At the open door he leaned towards her. He kissed her for the last time on her forehead, then on both cheeks, then on her lips, as he had kissed her that first time by the Thames. She kissed him lightly, just for a moment, and only on his lips. With their voices fractured and choking, they whispered their goodbyes.

He stepped down onto the platform, turned round, closed the carriage door. She stood at the open window. The crowds seeing off their friends and relatives stood back. Infinitely slowly, the train began to move.

He saw her raise one hand. She made what he thought was a little wave. For a moment, no more, he thought he saw a small, uncertain smile as she looked towards him for the last time.

This wave and this smile were burned deeply into his memory. So deep were they that, whenever he thought of her in later years, he could recall them as clearly as if he had just seen them. And, just as often, when he least expected them, they leaped into his mind with that same overwhelming clarity.

As the train began to move less slowly, she saw him return her wave with an almost imperceptible wave of his own. She, too, could recall it in later life with total and undiminished clarity. She, too, found it flashed uninvited into her mind, even when she was at the extremes of intimacy with another man.

After a couple of minutes, perhaps more, perhaps less, in which it had begun to gather speed, the train pulled out of the Gare du Nord. Except in their memories, they could no longer see each other.

The two leaves they had talked about in their weeks together had been torn apart. They had sunk without trace. What for both of them had been the greatest relationship of their lives now belonged only to their past.

Whatever future they might have, the one certainty was that it would not be a future together. Their love story had ended in tears – not of joy, but of desolation.

CHAPTER TEN

'Stephen?'

He turns round in total disbelief outside the tube station at the corner of High Holborn and Kingsway. For he has just heard a voice he remembers so clearly.

It is a voice he has replayed in his memory so many thousands, if not tens of thousands, of times over the years. It is a voice that is gentle and uncertain. And it has hardly changed or, perhaps, changed not at all, since he last heard it.

As he turns, he catches sight of the face he last saw all those years ago when they parted in tears of desolation at the Gare du Nord. It is a little older, a little fuller. It has not, though, suffered significantly from the ravages of time.

And, so he sees in these first few seconds, it has lost none of the kaleidoscope of expressions that so entranced him in those few weeks in England and those few days in France when they were together.

Her green eyes are, maybe, even quieter than they were. But they still flash and sparkle as they used to do. The dark brown of her hair has lost some of its richness. But it still falls profusely and wildly over her black leather jacket.

'Jo!'

She remembers so very clearly the voice she last heard when they said their goodbyes in broken whispers at the station. It is a little deeper now. Yet, even with one single word, it opens a huge floodgate of memories.

These pour in an uncontrolled torrent through her mind as she looks at his face. It is more lined than she remembers it, more worn. It is not, though, at least as far as she can see, much more careworn.

His black hair is now even shorter than it was. Especially above his ears, it is flecked with grey. Yet those deep-set brown eyes look at her with an intensity that has lost none of the depth that captivated her all those years ago.

He is, or so she thinks, wearing the same brown suede jacket he had on when they first met. She suspects, too, he is wearing the same navy blue trousers he had on when they walked along the canal.

'Can it be...' she asks hesitantly. 'Can it be twenty years?'

They stand facing each other on the edge of the pavement. Early-spring shoppers surround them at the traffic lights. Street tradesmen close by offer their fruit and vegetables and flowers, their newspapers and magazines. Cars, taxis, buses, lorries edge past.

His heart is racing out of control. His throat is suddenly dust-dry. Without thinking whether she would want him to or not, he puts his arms round her shoulders. In response, and blushing and shaking as she has not done for many years, she puts her arms round his waist. As he first did that afternoon when they met outside her school, he pulls her gently towards him and kisses her on her forehead.

He feels her soft skin that he last kissed that terrible evening in Paris. He smells the same perfume he used to know so well. It is a perfume that, whenever he has smelled it in the years after their parting, has overwhelmed him with memories.

'Yes,' he replies. 'It must be twenty years. Perhaps a little less than that since we parted. Perhaps a little more than that since we met.'

She feels his lips, dry yet soft, on her forehead. She feels his heart beating against her breasts, with his body firm against hers. She remembers those lips that once kissed her with a passion she had never known before in her life and has never known since. She remembers that heart pounding faster and faster until it suddenly quietened.

She remembers that body exciting her and filling her with delight. It was, she realises, all little less than half a lifetime – or at least little less than half her lifetime – ago.

'I can't begin to believe we've met each other again,' she whispers.

'I can't believe it's so long ago since we were together.'

He stands back and looks at her as she smiles. It is a smile which is just as he remembers it. She listens to him as he laughs. It is that soft laugh she has heard so often in her memory.

'In some ways, Stephen,' she tells him, 'it's as if we parted in another century. In another life.'

'But in other ways, Jo,' he replies, 'it's as if it was only yesterday.' After a moment of silence he adds: 'Though this must sound ridiculous and nonsensical – and that's probably exactly what it is – in these ways it's as if there's been no twenty years between now and then.'

'What happened to you after that awful goodbye?' she asks. 'Did you stay on in Paris as you said you would? And what did you do then?'

'What did you do on your journey after the train pulled out?' he asks in return. 'And what did you do when you got back to London?'

These – and many other – questions they ask each other as they walk together down Kingsway, along Bow Street where they pass the Royal Opera House, and through Covent Garden where she remembers her visits to listen to street music during her student days. He is looking almost all the time at her. She is looking both at him and, though he does not notice, around them.

He has suggested that the Nell Gwynne is as good a place as any to celebrate their chance meeting. She, with a mixture of delight and uncertainty, has agreed that, for old times' sake, nowhere could be better.

When they reach the Nell Gwynne – along one street where, so they discover, Jane Austen had stayed, and by another where Charles Dickens had worked – they sit down at the same corner table where they sat on their last visit.

The table is still copper-topped, still with iron legs. The windows still seem to let in little light. Though they are now orange, the lamps are still dim. Though there is now a large television set in one corner, it is switched off, and the pub is as dark now as it was then.

He has bought her a campari and soda, and himself a draught bitter. These are, he remembers, the very same drinks they had on their first meeting that Easter Saturday.

For a few minutes they sit in silence, overcome by what has happened. They look at each other, seeing both what has changed in their faces after twenty years and what has not.

What they see of each other becomes imprinted on their minds. But these are already teeming with memories of those weeks together, between their meeting in front of *Venus and Mars* and their parting at the Gare du Nord.

'There are hundreds if not thousands of questions I want to ask you,' he tells her. 'But there's one I've got to ask you first.'

'And what's that?'

He hesitates, not knowing if it is something he should ask her now, or later, or never. 'Did you ever write to me at that flat I used to have in Kensal Rise? Did you ever try to phone me at my chambers in Lincoln's Inn?'

She replies – and not for the first time since they first met – with a question rather than an answer: 'We've got much bigger and better things to talk about. But did you ever try to contact me?'

Instead of giving her an answer, he follows her example and asks another question. 'I've got something much more awkward to ask you.' Again he hesitates. Then, in a whisper, he asks her what he has asked himself so often. 'Did you soon find someone else?'

Her cheeks redden, as he has so often seen them redden before. Her eyes look down at her empty glass. She is very conscious she is about to tread on ground he might find painful in the extreme. Yet she replies with yet another question of her own. It is the question she has asked herself more than any other.

'Did you...' For a minute she loses her voice. 'Did you go back to your wife as you said you would?'

He closes his eyes. His face becomes, in an instant, much older. It does, but not to the same extent, what it did that day in Giroux after he had read that final letter from her.

'I don't think this is the time for answers,' he replies. 'At least not answers to the sorts of questions we're asking each other.'

'With this,' she agrees, 'I'm with you all the way.'

Just as suddenly, his face brightens. It becomes younger again. 'I've got an idea. It's absurd in the extreme. And if you say *no* you'll be saying what anyone in her right mind would say. You'll be avoiding making a mistake anyone in her right mind would be sure to avoid.'

'So what is it?' she asks. 'What is this absurd idea of yours?'

She looks at him quizzically, as she so often used to do in their past.

'It's to ask you to have dinner with me this evening.'

For a moment, she is confused and agitated. Then she bursts out laughing. 'As I said to you once before, a long time ago, being asked isn't the mistake. The mistake is in agreeing.'

'So, as I once asked you, will you make the mistake?'

'And, as I answered you then, it's not that I will. It's that I already have.'

They laugh together. They both remember that first exchange of theirs in front of Botticelli's painting.

'But I'm a bit wiser to the ways of the world than I was when I was in my mid twenties. I will come to dinner with you. Only, though, on two conditions.'

'The first?'

'It's that, if you've got a few minutes to spare in whatever you're doing in life these days, we walk along to the National Gallery. And we look at a painting which is, for better or for worse, very special for both of us.'

More memories dash through his mind. They jostle each other as they race around.

'Agreed,' he replies. 'And the second?'

'I reckon it's the same time of year, given a week or two, as when we first met. My second condition is that we have another drink... to celebrate your birthday.'

'What a beautiful face,' she whispers, though looking as she did twenty years ago at the body of the vanquished Mars.

'What a beautiful body,' he replies, though looking as he did then at the face of the victorious Venus.

'You've stolen my line!' she complains.

'Just as you've stolen mine!' he retorts.

They look at each other as they did when they last stood together in front of *Venus and Mars*. Just as they did then, they burst out laughing.

'Is this the first time you've seen it since that Easter Saturday,' she asks him.

'Not the first time. Nor the second. Nor the twenty second. I've come here to see it so often I can't remember how often it's been.'

He believes what he has just said is a statement of the obvious. For her, however, it is a statement that is far from obvious.

'If it's not too hard a question for you to answer,' she asks, 'can you tell me why?'

'I could tell you, as I've told you before, it's because Renaissance paintings are my favourites. And there are so many of these favourites of mine here. I could tell you I'd hardly be able to avoid coming to see this one even if I wanted to. I could tell you it's because the painting is so brilliant I have to look at it again and again. But that's not the real truth. I'll be as honest with you as you always were with me. It's as far from the real truth as it could be.'

'So what is the real truth? Why have you come to see it again and again?'

She fears she is crossing a boundary into his private world. She expects he will reply with silence, or with that look into the far distance, or with both. He looks, however, directly at her. He is silent for no more than a moment.

'I don't come here so much because of the painting. I come because of the memories it opens up for me. I could very easily have thought of you, thought of us, anywhere and at any time. And, of course, I did.'

He feels for her hand, holds it, tightens his grip. 'It may sound rather strange to you, but when I stand here in front of *Venus and Mars*, I remember every word we said to each other then. Whether I like it or not, it gives another dimension, a greater depth, to my memories.

'Just like those countless times when I've been on the towpath by Hammersmith Bridge. When I've sat in Lincoln's Inn gardens. When I've gone along the canal to Little Venice. When I've walked around Oxford. When I've trekked in Dentdale.'

He releases his grip. Instead, he puts an arm round her shoulder. 'And for you, Jo? Is it the same?'

She can hardly believe what she has heard. She cannot think how to reply. She can manage, as she begins to blush again, only to repeat one of her replies from one of their early encounters.

'*Yes*, Stephen. *Yes and no.*'

After a minute or more, in which his arm has stayed round her shoulder and has, perhaps, pulled her a little closer to him, she feels able to give him her answer.

'I've never been here again. Nor by the Thames. Nor – except once – in Lincoln's Inn. Nor by the canal. Nor – except to go to my dad's funeral and to visit my mum at Christmas – to Oxford. And never again to any of the dales.'

She looks at his face. She sees it is saddened by what she has told him. He looks at her face. He tries to decode at least some of the messages he can see flickering across it.

'It's not that I didn't want to go,' she continues. 'It's not that I wanted to wipe the slate clean. Block out the memories.'

'So why not? Why didn't you go?'

She begins to blush even more. She looks away from him as she replies.

'To have gone again with you would have been beyond my wildest dreams. To have gone again without you would have been nothing short of a nightmare. But that's only part of the story. And it's not the most important part.'

He looks at her, frowns. He raises his eyebrows in the hope this will encourage her to go on.

'I haven't needed to. I can recreate every time we were together, everything we did and said together, in my mind. I can recreate them in technicolour and stereophonic sound without any prompt from offstage. And just like you, perhaps for all I know even more than you, that's what I did.'

Oblivious of the visitors who are standing around them and studying the painting, they embrace.

'For me,' she whispers, I can remember *then* without any help from *now*.'

'Just as I can,' he whispers in reply. '*Now*, though, helps me to remember *then* more clearly. I'm sure it must sound absurd to anybody except the two of us. But for both of us, from what we've just been saying to each other, *then* is still alive and well.'

'Now we've fulfilled both of your conditions, are we still on for dinner this evening?' he asks as they stand outside the National Gallery in a corner of Trafalgar Square.

'Tell me when and where, and I'll be there.'

He answers without a moment's hesitation. It is as if he has already rehearsed what he will say. 'Seven thirty. On the Euston Road outside St Pancras Station. Dinner will be at my flat a few minutes' walk away.'

They look at each other. From what he has just said, she now has the answer to one of the questions she has most wanted to ask him. Whether he went back to his wife after their parting at the Gare du Nord she does not yet know. But what she does know is that he is not living with her now. He understands what she is thinking and nods.

They kiss again. She begins to walk away from him. Then she turns round and calls back to him: 'This is my luckiest of days!'

To this he shouts his reply: 'The good luck, dear Jo, is wholly and exclusively mine!'

She walks across Trafalgar Square, which is littered with the inevitable tourists and pigeons, towards Charing Cross. Once again he does not notice she is looking around her. As she reaches one of the fountains she turns and waves.

It is a wave he has thought about almost every day since that final farewell of theirs twenty years ago. It is, too, a wave he has never, until today, had any real hope of seeing again.

'Hullo, Jo of the beautiful face!' he greets her as he walks up to her. She is standing on the road outside St Pancras Station, wearing now an elegant and striking white dress, at exactly the time he suggested that morning.

'Hullo, Stephen of the beautiful body!' she replies. She is stopped from saying more by his kisses – first on her forehead, then on each cheek, finally on her lips.

'It won't take us more than a few minutes to walk back,' he tells her.

'It won't worry me how long it takes,' she responds.

As they set off along the Euston Road, however, and as he once more fails to notice, she looks around her several times.

They stride, holding hands, past the huge hotel they last saw together in the distance as they began their walk along the Grand Union Canal. He stops her and points at its intricate Victorian brickwork, its elaborate gothic arches and ornate chimneys.

'When we saw that from the canal towpath,' he explains, 'it hadn't seen a guest for decades. Now, I guess, it's as full as it was empty then.'

They carry on until just before the British Library. They cross the road that is still crammed with traffic crawling along to the east and the west. He takes her down into Judd Street and then on into Hunter Street, both dominated by a succession of redbrick mansion blocks.

'Why did you settle on this part of town?' she asks.

'Not for its night life. Though the streets around King's Cross can, of a late evening, be more than a little interesting. Not for its restaurants or pubs. Though I've come to like one or two of them – including the Skinner's Arms we've just passed. That's where I sometimes call in for a late-night beer. Not for its cinemas or theatres. Though there are at least a couple nearby.'

'Not for this. Not for that. Not for the other. So,' she chides him, 'stop telling me why not. Tell me why!'

'For one thing, it's within easy walking distance of my chambers. I only get on a bus to go to work when the weather's too awful. Or when I'm too late to walk.

'For another thing, it's within even easier walking distance of the British Library back there, and of the British Museum. I go to them as often as I can, and perhaps more often than I should. And spend many a happy hour in both.

'But maybe my biggest reason for coming here was that I found a flat which, or so I thought at the time, suited me down to the ground. And at a price that wasn't sky high and didn't cripple me for years.'

They turn into Handel Street and cross the road. After a few yards he stops her again. He points up at some first-floor windows in a row of houses whose bricks were once ochre, but are now grey.

'That's it!' he announces. 'The place I'm more than happy to call my home.'

They climb up the stone steps from the street. He pushes open the front door. They climb more steps up to the first floor.

'Welcome to my home!' He tightens his grip of her hand and edges closer to her. 'And, Jo, you're just as welcome here now as you were in that bedsit of mine twenty years ago.'

He unlocks the door. Still hand in hand, they walk into the narrow hallway.

On her left she sees two framed photos. The first: a

brilliantly blue butterfly in what looks to her like a dark forest. The second: a dolphin rising from the water of what looks to her like an incredibly wide river.

On her right she sees two more photos. One is of a spider, its legs as hairy as its body, coming out of a hole in the ground. The other is of a monkey with an open mouth that is crouching on the branch of a tree.

'Are these your photos?' she asks.

'All my own work,' he replies. 'I told you when we first met I was a glutton for natural history. And added for good measure that it was for anything that wasn't human.'

'So where did you take them? And what are they all?'

'They're all from a journey I made along the Amazon just a few years back. The butterfly's a morpho. The biggest and brightest I've ever seen. Or am ever likely to see. The next's a pink dolphin that played around the boat I was on. And came so close I thought it was trying to jump on board.'

'And the others?'

'The spider's a tarantula that's bigger than you can ever imagine. It was, I'm glad to say, more concerned with finding its next meal than with attacking me. The monkey's a howler that you're much more likely to hear than to see. And no wonder when its call carries for miles through the rain forest.'

She examines each photo carefully, full of admiration, until he stops her.

'Come on!' he tells her. 'You've seen more than enough of these. And there are other photos around that'll mean much more to you.'

From the hallway he guides her into his living room. By one window is a table not much bigger than the one she remembers in Kensal Rise where they had their first breakfast together. Around it are just four chairs. Facing the other window is a small sofa. Close to the fireplace are two equally modest easy chairs. Against the wall next to the door from the hallway is a long, plain sideboard.

On the table she sees two places set for dinner. On the sideboard she notices a collection of photos, including the photo of college freshmen she had seen during their first night together. Above the sideboard are shelves crammed with books and CDs. Among them, she finds Gilbert White's *The Natural History of Selborne* and Charles Darwin's *The Origin of Species*.

There is no carpet on the polished wooden floor, and only a small rug by the fireplace. On the sofa and the easy chairs there are no cushions. There are only plain green curtains on the windows. The flat is, she thinks, even more austere than she expected it to be. It is, as she sees it, the home of an academic or a scientist... or, perhaps, of a lawyer.

When, however, she looks round at the walls of his living room, she is confronted by prints of paintings that are very far from austere, and that she thinks – though she is not sure – she recognises.

One is of a skein of wild geese flying in a v-shaped formation over a mudflat. Another is of a huge bull elephant, its ears flared, its tusks so long that they almost meet in front of its trunk. The third is of a hare sitting alone, its front paws together, its long ears raised. The fourth is of a single sloping pine tree with the sea behind it and with mountains in the distance.

'Do you like them?' he asks as he walks in from his kitchen with two wine glasses.

She nods enthusiastically. 'But why these?' she asks as they sit down on the sofa.

'It's that natural history thing yet again. Just as those Amazon photos you were looking at are. And though they were painted by humans, there's not a single human in sight. Not one!'

He stands up. He walks from the sofa to the shelf stacked with CDs. He picks out Beethoven's *Eroica* and puts it on his CD player. With the first movement just beginning, he goes over to the sideboard. He takes a bottle of Burgundy from the wine rack in one of its cupboards and opens it. He fills the two glasses and carries them back to the sofa. He gives her one of them.

'To Beatrice.'

'To Benedick.'

They raise their glasses to each other. Both of them are still overpowered by everything that has happened today. They drink a large mouthful before they put their glasses down on the wooden floor.

'But that's more than enough about my obsession with natural history. What about that obsession you used to have – and that I always thought to myself was highly improbable – with poetry?'

'As alive and well as your interest in everything non-human seems to be.'

'So are you still reading those early English poems?'

'Still reading them. And with as much delight as ever, if not more. But not only that.'

He raises his eyebrows and looks at her enquiringly.

'What, then, as well as reading them?'

'I give the odd talks – some very odd – whenever I'm asked. I'm going to run a course of evening classes on them this coming autumn. That's if there are enough takers.

'I've also heard from an obscure firm of publishers that they might be interested in a book of translations into modern English of some of the most obscure of Anglo-Saxon poems. The same idea as Seamus Heaney's translation of *Beowulf*. But sadly without any of his genius.'

'You told me when we first met you weren't dedicated enough as a teacher. You told me you'd do it for a few years but not for ever. So,' he asks, 'are you still teaching?'

'The answer's simple. It's what I've said to you before in answer to another of your questions. It's *yes and no*.'

He raises both arms in a gesture of simulated frustration. 'I can understand the answer *yes*. I can understand the answer *no*. And, when I think back to the way you used to play with words and avoid answering even the simplest of my questions, I can even understand *yes or no*.'

He raises both arms again. 'But when you tell me it's *yes and no* I'm none the wiser. And maybe, now I come to think of it, that's just what you want me to be.'

'If you'd spend more time thinking how to word your questions – though that may be asking too much of you! – you wouldn't have any problem at all.'

'Please, Jo, just give me an answer I can understand. If that's not asking too much of you.'

'In spite of what I once told you about my dedication – or lack of it – I'm still in teaching. But the most I ever teach these days is a lesson or so a week.'

'So have you gone part time?'

'As a classroom teacher, the answer's *yes*. But I'm still full time at a school.'

He makes yet another gesture of frustration. This is even more simulated than his gesture of a moment before. 'I may be able to understand some of the more obscure corners of the theft acts. On a good day I may even understand the backwaters of the divorce laws. But what you're telling me sounds very much like a riddle. And it's one I'm failing miserably to solve.'

'It's simple. I'm a head teacher. And back in the very same school where we met before that walk of ours by the Thames. As well as that, though I can never believe it whenever I think about it, I've been doing the job for almost five years.'

He raises his glass again. With a broad smile playing across his face, he proposes a toast.

'To Joanna. Once mistress. Now head mistress.'

'And you?' she asks after he has poured her a second glass of wine and put bowls of olives and nuts between them on the sofa.

'There's so much else I've wanted to do in life. So much else I want to do now, even after I've crawled into my fifties. But I'm still in the law. Still in the same chambers I was in when we met that day at Lincoln's Inn.'

'Still performing in the courts?'

He smiles and tries – though unsuccessfully – to stop himself from laughing. 'To repeat what you've already said, and not for the first time, the answer's *yes and no.*'

She looks at him quizzically once again. She finds herself laughing as loudly as he is. 'At least,' she exclaims in between fits of laughter, 'you can't be a headmistress!'

'No. It's worse than that.'

He walks over to a photo of himself in full legal regalia on the sideboard. He picks it up and shows it to her.

'You're not what they call a Queen's Counsel, are you?'

'Yes I am,' he sighs. 'And have been for quite a few years. But, if I'm going to tell you the truth, the whole truth and nothing but the truth, there's even worse to come.'

He sees only the grimace she puts on. He sees nothing of the feeling she has that what is to come will delight her.

'Have you retired on your ill-gotten gains? Or are you a gentleman of leisure who works from time to time when there's a case that interests you and promises you an astronomical fee?'

'Retired from the law? No. But gone part time as a barrister? Yes.'

'Oh no!' She has a sudden flash of inspiration. She looks at him with an expression of amazement. 'You're not some sort of judge, are you?'

It is now his turn to blush. This is partly with embarrassment. It is also partly, as he admits to himself, with pleasure. 'I plead guilty. But I'm only a very junior one, a recorder. And it's only for a few days a month. I guess it's when they can't find anyone else to do the work.'

She looks at him and raises her glass. She shares his pleasure though not his embarrassment. 'To Stephen, QC and judge. And, from my memories...' She puts her hand on his knees. '...very much more besides.'

CHAPTER ELEVEN

There is a succession of knocks, quiet but at the same time insistent, on the door of Stephen's flat.

He puts down his glass of wine on the table where he and Joanna are sitting. They have already eaten a plate of smoked salmon which, as he has reminded her, was what they ate at their picnic lunch in Lincoln's Inn. He has already put out on the table for later the tiramisu that is another reminder of their first meal together. What they are waiting for now is the lasagne that is still in the oven, but is almost ready for the two of them to eat.

'I don't know who it can be,' he tells her. 'I know for sure I'm not expecting anyone. The trouble is that the entryphone's broken. And my neighbours in the flats upstairs and downstairs aren't locking the front door. So it could be anyone.'

He stands up, pushes back his chair. He walks round to her and kisses her once again on her forehead. 'I won't be a moment.'

He walks into the hall and opens the door. He finds to his surprise a man he has never seen before standing outside. The man, dressed in a grey pinstripe suit, a white shirt, a blue tie and black shoes, says nothing. To his even greater surprise, the man strides slowly and deliberately past him, along the hallway and into the living room.

The man looks long and hard at some of the photos of Stephen on the sideboard. Of him in the sixth form at Sedbergh. Of him as a Cambridge graduate in his gown and mortar board. The man then picks up the photo of him in his gown and wig that was taken on the day he became a QC, and that he showed Joanna just a few minutes earlier.

Stephen's face shows utter bewilderment at this bizarre performance. So shocked is he that he says nothing, does nothing. Her face, which he glimpses for a moment as he looks away from the man and towards her, shows nothing short of horror.

'No, Jack! Please,' she implores him. 'No.'

The man still says nothing. He walks calmly, almost nonchalantly, across the room to the table where she is sitting. He stands opposite her. His hands are on his hips. His feet are a little apart. She can see on his face that tight, purposeful smile she has come to know so well.

'No, Jack! Please.'

Slowly, very slowly, he picks up the bottle of wine. He leans over the table and fills her empty glass. He takes the glass, raises it to his nose. He smells the wine carefully. Just as carefully, he takes a small sip.

'No, Jack!'

Stephen is still standing, wholly perplexed, at the door of his living room. He is seeing everything, but is understanding nothing. He looks at the scene in front of him as if he is watching a play in which an unknown character has made an unexpected appearance on stage.

He looks closely at the man's face with its heavy jowls and its hint of a five o'clock shadow. He looks at his cold blue eyes, at his thin and almost colourless lips. It is, he thinks, a mask without expression from which he can decode nothing of who the man is or why he is here.

He looks, too, at Joanna's face. He remembers it as sometimes pale and sometimes nervous. But it is now frozen with fear as he has never seen it. He is, he feels, looking at an animal caught in the headlights of a car that is racing at top speed towards it.

'No!' she cries.

The man takes another slow, careful sip of wine from the glass. Almost casually, almost as an afterthought, he throws the rest of the wine over her.

Stephen watches, just as frozen as she is, as the wine cascades off her hair, down her face, her neck, her shoulders, her arms. The red stain covers her white dress which now clings to her breasts and her stomach. Before the unexpected visitor arrived, she looked as if she was in the best of health. Now her face looks as if she is the victim of some awful disease.

The man puts the empty glass down on the table as deliberately as he filled it a few minutes ago. Behind the tight smile there is just the hint of laughter.

'*Blood of Christ*,' he declares in a deep, resonant voice.

He crosses himself, like a priest at the high altar, with his right hand. He turns his back on her. Without another word, as if he is at the end of some religious ceremony, he walks slowly towards the hall and the front door.

Stephen is still wholly uncertain of the meaning of what he has just witnessed. He still says and does nothing – except, in an instinctive movement, he steps aside to let the man pass.

The man strides past him without as much as a glance. With *Eroica* still playing in the background, Stephen hears him walk down the stairs. The front door of the house bangs shut. After a moment, the sound of his footsteps dies away.

'Christ Almighty!' Stephen says to himself.

He goes over to where Joanna is sitting and stands behind her. He puts both of his hands lightly on her shoulders. He lifts one hand to her head and strokes her wet hair gently with the tips of his fingers.

He feels her body shudder violently once, twice, three times. These are deep tremors of movement over which she has no control. He hears her breathing, which is already heavy, become faster. Her tears begin to flow and fall onto the stains that cover much of the front of her dress.

'Come with me,' he tells her.

He puts an arm round her shoulders. He guides her to the sofa where they drank their first two glasses of wine. He sits her down. She leans forward, her elbows on her knees, her face cupped in her hands.

With one arm still round her shoulders, he pulls her closer to him. He strokes her shoulder and her hands until her breathing begins to quieten and slow down, until her sobbing begins to subside.

'Who the hell was he?' he gasps. He is still totally baffled by what he has seen and heard. 'And what the hell was he doing here?'

He looks at her face in the hope he will find an answer in her eyes. But her hair has fallen across her face, and hides them from him. He adds, almost as an afterthought: 'And, whoever he may be, how did he know you'd be here?'

She stares in front of her. The black-leaded fireplace, the photos on the wall, the clock on the marble mantelpiece, the table where they were having their dinner: all are out of focus. Somewhere inside her body she feels a deadweight. It is as if she has become, over these last few minutes, so much heavier. In her head, his questions repeat themselves until she cannot distinguish between them.

'Please tell me,' he whispers. 'Please try.'

Without moving her hands away from her face, without lifting her head, without turning towards him, she does her best to give him her answers.

'There are times, too many times, when he has me followed,' she begins quietly. 'Sometimes I know I'm being followed. Sometimes I don't. Today – though I don't think you noticed – I checked if this was happening time after time.

'From the moment we met at Holborn to when we walked into the Nell Gwynne. From the moment we left the pub to when we said goodbye outside the National Gallery and I walked off across Trafalgar Square. And, again, between St Pancras and your flat. I thought I was on my own. Not for the first time, I was wrong.'

She shudders as she remembers some of those other times. They were never, though, as she also remembers, when she was with another man.

'But why does he have you followed?'

'He wants to know where I am every hour of the day. And every hour of the night. Most of the time he's got no problem. But when I'm out on my own, that's different. At best it's because he wants to be sure I'm safe. At worst it's because he wants to be in control of me even when I'm not with him.'

He frowns as he tries to interpret what she has just said. 'So do you live with that man?' he asks her.

'More than that,' she replies, and her voice becomes

even quieter. 'Jack's my husband. And has been for more than ten years.'

She looks away from him. She is uncertain how he will react.

'Good God, Jo! Then why did he throw the wine over you?' he asks, looking at the stains on her dress. 'Was it because you were here with me?'

She stares at the clock. Its second hand creeps round the face. She stares once again at the photos of him on the wall. '*Yes and no.* That usual answer of mine. I'm sure he wanted you to see how he dominates me. He wants everybody to see that. And he makes very sure everybody does.'

She begins to talk to him less hesitantly. For the first time since she sat down on the sofa, she looks directly into his eyes. 'But you were incidental. At most you had a walk-on part. At least you had an end-of-row seat in the upper circle. He wanted to remind me of his power over me. Wherever I am. Whatever I'm doing. Whoever I'm with. And, if he's acting true to form, this won't be the last reminder he'll be giving me.'

'Does he often treat you like that?'

'When he wants to, he does. But the only reason I was so hurt this evening was that you had to see it all. The last thing I want is to have anybody seeing me being humiliated. And the worst of all was that it was you.'

'For heaven's sake!' he exclaims as memories of what she told him when they were together suddenly flood back. 'Not another man like some of those men you knew before we met? Surely not!'

She does not reply at once. They sit together, motionless and silent. They are like two actors at the end of a Beckett play who are waiting for the curtain to fall.

Almost inaudibly, she delivers her final lines. 'Then and now, Stephen. Now just like then.'

Joanna's words remind him so clearly of so much that – though sometimes reluctantly and piecemeal – she had told him about her past when they were together. In response he kisses her as he has done so often: first on her forehead, then on her cheeks, finally on her lips.

'And now?' he asks. 'Do you think you'll go back to him tonight after...?'

'... after what he did here this evening?'

She tries to collect her dislocated thoughts. She tries to decide what she should do. After several minutes of agitated thinking, she breaks her silence. 'I can't go back to him. I won't go back. Not now.'

'So would you like to stay here for the night?'

She avoids his gaze and does not reply. She tries – and with great difficulty – to think through at least some of the implications of his offer.

'If you aren't going to go back to him tonight,' he asks, 'and if you don't stay here, where are you going to go?'

She bites her lower lip, closes her eyes tightly. She runs her fingers through her wet hair, scratches the back of her head. She is thinking as best she can. She is searching for clarity but finding only confusion. She is failing to find any answer to his question.

'I don't know,' she admits with a deep sigh.

He stands up, puts his hand briefly on her shoulder, walks into his kitchen. He opens another bottle of red wine he has taken from his wine rack. He fills both their glasses. 'Drink this,' he tells her when he returns.

While he has been opening the bottle and filling their glasses in the kitchen, she has continued to think where she might stay the night, where she might find a refuge. After she has swallowed her first mouthful of the wine, she admits she is defeated. She shakes her head slowly from side to side.

'I can't think of anywhere I can go. Anyone I can stay with. There's nowhere, nobody at all. Certainly not at this time of night.'

'So will you stay here?' he asks, at the same time thinking of the possible consequences for them both of her accepting his offer. 'Will you stay with me?'

She takes hold of his hand, at first tentatively, then more firmly. She has, at last, decided what she will do. 'It's what I told you when we first met, and as I told you again this morning. Being asked isn't the mistake. The mistake is in agreeing.'

'So are you going to make yet another mistake?' he asks. He recognises, as she does, that she could be walking towards a minefield – as, quite possibly, could he.

She pauses, looks directly at him. For a moment, a hint of a smile crosses her face before she replies. 'It's not that I'm going to. For better or for worse, as I've told you whenever you've asked me the question, it's that I already have.'

'What did you do after we said our farewells that evening?' he asks as they sit close together on his sofa.

The glasses they are holding are both more than half empty. The bottle of wine in front of them on the floor is also more than half empty.

His voice breaks, and he struggles with his emotions to finish his question. 'After the train began to leave the Gare du Nord?'

She runs her index finger slowly round the rim of her

glass. She dips it into what is left of the wine. She licks it until all taste and smell of the wine have gone.

'From the time I left you till the time I reached Calais I did nothing but cry. Not so that the other passengers could see. But deep inside me. Like the victim of an accident who, on the surface, seems to have suffered not a single injury. But a victim who, inside, is bleeding to death.'

She stops as the events she has pushed so far into the distant recesses of her memory tumble back into her consciousness. They are, she thinks, like rocks cascading down a steep mountainside.

She swallows what is left of her drink, too much and too quickly. She coughs violently and splutters. She scatters red splashes over the sofa, and adds even more red stains to her dress.

'Whenever I closed my eyes I could see you there on the seat opposite me. Your face was empty, blank. It said nothing to me. It was dead. You were with me and I wanted you gone.' For a minute or more she is silent. 'Whenever I opened my eyes I could see you weren't there. You were gone and I wanted you with me.'

She stops again, muted as the rocks in her mind hurtle onto the valley floor. She holds the new glass of wine he has poured for her. She looks into it, then shakes it so the reflection of herself she sees on the surface is distorted.

'On the ferry back to Dover I felt sick. Not from the sea which was as calm as I've ever seen it. But from the turmoil going on inside me. Then, as well as feeling so awful, I was sick as a parrot over the side and into the Channel. To the disgust of a gang of wheeling gulls. After that I hoped I'd feel better. The truth was the opposite. I felt much worse.'

She stops yet again, so unused is she to talking about what happened that day. She is, she feels, like a rusty bicycle whose pedals grind round and, after a few turns, seize up. She holds her glass up in front of her eyes and looks through it at his face. Through the rich red of the wine, what she sees is deformed and discoloured.

She puts her glass down on the floor beside the now empty bottle. With her head bowed, she holds it between her hands. Except for her quick breathing, she sits silent and still. She makes an immense effort to control herself. With her voice breaking, she completes her account of that day when they parted.

'On the train to Victoria it was the worst of all. You may not have realised it, but you'd filled me with yourself as nobody had ever done before. I'd depended on you more than I'd ever depended on anyone.

'When I'd looked around me, it was through your eyes as much as through my own. When I'd listened, it was with your ears as much as with mine. When I'd thought and felt, it was with your mind and with your heart next to mine.'

He has listened very carefully to each word. He is beginning to discover at last what he has wanted to know for the past twenty years. He puts his arm round her again, pulls her towards him. He helps her to rest her head on his shoulder.

'I was, I suppose, so concerned with myself and my problems I didn't think anything like enough about you. But I never dreamed it would be so bad for you.'

He feels profoundly guilty at the damage he wreaked. Yet still he finds it difficult to believe this damage could have been so dreadful. 'Was everything, though, as black as you've just painted it?'

'For me, everything was black. Black as the ace of spades.'

'I never dreamed, never imagined, I could have meant so much to you. Surely I hadn't filled your life quite as completely as you've told me I had.'

'For me, whether you like it or not, you were everything. You were my north and south and east and west – and every other point of the compass. But this, so I understood more and more, was all behind me. As that first train sped away from Paris. And as that second train sped towards London. It was all left at the Gare du Nord like abandoned baggage on the edge of the platform. In front of me I saw nobody and nothing.'

He holds her cheeks gently between his open hands. He puts his lips, just as gently, against hers. He kisses her affectionately. The tip of his tongue moves slowly into her mouth. It touches her tongue, plays with it. It retreats as her tongue advances.

'So you'll be spending the night here, Jo.'

'Yes. As long as you're happy to have me here.'

'Are you sure?' he asks, looking carefully into her eyes.

'Mistake or no mistake, quite sure.'

He moves his hands away from her face, down her neck, over the front of her stained dress. Through the cotton he feels her breasts, her belly. He is excited, though not by a new experience, not by a prelude to one of his first-night adventures. He is excited by the rediscovery of what he experienced twenty years ago. Before he replies he hesitates, not sure how directly to frame his next question.

'Do you want to spend the night here…' He hesitates again. '… as an old friend might spend it?'

'I do want to spend the night here. And I am an old friend. So there's only one answer. And, quite simply, it's *yes.*'

He abandons one euphemism. He recalls her pleasure when they played games with words, and tries another. 'You know what I'm trying to ask you. Do you want us to spend the night together?'

'After those nights when we were together, even if they were twenty years ago, I can't think of any other way to spend tonight than together with you. And...' It is now her turn to hesitate, though only for a few seconds. '... as more than an old friend.'

He feels her hands begin, softly but firmly, and without inhibitions, to explore his body through his shirt and trousers. His memory flashes back to those nights with their glorious mixture of passion and exhaustion. Passion dominating them until the early hours and often later. Exhaustion overwhelming them before – though sometimes not much before – dawn.

'You want us to sleep together?' he asks. He is still trying to be sure of what she is telling him. He is still unable to believe this is really what she wants.

'If you haven't worked that out by now, your brain must have atrophied more than I'd have thought possible.'

He remembers once again those first exchanges of theirs in the National Gallery, in the Nell Gwynne, on the Thames towpath. He notices to his delight that she has lost none of the sharpness of her repartees, none of her Beatrice to his Benedick.

'It's just that when we were together, I was the one who was married. You were the one who was single. Or, as you put it that first Saturday, very single. Now the shoe's on the other foot. As well as that, and after what's happened here this evening, I don't want to take advantage of you. I want whatever you do to be your decision and not mine.'

'I've made my decision. I'm not going to change my mind. And,' she adds with the smile he remembers so well, 'I'll be taking advantage of you at least as much as you'll be taking advantage of me.'

With one hand holding his glass, he drums the fingers of his other hand nervously on the arm of the sofa. He is waiting for, though not wanting, the question he knows she will ask him.

'And you, Stephen, what did you do that evening, that night? One minute you were standing there on the edge of the platform. Your hand partly raised, a half salute. The next minute the train was out of the station. You were out of sight.'

He forces himself, just as she has forced herself, to remember what he has tried over the years – but only sometimes successfully – to push into the depths of his memory.

'I walked with my bags all the way from the Gare du Nord down to the Seine by Notre Dame. I sat on a wall, watching the water sliding past. Watching the flotsam of twisted plastic and broken wood bobbing on the surface.'

He pauses, looks at her. He touches her uncertainly and just for a moment on her forearm. He is for a time, as she was a few minutes ago, silenced by his emotions. These are, he feels, rising in streams of bubbles to the surface, and exploding in rapid succession into his consciousness.

'But my mind that evening was far, far away. I was thinking of you. Hating myself for what I'd done to you. Cursing myself for the decision I'd made and for the reasons why I'd made it. And, above all, I was in despair that I wasn't with you.'

Although he is unaware of what he is doing, his fingers begin to beat a slow, deliberate, agitated rhythm on his knee.

'My head was filled with the heavy weight of Mozart's *Requiem Mass*. I tried to stop it. To fill my head instead with the joys of Beethoven's *Pastoral*. But it was no contest. Wolfgang Amadeus won hands down, however much I wanted him to lose.'

She puts her hand on his. Though he does not know it, his fingers become still.

'I must have sat there by the Seine for hours. Past sunset. Into night. I walked along by the river as slowly as any courting couple. I watched the reflections of the street lights shivering in the water.

'I remembered in short but vivid flashes my first visit to Paris, my transition from schoolboy to student. Girls parading themselves in their g-strings in a sweaty strip club at the cheap end of Montmartre. Girls offering mysterious and, to me at that time, unknown delights at late-night street corners.'

He puts his head in his hands. The tips of his fingers are on his forehead. The ends of his thumbs are on his cheekbones. He is silent again. He is as unaccustomed as she was a few minutes earlier to recounting the events of that day.

He is, as much as she thought she was, a rusty bicycle. Yet he is finding he is able to give her some idea, however overstated it might be, of what he did.

'But I was also remembering Erica. Who'd pushed me into despair. Who'd taken me closer to the horrors of hell more than anyone had ever done. And who was the woman I'd decided I had to go back to.

'I was, of course, remembering you as well. Who'd given me the greatest delights I'd ever known. Who'd shown me some of the pleasures of paradise. And who was the woman I'd decided I had to abandon.'

He begins, again unaware of what he is doing, to drum his fingers, this time on his forehead.

'I tried to imagine you. Your hands caressing me. Your lips kissing me. Your body beside mine. Instead I saw the blood running down my legs from her kicks. I felt the bruises throbbing on my face from her punches.'

She remembers as he talks what he told her on their last evening in Giroux, before he left her on her own by the unlit fire and shuffled across the room to the stairs.

'I know you told me how much I meant to you. But I've always feared you'd decided your wife meant more.'

'No. Not at all. It's just as I tried to tell you that last evening. My decision to go back to her had nothing to do with what she meant to me. It was everything to do with what she was threatening to do to herself.'

'So are you saying, when we said our last goodbyes in Paris, you still loved me?'

'More than at any time since we'd met. Though I didn't have the strength or the words to tell you.'

As she watches his face, she sees one tear, then another, trickle slowly down between his cheeks and his nose.

'I'd had to choose between your love and her blackmail. What I did, I now know and understand, was an act that was weak and cowardly. And, of course, it was totally stupid. I chose her blackmail.'

She leans over, puts her arms round him, tries to console him. She kisses him lightly. With their lips just a little apart, the tips of their tongues meet again.

'Did you ever try to find me?' she asks.

'After I went back to her, I did everything I could to help her. To make it work with her. Apart from my job, and for months on end, I excluded everybody, everything. Even you, hard as that was.

'It was only after I'd left her again, fully and finally, I phoned your flat. But I found myself talking to somebody whose English I couldn't begin to understand. It was only then I phoned your school and found you'd moved to another job. Where it was, though, nobody there could – or would – tell me.'

He thinks back to those early days and weeks when he was on his own again. He remembers when his hopes of finding her reached a dead end.

'And you, Jo? Did you ever do anything to contact me?'

'I lifted up the phone a couple of times in those first weeks back in London. I dialled your Lincoln's Inn number. I even listened to your phone ringing. Then, though I'm still not sure why, I forced myself to go no further. I put my phone back down.

'Once I went to Lincoln's Inn. I saw your name on the board at the bottom of the steps. I even began to walk up them. But, again, I forced myself to go no further. And, though again I didn't know why, I retreated back down the steps.

'Sometimes I found myself trying not to think about you. But, in spite of this, I remembered you every day. At other times I found myself hoping not to see you. But, at the same time, I was looking out for you every day.'

Though he is far from certain, he thinks he can understand these paradoxes. But he knows he cannot fully understand why she abandoned her phone calls or her visit to him.

'When you heard the dialling tone,' he asks her, 'why didn't you wait for me to answer?'

'There's nothing sensible, nothing rational I can say to you. I don't know why I did what I did. I just did it.'

'And when you came to Lincoln's Inn, when you started to walk up the steps to my chambers, why didn't you come in and see me? Or is your answer the same?'

'Just the same. Just the same. Though I can't begin to explain why, I wanted to be with you only in my imagination. I wanted you to be feeling for me as you were when we were together.

'I didn't want you to be feeling for her as I was sure you'd be when you were back with her. And after that there were other reasons why I didn't try to contact you again. Reasons I'm sure you'll discover before too long.'

She looks at him, and at the same time beyond him. As his eyes did in the Nell Gwynne that first morning twenty years ago, her eyes focus on some point in the far distance behind him.

CHAPTER TWELVE

Joanna and Stephen are now standing together by the window of his bedroom. On the wall next to the door she sees those Mucha prints she last saw in his Kensal Rise flat on their first night together. On the other walls she sees four larger prints.

One is of Michaelangelo's *Creation of Adam*, part of the unforgettable ceiling fresco she had seen with her husband on a visit to the Sistine Chapel. Another is da Vinci's *Mona Lisa*, with her gaze as inscrutable as it was when she saw it in the Louvre on a school trip to Paris.

She sees, too, Masaccio's fresco of Adam and Eve – *The Expulsion from the Garden of Eden* – that she has never seen before. But the painting she sees with most surprise and delight is Botticelli's *Venus and Mars*.

'Why these?' she asks as she walks round the bedroom.

'It's what I told you this morning. For better or for worse, Renaissance paintings are my favourites. And there's one that's my favourite above all.' He walks over to *Venus and Mars*, turns to her, smiles. 'Though the reason this is my very favourite isn't, as you well know, just because it's so brilliant. It's because…'

She runs across to him, puts a finger to his lips. 'I know what you're going to say to me. And it's exactly what I'd say to you if you'd give me half a chance!'

'Is something wrong?' she asks a little later as they are sitting, looking at each other, on the edge of his bed. She sees on his face an expression of dismay. It is as if, so she thinks, he has had some unexpected or unwelcome thoughts.

'It's something I've only just realised,' he tells her, his face now registering both puzzlement and amusement. 'Something that's so obvious. But something I've never thought about before.'

'So what is it?'

As she watches him, she sees the beginning of a smile, perhaps more wry than broad.

'I've imagined being in bed with you thousands and thousands of times since we said goodbye. I've imagined it when I've been on my way between my flat and Lincoln's Inn. In chambers with clients. In court before or after a case. Very occasionally, in the courtroom itself. Even when I was in the middle of my cross-examination of a witness.'

She sees now no dismay, less puzzlement and more, much more, amusement.

'I've always thought of myself in bed with you as I was when we were together. In reasonably good shape. Even if not ultra-fit. Under eleven stone. Even if not by much. Still young and not only at heart. Even if I'd already reached thirty.'

'So what?'

With his smile even broader, he starts to laugh at himself, make fun of himself. 'I'd never thought of myself in bed with you weighing in at well over twelve stone and still rising. Being the wrong side of fifty and further on the wrong side of it with every day that passes.

'Having a stomach that's got so big I can only see whatever's below my midriff by looking at myself in a mirror. With hair that's been migrating down from my head to my back and my chest for longer than I care to remember. And, to add insult to injury, turning from black to grey in the process. I am, to put it quite simply, growing old. And that's what I'm trying to reconcile myself with right now.'

'Why does it bother you?' she asks.

Instead of giving her his answer, he stands up, walks away from the bed. He starts to undress. He looks at her quietly, softly, more than a little sadly.

'In my mind, in my imagination, I'm as young as I was then. Whenever I've thought of you, I've been the young – or almost young – man I used to be. But the reality, as you can see for yourself, is quite different.'

He stands self-consciously, shyly in front of her. He looks not at her but at the floor in front of him. It is the first time she has seen him undressed since they stood together by the doorway in Giroux and listened to the nightingale. He is, she thinks, both right and wrong about what he has said of himself.

True, she does not see in every detail the young body she remembers. Those powerful muscles on his arms and legs. Those strong shoulders. That broad chest. That tight stomach. But, as she looks at him, she can still see much of the man she used to know.

The muscles on his arms and legs have lost only a little of their power and firmness. His shoulders look almost as burly as they used to look. His chest, even though it is covered with a coat of greying hair, is still broad and strong. His stomach, though not as flat and tight as it was, is much smaller than he has just described it to her.

She stands up, slowly and deliberately, and steps towards him. She touches his hands and arms with her fingers. She moves them lightly over his shoulders, across his chest, down to his stomach. She feels how, involuntarily, his body tightens as her fingers brush across his skin.

She kneels in front of him, between the bed and the window. She strokes his feet, his legs, his thighs with her fingers. She kisses his body gently as she puts her arms round his waist and pulls him towards her.

For some time, neither of them says a word. Both are enjoying the rediscovery of passions from their past together. Even more, they are enjoying the discovery that these are in no way passions that belong only to their past.

'And you, how did you think about me?' he asks.

'I thought about you and how you looked so often. Even after those first months and then years when we were apart. Sometimes deliberately. Sometimes whether I wanted to or not. And in situations just as bizarre as when you thought about me.

'Even when I was reading some of my favourite poems. Even when I was reading the class an afternoon story. You as Daddy Bear, Piglet, Mole. Even – though I'm more than embarrassed to admit it – when I was in bed with some man or other.'

'Was I as you remembered me then? Or did you try to update me as time passed?'

She looks up, brushes her hair away from her face, smiles at him. Her eyes are full of understanding of what he has told her. She knows, too, what he would like her to tell him.

'In this, if in nothing else, I may have been more realistic than romantic. And certainly more realistic than you've been about yourself. I suppose I thought of you as not quite so youthful. And less and less youthful as the years passed. Yet, in spite of the inevitable damage inflicted on you by time, as not so very different.

'I may have thought of you with a body in gentle decline. I also thought of you, though, with a mind and an imagination intact. In this, if in nothing else, unchanged.'

She hesitates after she has given him this account of how she thought. She stands up and throws back at him the question he has asked her. 'And you, how did you think about me?'

'Just as you were then. In every way unchanged. A heart so full of love for me it almost hurt me. A mind wise beyond its years and yet so full of fun. A body at its very best. Floating deliciously between girl and woman.'

He sees her smile again. He watches her as she turns away from him, though only slightly. It is what he can only interpret as an act, however ineffective, of modesty. He watches her keenly as she unbuttons her dress and lets it fall to the ground.

'And whenever you imagined us together,' he asks her, 'how did you imagine yourself?'

He watches her with growing excitement as she takes off her wine-stained slip and rolls her tights down to her feet before kicking them away from her. She smiles again. For the first time since her husband's visit, her eyes, her mouth, her whole face are laughing.

'Body damaged by time and by what I'd done to it. My self-inflicted wounds. More and more layers of fat over my bottom and my belly and everywhere around them. Breasts less pert than pendulous. And in more and more need of support...'

She hesitates yet again. Much as she wants to complete this account of herself, she is unsure how to do this. '... Feelings dulled, anaesthetised. Maybe as you told me yours used to be. My way of coping with everything that's happened to me over the years. But deep inside, unless I'm much mistaken, much as I was then.'

He stares at her as she takes off the last of her clothes, and makes a pile of them on his carpet. He sees a body no longer floating – as he has just told her he thought it did when he first saw her undressed – between girl and woman. It is, he thinks, a body that has clearly completed its transition to womanhood, and some years ago.

Her breasts are fuller. Her hips are broader. Her stomach is rounder, as is her bottom. Yet there is still so much of the woman he remembers. He is, he finds to his delight, still strongly attracted by her body. It attracts him now at least as much it did then, when it was only partly formed.

As he did on that first night twenty years ago, he touches her neck, which he strokes again and again. His fingertips glide from her shoulders onto her breasts, and on across her belly.

And, as he did then and as she did just a few minutes ago, he goes down on his knees in front of her. He strokes her from her toes to her calves. He holds her bottom in his hands before he slides them round her thighs. He embraces her with his arms round her waist. He kisses her skin, as soft now as it was then.

He has made a proposal, now they have undressed, now they are by his bed. It is that they should do what both of them have thought about for the last twenty years. She has agreed. For she is every bit as eager as he is for them to go to bed together.

She has, however, made a counter-proposal. Before they make love, she suggests, they should let a little more time pass. They should, in the aftermath of her husband's unwelcome visit, recover just a little more.

She suggests, too, each should discover a little more about what the other did after they parted. He agrees, and tells her how much he wants to hear what happened to her. But before that, he offers to tell her more of his own story.

'After our first night apart I stayed on in Paris for a couple of days. I went to some of the places I'd been to as a student. I went back to the Cité Universitaire where I'd half heard and quarter understood – and not only because of my abysmal French – a handful of morning lectures on European civilisation.

'I revisited the Théâtre de la Huchette on the Left Bank where I watched the same two plays I'd watched ten or more years before. Ionesco's *La Leçon* and the *Cantatrice Chauve*. I stayed yet again at the Hôtel d'Aguesseau. Hidden away in a courtyard off the Rue Boissy d'Anglas. Where I'd slept for a few francs a night, service and bedbugs included.

'As well as these, I went to some of the places I'd so much wanted to go to with you. The Impressionist galleries at the Orangerie. Monets in room after room. Echoes of Giverny summers. Waterlilies in overabundance.

'I went to Bofinger's to start with a plate of oysters. To move on to a roast leg of lamb. To drink a bottle of rich, dry Burgundy. To lose myself in the magnificent excesses of its Belle Époque decor and its glass-domed ceiling.'

He brings instantly and easily to mind the plays, the

paintings, the oysters and lamb and stained glass. The islands of delight he inhabited during the hours he was enjoying them. He brings to mind, too, the ocean of despair to which he was forced to return after each island visit.

'I was, I suppose, like a young boy playing frantically on the beach on the last afternoon of his family's summer holiday. Making sandcastles with his bucket and spade. Dashing in and out of the sea like a puppy that has just been taken off its lead. Burying his legs in the sand. Turning cartwheels at the water's edge. Evading in every way he can any thought of school, assembly, lessons, homework that will begin again next week.

'I was, I guess, trying as best I could to forget what I'd decided to do. Trying, in every way I could devise, to avoid thinking about where I'd be, what I'd be doing, above all the woman I'd be with, in just a few days' time.'

He recollects those precious hours he spent in the calm and quiet of Notre Dame before the daily tourist invasion. In the bright gothic world of the Sainte Chapelle. In St Denis where he revisited the beginning of the end of the Romanesque world. More islands of delight, but still surrounded by that boundless and inescapable ocean.

'After I got back from Paris, and before I began what I saw more and more starkly as my prison sentence, I still didn't go back to her. I walked about endlessly. I went to all the places in London you and I'd been to in those few and infinitely precious weeks we'd been together.

'Partly I went to those places, our places, to remember the past. Still not wanting to believe it was really past. But I've got to be honest with myself – and with you. I went there as much if not more to avoid having to think about the future.'

His memories of those visits on his own to places where, just weeks earlier, they had been together are extremely clear. Where they kissed. Where they picnicked. Where they walked.

Just are clear are his memories of how he felt sick each time his retreats into their past together ended. And of how, from the moment he woke up to the moment he fell asleep, he was overwhelmed by a deep emptiness and loneliness.

'Then, after a couple of days, when I'd built up enough courage or at least enough bravado, I phoned her. Said to her, as calmly as I could, I'd spent a lot of time thinking about everything she'd written in her last letter. Fully understood what she'd written and what she meant. Told her, because of what she'd written, and come what may, I'd be back with her that same evening.

'Didn't say I'd thrown away every shred of hope of a happy future. Didn't say I was looking forward to going back to her as much – or as little – as a convicted murderer facing the gallows.'

He cannot forget the voice he heard when his wife answered the phone. She spoke in monosyllables after what seemed to him like minutes of silence. Nor can he forget how his emptiness and loneliness reached new and even more awful depths. And this when the woman he was talking to was the very woman he had spent more time with than anyone he had ever known.

'I packed my bags as slowly as I could. Zipped them up one by one. Locked the door of the Kensal Rise flat where you and I spent that first night of ours together. Walked down the stairs and into the street. Got on the tube. More on autopilot than in control of what I was doing. More an automaton than a man.

'As it had been when I'd left, so it was when I returned. No drama. No grand flourish. No climax. Just sotto voce. Unobtrusively. Tail even more between legs. And heart so heavy, spirit so low. Wanting more than anything to be anywhere on earth but back in that flat. And with anyone on earth but her.'

'A little while ago,' she told him, 'you said your decision to go back to your wife had everything to do with what she was threatening to do to herself.'

'Yes,' he sighs. 'That's what I said.'

'You said you had to choose between my love and her blackmail.'

'Yes,' he sighs again. 'Your love. Her blackmail. Some choice!'

'And you chose her blackmail.'

'Yes.'

'But if you were dreading to go back to her so deeply, so desperately, why did you tell me it was an act that was weak and cowardly? Wouldn't it have been more of an act like that if you'd stayed away...'

'... and if I'd stayed with you?'

She thinks for a moment before she replies. 'Yes.'

He is not at all sure he can explain himself. But, after he has worked out what he wants to say, he makes an attempt.

'From everything I knew of her, from what she'd done before, I was sure beyond any reasonable doubt she was capable of doing away with herself. Just as she'd threatened to do. I believed, by going back to her, by helping her as best I could, I'd be able to make sure she didn't harm herself.'

'And was that what overcame your dread of going

back?'

'That's what I persuaded myself in those long night hours after we parted. When I was drifting in and out of shallow sleep. In moments of brutal honesty, though, I told myself there were other reasons why I'd decided to go back.'

'So what were your other reasons?' she asks.

'One was what she'd written in her last letter I read you that terrible morning. That, if I'd gone back to her at any time, she wouldn't ever have been violent again. My years in the law should have totally destroyed whatever faith I ever had in human honesty. Yet I was gullible and foolish enough to believe she'd stand by what she'd written.'

'And the other reason?'

He looks at her. His face registers his distress. She understands he is trying to tell her something that is, to him, deeply significant.

'The other was, for me, just as important. It's what I told you when we sat opposite each other in Giroux that last evening. I decided to go back because I wouldn't have been able to live with myself, look at myself in the mirror, if I'd done anything else.

'What I did wasn't simply an act of altruism, of self-sacrifice. It was, as well as that, an act of self-interest. My concern wasn't only for her. It was also for myself.'

She realises he is extremely agitated and, perhaps, close to tears. She decides to ask him no more questions but, after she has been to the bathroom, to tell him more of her story.

In the bathroom she glances briefly at a spartan collection of toiletries. On the shelf above the basin: just a razor, a shaving brush, a toothbrush and toothpaste. By the bath: just some soap and a flannel and a towel.

What she sees on the bathroom walls, however, she can hardly believe. She stares, with her mouth wide open, at four black-and-white photos. At Hammersmith Bridge with the Thames towpath leading up to it. At the metal footbridge crossing the Grand Union Canal at Camden Lock. At Magdalen Bridge over the River Cherwell with the bell tower behind it. At the stone bridge over the River Dee with Dent beyond it.

'These photos in here,' she shouts from the bathroom. 'Whatever made you take them? And whatever made you put them up in your bathroom?'

He walks in from the bedroom, and thinks carefully before he gives her his answer. 'I've told you I've been back to every single place in England we went to together. I've told you that going back gave me a greater depth to my memories. These photos of bridges do exactly the same. Every morning when I'm getting ready for work. Every evening when I'm getting ready for bed.'

He stops, thinks again. 'There should, perhaps, have been a fifth photo.'

'Of what?' she asks.

'Of that little stone bridge at the far end of Giroux.'

'But?'

'But, if you remember, I never took a photo of it. And, unlike the other photos, my memories of it and of Giroux are bitter as well as sweet.'

There are several minutes of silence. In these she remembers those bridges they had stood on together. She remembers, too, how understanding a listener he had been twenty years before, and how he was the one and only man she had felt able to talk to about her past. She then begins to tell him more about this time: her life after her return to London.

'As soon as the train got me back to Victoria I phoned Susan. She was a girl I'd been friendly with at school in Oxford. We'd been in the same class each year. From when we were eleven to when we were eighteen.

'I wasn't as close to her as I'd been to Mary. And our friendship was purely platonic. But we'd been good friends. We told each other almost every schoolgirl secret we had. The surprises our own bodies were giving us as we crept into adolescence. The surprises our boyfriends' bodies were giving us as we floundered towards being adults.

'On the phone I gave her what must have sounded like a prize-winning sob story. That you and I had split up in Paris just a few hours before. That I couldn't bear to be alone in my empty flat. Not on that first night without you.

'She told me she'd moved into a top-floor flat in Maida Vale with a passable view over the Grand Union Canal. She added – which was very much more important to me at the time – that she had a spare bedroom. And this, if I wanted it, was mine for the asking.

'Everything in my mind and my heart was in turmoil. I felt, though, I'd begun to wade out of the wetlands I'd fallen into when we parted. And I'd begun to reach an island of solid ground – however small it might be.

'I stayed with her that night. The next day, and with few regrets, I gave up my own flat. The view over the canal was, to say the least, restricted. But I made that little room, with Susan in the bedroom next to mine, my home.'

As she begins to tell her story, she remembers the

room. Its narrow single bed that dipped dramatically in the middle. Its tiny bedside table piled with her poetry books. Its chest of drawers, just as tiny, that was crammed with her clothes. Its Muybridge photos of galloping horses that almost covered one wall. They are, she realises, memories she holds very dear. And this is in spite of, or perhaps because of, the chaos of her life after they parted.

'With half term over, I was back to teaching my class the very next week. I still didn't feel this was my vocation in life. Certainly not for ever and a day. Yet, once again, I felt at my school I'd reached another island of solid ground. I taught the children with more enthusiasm, even if not with more professionalism, than I'd ever managed to generate before.

'I made myself busy morning, noon and night. I was active every day of the week. It was part of my new life. Part of my attempt to live a whole day without imagining us together. You walking along the pavement towards me. Smiling at me on a street corner. Holding me tightly in your arms. Lying with me in bed as we made love.

'Teaching helped me a lot to think about you less. I was with a classroom of boys and girls who demanded my full concentration. From the start of the first lesson when I was still more asleep than awake. Through to the final bell of the day when I was often completely exhausted and ready to fall asleep as soon as I could.'

She thinks back to what were among the fondest of her memories of that time. They were of those crowded school days when she threw herself into her work as she had never done before. When she could see, from the expressions on the children's faces, their responses to the efforts she was making. When she could hear, from what they told her before they dashed off home, she had sparked the imaginations of at least some of them.

She thinks back, too, to those times – sometimes only a few minutes, sometimes several hours – when she was able to devote herself to her poetry. When her interest in poems from earlier and earlier centuries blossomed. When she became more and more excited by *The Canterbury Tales*, by *Piers Plowman*, by *Sir Gawain and the Green Knight* and, above all, by the glories of *Beowulf*.

'As well as giving me a room, Susan helped me in my attempts to forget. At her flat she introduced me to some of her inexhaustible stream of boyfriends – or, more accurately, menfriends. These visited her, so it seemed to me, almost every weekday evening.

'She introduced me to a never-ending succession of men at parties she took me to at weekends. These were parties that always went on into the early hours. And often went on until some time approaching dawn.

'Some of those men I'd met at the parties, even some of Susan's boyfriends, invited me to go out with them. I ate in West End restaurants whose food was, in comparison with anything I'd ever eaten in London before, spectacular. Lobster thermidor rather than fish and chips. Quail or partridge or grouse rather than chicken. Strawberries and cream rather than sponge pudding.

'After dinner I often went on with them to nightclubs and casinos. It was a world I'd never entered before. It was one I knew next to nothing about. The cocktails they gave me – with names as exotic and obscure as the names of the wines they'd ordered at dinner – were heavenly. The prices were nothing short of astronomical.'

She recalls those parties where the men wore their college or club ties with the same quiet confidence they wore their Savile Row suits and their well-practiced smiles. Those dinners where these same men chose the food and wine with much more assurance than any Bradford millionaire wore his silk hat. Those clubs where they seemed to know both staff and fellow members with equal and easy familiarity.

Her memories of these successions of late nights are clouded by the volume and variety of the drinks they encouraged her to try. Yet she recalls them with more pleasure than pain... apart from her inevitable hangover the morning after.

'The men themselves were almost always much older than I was. Often they had jobs in the City I couldn't begin to understand. Even after they'd explained in detail what they did. They were, though, in what they had to say to me, often interesting and sometimes amusing. Occasionally they were funny in the extreme. And not always intentionally.

'Whether I wanted it or not, sex followed dinner or cocktails or both as inevitably, I often thought to myself, as night follows day. Often, too, it was just as interesting as what they had to say to me. Especially whenever they made demands I can only describe as highly unorthodox. Or, at times, as highly idiosyncratic.

'As well as finding it interesting, I sometimes found it amusing - if that's the right word. This was when they played out with me as their plaything their more adolescent, even childish, fantasies. It was, occasionally, hilarious when the fantasies they'd been building up so carefully collapsed on them like a house of cards. Though they didn't always find it quite as hilarious as I did.'

She reminds herself, with a mixture of acute embarrassment and yet some measure of good humour, of some of the comedies where she was both a spectator with a front-row seat, and a performer with a role on stage.

'Many of the men gave me presents as well as an evening out. My collection of extravaganza grew to absurd proportions in that little bedroom of mine. There wasn't a single drawer or shelf or corner that wasn't crammed with the evidence of their generosity. And – not that I ever dreamed of asking for it – all of them gave me money.

'Some of them discreetly left a small pile of banknotes. Inside my poetry books on my bedside table. Under my pillow. Or between the clothes I'd been wearing and had discarded by my bed when I'd stripped for action.

'Others, and less discreetly, pressed the notes into my hand as they left. Or, as a final flourish, they tucked them inside my bra with all the enthusiasm of a guest pinning a banknote on the bride's dress at a Balkan wedding.

'I felt, in quite a different way from ever before, I was wanted. I gave them something, whatever it was, their wives or fiancées or girlfriends didn't or couldn't give them.

'As well as that I felt, in quite a new way, dependent on them. Not because of the dinners or the drinks or the presents or the money. Perhaps because they were helping me, even if only in a small way, in my efforts to relegate you to the deep recesses of my memory. Perhaps because, however perverse this may seem to me now, I wanted them – even needed them – to do everything they did to me.'

CHAPTER THIRTEEN

'Oh hell!'

'Stephen, what is it?'

He is staring at her with an expression she cannot be sure she is interpreting correctly. She thinks, though, it may be one of anger and hostility.

'It's what you've just been telling me, Jo. Over these last minutes my mind must have been working at half speed if not less. The full horror of it all's just beginning to dawn on me.'

She fears he is angry about what she did in those first months and more after they had parted. She asks herself whether he might be hostile to her after what she has told him. She also asks herself whether, because of this, their first night together again might also be their last.

'When we said goodbye,' he explains, 'I felt an enormous and overwhelming weight of guilt. Though you'd done absolutely nothing to deserve it, I was doing nothing less than abandoning you to your fate. Sailing with you to a desert island. Then leaving you there on your own.'

He turns his head away. He puts one of his hands over his eyes. After several minutes – or so it seems to her – he turns his head back towards her. He looks angrier than she has ever seen him look before.

'Why did you go with those men? Why did you accept their money, their presents, their dinners, their drinks? Why did you have to sleep with them?' He pauses. It is not to allow her to reply. It is to think how to word what he wants to say.

'It was, quite simply, because of me,' he tells her as he clenches and unclenches his fists in agitation. 'I'm feeling that weight of guilt again. But it's now so much heavier. The real blame for what those men did to you, what they made you do to them, isn't theirs, isn't yours. It's mine.'

She puts an arm round him to try to comfort him. He edges closer to her. His head rests on her breasts. He is at this moment more a boy than a man.

'In the most obvious sense,' she explains, 'you're quite right. If you hadn't made your decision to leave me and go back to your wife, I wouldn't have needed to find somewhere new to live. I wouldn't have gone to my girlfriend's flat. I wouldn't have been introduced to those men. I wouldn't have gone with them.'

He looks up at her. He is, if anything, even more angry with himself. For what she has just said appears to him to confirm his guilt.

'But in a much less obvious and a much deeper sense,' she tells him, 'you're totally wrong.'

'How?' he asks in disbelief. 'How in Christ's name could I be?'

'Do you remember me telling you how, whether I like it or not, one part of me wants to be utterly and completely dependent...'

He remembers what she has told him, and nods in agreement.

'... and how another part of me, however much I may

try to suppress it, wants to be, needs to be, violated.'

He nods again. He shudders as he recalls some of the stories she told him when they were together.

'You're not in the slightest way to blame for either of these. And you don't have the slightest reason to feel even minutely guilty.'

Holding hands, they lie beside each other in his bed. For a time they are silent, thinking about what they have just told each other. They are, too, more than a little shy.

They are, in a way, like two youngsters who are sunbathing next to each other on their first visit together to the seaside. Wholly unaware of everybody around them. Intensely aware of each other and of themselves.

'Until we met this morning,' she told him, 'I never thought we'd meet again. However often I imagined I was with you. However much – in spite of trying not to – I thought about you.'

'I hoped we'd meet again,' he replies. 'Somehow. Somewhere. Sometime. But, though I often thought of being in bed with you again, I never dared to hope it would be anything but a dream. A fantasy I'd created for myself out of a cruel mixture of memory and desire.'

She watches him roll over onto his side to face her. Now smiling again, he looks at her. She feels him touch her body again with the tips of his fingers, just as she has touched him.

She feels him taste her lips, her skin with his tongue as she has tasted him. She feels him smell her body and her hair as she has smelled him. She feels him listen to her heart beat with his head resting on her breasts.

'Will you?' she asks.

'Will I what?'

'Will you spare me from repeating that question I had to ask you when we went to bed that first night in the flat you used to have?' She hesitates, but only for a moment. 'Will you make love to me?'

They hold each other tightly. Their arms are round each other, one hand on the other's back, one on the other's bottom. Their legs are intertwined, with his between hers. Her belly is pressed against his, soft flesh against hard. His chest is pressed against her breasts, hard flesh against soft. It is their first such embrace since they made love together on the cushions in front of the Giroux fire.

'And will you spare me from repeating that question of mine?' His voice drops until she can only just hear him. 'Will you make love to me?'

'It's the first time I've heard that question since you last asked it. And it's a question that means as much to me now as it did almost half a lifetime ago.'

They kiss. Their tongues explore each other's lips and mouths with a juvenile eagerness. They pull each other even closer together. Their embrace becomes ever fiercer. The world around them, even the room, even the lilac sheets and pillows on the bed, even the Renaissance prints on the wall, retreat beyond the edges of their consciousness.

'It feels now just as it felt then,' he whispers. 'It's as if there's been no in-between.'

'Forget the in-between. Just remember then. Just live for now.'

Unhappy memories – of their parting at the Gare du Nord, of his return to his wife, of her husband's visit just a few hours ago – dissolve and disappear. Their happy memories, too, dissolve and disappear. Even of their first embrace by the Thames. Even of the delights of their first night together. Even of the magic of the nightingale's song after they had woken up in Giroux by the embers of the fire.

'And your answer to my question?' he asks. 'Will you make love to me?'

'I've only one answer. Far from original. But as heartfelt as any words I've ever spoken.' She lowers her voice to a whisper. *'Yes I said yes I will Yes.'*

Stephen, in the aftermath of love's labours, is not lost but fast asleep. Joanna, though her body echoes with those same labours, is wide awake and has long been so. The silence in the bedroom is broken by the abrupt buzzing of her mobile phone in the next room. A text message has arrived.

In an automatic response, she jumps quickly out of bed. She feels her way uncertainly in the early-hours darkness across the bedroom towards the door. She opens it, edges into the living room and towards her handbag. This she thinks, but is not sure, she has left on the dining table.

After finding first the sideboard and then the fireplace, she reaches the table. With her hands skimming nervously over it, she feels for her bag. She finds it, opens it and fumbles blindly through it. She pulls her mobile from under a jumble of keys and loose change, envelopes, lipsticks and perfumes.

With her thumbs working automatically, she opens the message and reads – to her utter dismay – the first lines on the screen. Her eyes are only a little more used to the darkness than they were when she jumped out of bed. But she runs back as fast as she can into the bedroom. On the way she bangs an elbow against the bedroom door and a knee against the wooden bed frame.

'Stephen!' she shouts in panic. 'For God's sake! Wake up!'

He rolls over slowly from his back onto his side. He switches on his bedside light. Though he is still much more asleep than awake, he sits up. To his dismay he sees her face is more like the face of Munch's *Scream* than the face he kissed before he fell asleep. It is as full of fear and horror as it was when her husband walked into his flat a few hours earlier.

'What's wrong?' he asks. 'What the hell's happened?'

Though one knee is throbbing with pain, she kneels on the carpet beside his bed. She is shivering uncontrollably as if she has just seen a fatal road accident. She sways backwards and forwards as if she is in a trance. She clutches her mobile tightly between her hands as if it is a prayer book.

'I've just had a message,' she tells him in a hoarse and breaking voice.

He looks first at her, then at her mobile. 'What does it say?' he asks. 'Read it to me.'

She looks down at the screen once again. She is mesmerised by the words that go in and out of focus in front of her. She says nothing. He leans over, puts his arm round her shoulder. Her body stops shivering and swaying, becomes still.

'Take your time,' he tells her. 'Read it to me when you feel you can.'

She lifts her mobile in front of her face, tries to focus on the screen. She begins to read the message in a voice so quiet that, in spite of the silence around them, he can hardly hear her.

'*If a man be found lying with a woman married to an husband, then...*' Her voice breaks in mid sentence. He hears only a dry and strangled croak in her throat.

'Go on. Read me the rest of it.'

She remains silent until she can once again focus on the screen. She then reads on in a hoarse whisper. '*... then they shall both of them die, both the man that lay with the woman, and the woman.*'

'Who the hell sent you this?' he demands angrily. 'And what in God's name does it mean?'

'Your first question. That's only too easy to answer. Jack sent it. Not a shadow of a doubt. None. It'll be one of those Biblical texts he's stored up to use whenever he thinks it's the right time.'

Her voice breaks again, but only for a moment. She looks away from the screen of her mobile, and forces herself to reply. 'Your second question. That's much more difficult. But, whatever it means, it's bad news. I've come to know – and all too well – how he plays games with people. One of the games he plays so well is to frighten them. Me included. He's also a genius at calculating when people might do something in response. And when, for whatever reason, they won't.'

As he begins to absorb what she has just said, and as he tries to think about it, she gives him more food for thought.

'The good news – if there is any – is that what he says isn't always what he means. Nor is it always what he does. That's also part of the game he plays so well.'

He looks directly, searchingly, into her eyes. His mouth is dry. His mind is racing. 'What should we be doing, Jo? What do you think?'

She looks first at him, then down at the floor. Her mind is at the same time hopelessly confused as well as deadened by her husband's message.

'I've got no idea. No idea at all. But if we go on talking about it we'll more than likely do nothing but go round in circles. Get nowhere fast.'

'Then do we do nothing?'

'We could try to get some more sleep. After all, we may be needing all the strength and stamina we've got. And, for all we know, that may be sooner rather than later. We're both wide awake, though. With little or no chance of getting any more sleep.'

'So?'

'We could, I suppose, try to tell each other more about what's happened to us in our last twenty years. You were the married man, and now you're single. I was the single woman, and now I'm married.'

He pushes himself up the bed with his elbows so that his back rests on his pillows. He moves her pillows so that she can be close beside him. At the same time, he thinks how best to take his story forward from the day he went back, tail between legs, to his wife.

'Do you remember what I told you that very first night of ours together? How, before I'd left Erica for the first time, I often walked out of our flat in the mornings to a barrage of shouts and screams? It was, in the first months after I went back to her – and, I suppose, just as I should have expected – no different at all.

'I might be shaving or showering. I might be having breakfast or getting dressed. I might be listening to the news on the radio or sorting through my papers to prepare myself for a day in court. I never knew when she'd begin.

Or what would trigger those shouts and screams.'

He has memories, as vivid as if they belonged only to yesterday, of those mornings, and of the horror he felt with the day's first explosion.

'I told you as well how I'd often gone back home in the evenings, after a day in chambers or in court, to lengthy accusations or silences. That wasn't any different, either, in the early months after my return.

'With each step I took as I walked back home, I became less and less concerned about the case I'd been working on that day. Just as with each step I became more and more concerned about the scene that might be played out after I'd closed the front door behind me.'

He recalls the hopes he sometimes had on his journey home of a good and happy evening. He recalls, too, how his hopes were so often shattered. At worst it was the moment he walked into their flat. At best it was a short time after his return.

'At weekends in those early months it was often as if the mornings and evenings were just two acts in complete operas, sometimes of what you once described as Wagnerian proportions.

'When exactly the next shouts and screams, the next accusations and silences would come, I never had the slightest idea. But what I knew for certain was that, sometime or other, they would come. And I knew I'd be no better able to cope with them than I'd been before I'd left her.'

He thinks of those late Saturday mornings when the first storm had already come and gone. This was when he looked forward – almost with a sense of relief, though with no certainty – to a calm weekend. He thinks as well of those late Sunday afternoons when the first storm had yet to arrive. This was when he waited in gloomy anticipation for the calm to end.

'I still had those painkillers I'd created for myself over the years to dull my feelings. One of these was, of course, my work. I threw myself into it lock, stock and barrel. Even when I hadn't the least interest in the cases themselves. Even when I hadn't the least liking for the clients I was representing.

'Although I often enjoyed being on my own, another of these painkillers were my friends. Some from Sedbergh. Some from Cambridge. Some from the Bar. These I met a couple of times a week or more for a lunchtime beer in the Seven Stars.

'A third were my walks, even in the worst of weathers. Round the gardens of Lincoln's Inn Fields where – at least in the summer – I looked at the butterflies flying over the flower beds. Through the narrow backstreets of the City where the sparrows and starlings were hunting on every pavement for scraps of food. Along the footpaths beside the Thames, with gulls wheeling above the river and following in the wake of every passing boat.'

As he talks, he remembers those days in chambers when he filled every minute he could with back-to-back work on his cases. Those pub lunches when he listened to his friends as they chattered noisily and exchanged bawdy anecdotes at their usual corner table. Those walks when he focussed all his attention on the natural world around him.

'I still hoped she's do what she'd said she would in that last letter of hers. I told myself that, by going back to her, I'd fulfilled my side of the bargain. I told myself as well that I'd expected her to fulfil her side of it. But the reality in those first months after my return was the same as it had been before. It was, to use – or abuse – one of your own lines, *now just like then.*'

'So why in Heaven's name did you let her do what she did to you?' she asks. She is saddened though not greatly surprised by his account of what happened to him after he returned to his wife.

'If I'd ever known when she'd fly off the handle, I suppose I could have done something to avoid it, to get out from under. There were times when I had a few minutes of advance warning. The sighting of a tsunami racing towards me over the horizon. But there was never enough time for me to race inland to safety before it hit the shore.'

'Then why didn't you talk to her about it? Try to get to the bottom of it? Try to find out why she wouldn't talk about it? Tell her how devastated you were by what she was doing to you?'

'I'd love to have talked to her about it. To have discussed it with her quietly and calmly. To have found out why she did what she did. To have given her some idea of the effect it had on me.'

'And wasn't that ever possible?'

'Totally and utterly impossible. It was, quite simply, a no-go area.'

'Why didn't you stop her? I just don't understand. You may not be a Maasai warrior, six feet or more tall and as strong as an ox. But you aren't exactly a Congo pygmy either.'

'I suppose I could have stopped her being violent to me. But I could only have done that by being violent myself. And, rightly or wrongly, that was never on my agenda. Never at the back let alone at the front of my mind. Even when I was feeling most sorry for myself.'

'Why didn't you remind her of what she'd written in that last letter of hers?'

'I could no more talk to her about that than I could talk to her about what she did to me and to herself. If I'd ever tried to talk about it she would, without a shadow of a doubt, have done just what she'd said in her letter she wouldn't ever do again.

'I also came to realise she mightn't have seen what she'd written as being her side of any bargain. And even if she'd seen it like that, she mightn't have seen she had any obligation to keep it.'

'So she mightn't have meant a word of it?'

'That's the conclusion I reached early on after I went back to her. What she wrote could have been, as anybody with any sense would have known without a second thought, and as you thought that last night in Giroux, no more and no less than a way of getting me back.

'I had to accept, however unwillingly, that what she'd written might have meant, in her books, absolutely nothing. I had, fool that I was – or so I thought at that time – been led up the garden path.'

She listens intently to him as he talks. Sometimes he is hesitating between words. Sometimes he is racing at breakneck speed from sentence to sentence. She listens as he becomes progressively quieter, until his voice is almost a whisper. Breaking as he mocks himself. Cracking as he forces himself not to cry.

'Why didn't you do something, anything, to retaliate? Even if what you'd have done to her wouldn't have been in the same league as what she'd been doing to you?'

'I could tell you I still believed I could help her to overcome her violence. I could tell you I still blamed myself for her violence. I could tell you I stood on the high ground of principle and reckoned I had no right to be violent. Neither to her, nor, for that matter, to anyone else.

'But I've got another and much less principled answer. It's that I couldn't have lived with myself if I'd done anything like that to retaliate. Some men, I'm sure, can beat their wives half unconscious. Go off for a few beers with their mates. Think no more of it.

'Just as I guess some men can spend an evening of so-called passion with their mistresses. Then go back home for a night of similar so-called passion with their wives. My bad luck is I'm not one of them.

'There's a third answer that's probably closest to the truth. It's that I feared if I retaliated she'd become even more violent. Towards me, of course. But also, which was what I feared most of all, towards herself.'

She feels his body become more and more tense. In the silence she hears his heartbeats become more rapid, and his breathing become shallower.

'Then why didn't you make more use of what you've called your painkillers? Go out more often with your friends after you'd finished work? Go off with them for weekends and for holidays? Even find yourself a girlfriend or two?'

'It may sound as if I'm putting myself forward as a candidate for minor sainthood. But if I'd accepted all their invitations to drink or to dinner, I'd have had so much less time to do whatever I could to help her.

'I was still hoping that, if I tried hard enough, put enough effort into it, I'd achieve a breakthrough. That I'd reach port after stormy sea. But to be more down to earth, if I'd accepted their invitations – and a bottle of red wine or a plate of tapas or both were quite sizeable temptations – there was one thing I was sure of. Even though I'd have been at home less of the time, she'd have been violent more of the time I'd have been there.

'And I'm not at all sure that a girlfriend or two would have helped all that much to kill the pain. It's more likely they'd have done the reverse. Make me aware there'd be no port after stormy sea. Just think back to the effect you had on me when we were together twenty years ago!'

She watches his face begin to light up as he remembers their weeks together. She listens to his voice as it begins to strengthen. She feels the power begin to return to his arms as he holds her close to him, and to his body as he lies over her. He then enters with her a world in which, for a few infinitely precious minutes, their memories of their pasts disintegrate, and they are aware only of each other.

CHAPTER FOURTEEN

Stephen knows all too well how pathetic the story he has just told Joanna must have sounded to her. He also knows how much his answers to her questions must have convinced her of his stupidity – if, that is, she was not already completely convinced of it.

She is not in the least surprised either by his story or by his answers. She has expected him to have changed in body over twenty years. She has not expected him to have changed in mind. Nor has she expected him to have overcome any of his vulnerability, any of his inability to cope with his wife's violence.

She has only one surprise, and this not very great. It is that he has remained so incapable of questioning his wife about her actions or, indeed, of talking to her about them. And this is in spite of his having had many more years' experience of questioning witnesses in court about their actions – often, she is sure, very rigorously.

He wonders whether she will tell the next episode of her story more successfully than he has told his. Whether she will be able to tell it as easily and calmly as she told him about her entry into the world she came to inhabit after her return from France.

Her concerns as she prepares to take her turn are quite

simple. Remembering how sympathetic he was – and is – to her life story, she wants to recount it just as it was. To tell it warts and all. She does not, however, want him to react as badly as he did earlier to her account of what she did after her return. Even more, she does not want him to blame himself for anything she has done.

'So by day I was a teacher. If not demure certainly not far from it. If not a wilting violet, then certainly not its opposite. Whatever that may be. I dressed quietly and unobtrusively. More likely to be wearing a calf-length skirt than designer jeans. More likely a loose pullover than a tightly fitting T-shirt.

'It was I, and no-one else on earth, who was responsible for a class of twenty five or more boys and girls. I was treated by their parents as a member – however junior – of the establishment. I was pigeonholed in the same category as a doctor or dentist or, I suppose, as a lawyer. Though, I suspect, as a solicitor rather than a barrister!

'By night, like it or not, I was somebody quite different. In no way was I an underage amateur parading around King's Cross. Open for business night and day like a twenty-four hour supermarket. Doing anything with anybody and anywhere to pay for her drugs.

'Nor, at the other end of the scale, was I a full-time professional. With a top-drawer clientele and running the business from a penthouse flat in St John's Wood. I was, perhaps, somewhere between these two extremes. Though, or so I'd like to think, I was significantly closer to St John's Wood than to King's Cross.

'I might call the men I was with my boyfriends or menfriends. I might say they were just taking me out to dinner and giving me a good time. I might describe everything they gave me – including the money – as generous gifts. I might think of myself as a teacher and tell anybody who cared to ask that this was my profession. I was also, though, at the end of the day, and again whether I liked it or not, a hooker, a common tart.'

She thinks back to those schoolday afternoons. When, after the children in her class had left, she cleared her desk of the textbooks she had been using. When she travelled back from Shepherd's Bush to Susan's flat by bus and tube.

She thinks back, too, to those early evenings. When she was sitting by her bedroom window reading a few lines of poetry until the phone began to ring. When she arranged to meet one of her menfriends later on. When she agreed with him when he would come round to pick her up.

'I lived this double life for a couple of years or more. A long time, whenever I think about it. Which, these days, is hardly ever. But it was a time that wasn't without its changes in the work I did, both in the daytime and at night.

'Each July I lost one class of children, with most of them looking so much older than when they'd arrived. Perhaps still – if you'll forgive the quotation! – with *satchel and shining morning face* they'd been *creeping like snail unwillingly to school*. But they certainly knew so much more than they did when I'd begun to teach them the previous autumn.

'Each September I gained another class. Most of them had done with *mewling and puking in the nurse's arms*. But they all looked so much younger than the ones who'd gone on to the next year. And they seemed to know so little.'

She recollects the mixture of relief and regret she felt

on the last day of each school year. True, there were one or two exceptions she was glad to see the back of. Yet she was sadder than she thought possible to be losing boys and girls she had got to know so well. For these were children whose lives she had helped – perhaps more than she recognised at the time – to shape.

At the same time she recollects her eager anticipation, only slightly tinged with uncertainty, on the first day of the new school year. She recalls looking at the faces in front of her, and wondering about her work with them. Which of the children would respond wholeheartedly to what she taught them? Which would have their own very different and possibly disruptive agendas?

'After a few months some of my menfriends also moved on. Exiting the stage where they – and even at times I – had been such enthusiastic and dedicated performers.

'Perhaps to return to the safer world inhabited by their wives or fiancées or girlfriends. Perhaps to move on to another stage and another actress. To someone who offered new theatrical excitements, new releases for their fantasies. Or to someone who was just a new alternative to their long-term partners. Perhaps – though from what I knew of them I very much doubted it! – to retreat into celibacy or abstinence.

'But as some of them exited the stage, so others walked on to play their parts. Occasionally I saw these performances of theirs as tragedy with a dash of melodrama. More often, though, they were comedy with a dash of farce.'

Unlike what she did for most of the children in her class, she understands she did little to shape her menfriends' lives. Indeed, she understands they taught her more and shaped her life more than she did theirs.

From those she met only once or twice, she gained little or no understanding of them. But from those with whom she spent a full term, and even a full year, she gained a wealth of insights into their professional and private worlds. And, in spite of how she had gained these insights, she felt more lucky than unlucky to have done so.

They may have shared with her the secrets of their lives, just as she shared with them the secrets of her body. She is, though, very aware that her life and how she really felt about them remained a closed book which none of them managed to open.

'In some weeks there were performances on most evenings. Even if not on every one. In other weeks the curtain rose only once or twice. Or, at short notice, the performance was cancelled or postponed when the male lead failed to materialise. And when there was no stand-in to take his place.

'At weekends there were often matinées, and on Sundays as well as Saturdays. There were even times when the matinées continued without a break into the evenings. And, once or twice, the cast changed between performances.'

She is both amused and embarrassed when she recalls those weekends when she met more than one of them. These were weekends when – though without their knowing or even suspecting it – she had to organise their comings and goings with almost military precision.

'Some, perhaps most, of the men I went with had needs that were highly conventional and wholly predictable. Often, I suppose, like the men themselves. Merchant bankers, stockbrokers, company directors, army officers, corporate lawyers, surgeons, even the odd clergyman. Though, as far as I knew, not a single rabbi or imam.

'Their needs made few if any demands on my imagination. Or, for that matter, on my body. They themselves would have won the wholehearted approval of any nineteenth-century missionary in Africa. Not for their infidelities, of course. But for the ultra-orthodoxy of the position they automatically adopted. And expected me to adopt as well. Which, now I come to think of it, is just what you were telling me about yourself and your first conquest at Cambridge.'

These men may for all she knew have been at the cutting edge of new thinking in their professions, radical and inventive in the extreme. But after they put down their briefcases and took off their dark suits and more besides, it was very different. They conformed – at least as she saw it – to every instruction a Victorian father might have given his son on the eve of his wedding to prepare him for the night to come.

'Others – and some of these were also bankers, stockbrokers, directors, officers, lawyers, surgeons, clergyman – had needs that were, to put it mildly, less conventional. When I first went with them, their demands pushed my imagination to its limits.

'And my body was pushed into positions that would have qualified me as a professional contortionist. But once I'd got to know them, they – and their demands – were no less predictable than the others.

'Just as predictable as the men's needs were my own. To make them dependent on me for their delight. And, in turn, to be dependent on them. Even when the stage directions on their scripts required them to exercise their fantasies of flagellation.'

Her mind is flooded with memories of the gymnastic exercises these men attempted to perform. As she tells Stephen about them, she cannot hold back the mirth she felt then even more than she does now.

It was, though, when she was with them, mirth she had to make enormous efforts to hide. She also has memories of their canes and rulers and slippers, many – but not all – of which gave her at least as much pleasure as pain.

'One of the latecomers onto the stage was Jack. He became the most prolific – and at the same time the most generous – of all the actors in my dramas.

'He gave me a succession of earrings, bracelets and necklaces. Echoes, now I come to think of it, of the presents her clients gave Fanny Hill two hundred and fifty or so years earlier. As well as these, he bought me a little MG sports car. It was bright green and with an engine that roared at the least provocation.

'One evening we had dinner – lobster bisque followed by baked bream – at his favourite fish restaurant behind Leicester Square. After we'd finished, he told me he had a surprise for me. He took me to his car, a black Mercedes whose engine did no more than purr like a contented cat. He drove me to a small block of flats on the edge of South Kensington.

'Here he greeted the doorman as if they were old friends. He escorted me in a lift to the top floor. He invited me into what he described with a laugh as a room with a view and a half. This was, I told him, a serious understatement.

'He then stopped me in my tracks. He revealed to me – and to my utter amazement – that it, together with the bedroom, bathroom, kitchen and balcony, not to mention the garage space in the basement, was all mine.'

She reminds herself of the shock and delight she had felt when Jack had handed her the keys of the MG. She remembers, even more so, how shocked and delighted she was when he handed her the keys to the flat. She could not believe her good fortune. Not only did she have her own car and her own flat. She also had him, generous to a fault, as well.

'His demands weren't exactly the most conventional. But nor were they at the other end of the spectrum. Sometimes he brought one or other of his menfriends with him, though never any other girls.

'Their demands, like his, were ones I had no problems with. Especially as these were, as you might put it, consecutive rather than simultaneous. And, of course, they contributed as he did to paying for a lifestyle most teachers could never dream they'd have.

'After a couple of months, almost as if it was on cue, all my other menfriends faded away. Whether to return to their regular pastures or to move on to pastures new I didn't know. Nor did I ever try to ask.'

She remembers the moments of regret – though at the same time relief – she felt when all the other men she had known disappeared from her life. But far outweighing her regret at losing them was her joy at gaining Jack. For he was as agreeable as any of them had been. And, as far as she could judge, he had a successful business career from which she benefited.

'So, when he moved in and provided for me rather than paying for my services, it wasn't in any way awkward. Nor did it feel anything but natural that we were in bed together throughout the night and not just in the evening. And that we had breakfast and not just dinner together.

'I became more and more dependent on him. More and more needing and enjoying what he did. Including those marks on my bottom! Then, one New Year's Eve, we were standing on the balcony at midnight listening to the church bells around us. It felt only natural when he told me he wanted to marry me as soon as his divorce advanced from nisi to absolute. And it felt just as natural when I told him my answer was *yes*.'

'Even though it wasn't any of my business, Jo, I asked you a little while ago why you went with those men. Why you accepted their money, their presents, their dinners, their drinks.

'I now realise that, as soon as I'd asked you the questions, I gave you my own answers. That it was because of me. Because I'd deserted you. I never gave you a chance to give me your answers. Or even to tell me to mind my own business.'

'I did give you parts of an answer, you know. When I said you were, in the most obvious sense, right. When I added that you were, in a much less obvious sense, wrong. And I did try – even if it was far from fully – to explain why.

'There is, I suppose, much more to tell. I've got to warn you, though, I may not be too fluent in the telling. It's not because I don't want to tell you. It's because, as I've already said, I hardly ever think about those days. And this'll be the very first time in my life I'll really have talked about them to anybody.'

He sits up, startled. He becomes for a moment the lawyer who has just had an unexpected answer from a client in chambers or from a witness in court.

'Didn't you ever talk about those days to your Maida

Vale girlfriend? The one who gave you your entry visa into that world?'

'Never. Though Susan knew perfectly well what I'd been doing. And she knew as well as I did, if not better, quite a few of the men I'd been doing it with.'

'Didn't you ever talk about those days to your husband? After all, he shared quite a few of them with you. And he gave you your exit permit from them.'

'Never. Though he knew more than enough about my past. And, as I discovered during our years together, he knew much more than was good for them about some of those men.'

He looks at her. He is finding it difficult to believe she has been so silent about that part of her past, and for so long. He is also finding in her silence a reflection of his own silence about much of his past.

As he has done so often that evening, and as he had done so often when they were together before, he strokes her hair. He kisses her on her forehead. He holds her head in his hands.

She edges across the bed. She pushes herself against him. At this moment she is as much a child seeking warmth and shelter and protection as an adult. He puts his arms round her. This is, however, not as a prelude to passion. It is as an encouragement to her to answer more of his questions.

'Why,' he asks her, 'even though you weren't in any way a full-time professional, did you go with those men so often? Why, even though you didn't go with all and sundry, did you go with so many?'

'There's a very simple answer. It's that I got into the rhythm of it. They started phoning me from their offices as soon as I got back from school. I fixed up to meet one of them. And that was it. Day after day. Week after week. Month after month.'

'And is that the only answer?'

'Of course it isn't. As I've told you, I found it interesting to go to the bars and restaurants and clubs that otherwise I'd never have dreamed of visiting. I found it interesting to talk to them. Even, perhaps perversely, to hear what they had to tell me about their wives and fiancées and mistresses.'

'And was that all you talked about?'

'We talked, inevitably, about sex. What I heard about their sex lives could have filled volumes. What I heard about their fantasies could have filled whole libraries. As well as that, they used language that, from navvies in a public bar at closing time on a Saturday night, might have sounded quite natural. But, from men deeply embedded in the English establishment, it sounded odd in the extreme.'

'And the sex itself?'

'For me it was usually more of an afterthought than the big idea. I was interested to find out what they wanted from me. And how they went about getting what they wanted. But, however enthusiastic I appeared to them to be, there wasn't – well, only rarely – any passion. I was usually – though I've got to admit not always – less a participant than an observer.'

As she talks, she thinks back to those evenings when she lay back and thought of England. When she thought of every country she had ever visited, and even of many she had not. When she thought of the *fair field full of folk* in *Piers Plowman*, of the heroism of Beowulf when he fought first against the giant Grendel, then against Grendel's mother. When her body and mind were in perfect disharmony. Feelings firmly in cold storage.

She also thinks back to other evenings, few and far between but still clear in her memory. These were when she was as much a participant as the man she was with. When, perhaps in spite of herself, she felt she was dancing towards the gates of ecstasy.

He listens with some remnants of the horror, revulsion, nausea he felt when she first told him about her double life. He also finds himself listening to her with a growing fascination.

'How easy was it to cope with your dual life? By day a teacher. By night, to use your own description of yourself, a common tart?'

'Physically I was always tired. Often exhausted. Sometimes absolutely shattered. As well as that, I was sometimes in a bit of pain after a caning had become a little too enthusiastic. Or after an evening had developed into a sex olympics when I found myself competing for a gold medal in endurance.'

'And in your mind?'

'It wasn't, as I remember it, too difficult. Certainly not as difficult as you seem to think it was. Certainly easier than if I'd been doing it because I had to get my hands on heroin. Certainly easier than if I was being forced by some man or other to sell myself to every Tom, Dick and Harry who'd found my card in a West End phone box. And beaten up or worse if I didn't.

'After a time it felt a natural and normal way of life. As I've just told you, I'd got into the rhythm of it. Whenever, for some reason or another, I had to put my double life on hold for a few days, I've got to admit I missed it. And when I started off again, it was usually with a light rather than a heavy heart. It might be difficult for you to understand. But I found I was looking forward to, rather than dreading, my first evening's adventure.'

She is revealing more of her life in those days than ever before. Yet she feels at the same time less and less self-conscious, more and more confident. He, too, feels more confident. He even begins to ask her questions he would have avoided just a few minutes ago.

'Why,' he asks, 'did you agree to satisfy the demands that some of those men made? Demands you've called less conventional?'

'I could simply say I'm a masochist. But I think I can do better than that. I've already tried to explain that, among the raft of needs I've had in life, one's been to be dependent.

'Another's been to be at the receiving end of violence. To continue, perhaps, what began when I was a child. When I wanted to be dependent on my parents. When, by beating me, my father was at least paying me some attention.

'That I've already told you. I've also told you I've enjoyed the violence at least some of the time. The hand or slipper or cane hitting my bare flesh as I knelt on the floor or crouched on the bed. However perverse it may sound, finding pleasure by being at the receiving end of pain.'

He accepts he now knows more about her than he has ever known. He decides, though reluctantly, he must give her time to recover from his interrogation.

'One last question before I let you stand down from the witness box I feel I've put you into. How is it you're able to talk so dispassionately to me about the life you led? That you often seem to be talking about somebody else and not about yourself? That you can even laugh at what you got up to, treat it as comedy?'

'If I was to tell you I'm schizophrenic that might satisfy you. But a friend of mine who's a psychiatrist assures me I'm not. So I'll try two other answers. One is that it's you I'm talking to, and I don't need to put on an act.

'The other is that I'm talking about a long time ago. About another me. About distant memories I hardly ever recall. And, to be honest, about some things I can only laugh about. I saw them as comedy at the time. I still see them that way if ever I think about them.

'Perhaps I can talk dispassionately because, though flagellation certainly figured in my repertoire, I'm not in the business of self-flagellation. I'm not at all sure I was right to do everything I did. There are odd moments when I fear what I did was dreadfully wrong. And one day I may come to regret some or all of what I did in those years. But it's a day that hasn't arrived. At least not yet.'

He puts his arms round her as they lie together. He holds her, kisses her. She feels his fingers begin to caress her breasts, to explore the cleavage between them. She is filled with delight that he is touching her, and that he is touching her there.

'Will you, Stephen?'

With the same delight of being touched, he feels her fingers slide along the cleft between his buttocks.

'Again?' he whispers.

'Yes,' she replies. 'Again.'

She feels his hands move slowly over her belly, down below her navel. What she senses now is both the delight of his touch and a growing excitement.

'And you, Jo, will you?'

With the same mixture of delight and excitement, he feels her hands move, just as slowly as his are moving, round from his buttocks.

'Yes. Again.'

She feels his body on hers, pressing down on her, pinning her against him.

'*Now just like then?*' he whispers.

'Yes,' she whispers in reply. '*Now just like then.*'

CHAPTER FIFTEEN

Joanna and Stephen lie together, both fast asleep after they have made love. They are like two survivors of a shipwreck who sprawl unconscious on a sandy shore after a storm at sea.

In the depths of his sleep, he hears a succession of knocks on the door of his flat. The first three knocks are rapid and light. The next knock, after a gap of no more than a second, is heavy. These knocks are repeated several times: a hollow reminder of the opening bars of Beethoven's *Fifth*.

He sits up, switches on his bedside light. He clambers out of bed as quickly as he can. He picks up his dressing gown from the floor, puts it over his shoulders. Still far from awake, he stumbles barefooted across the bedroom, through the living room, along the hallway, to the door.

He unlocks it. With more than a little caution, and with no idea at all of who might be outside, he opens it inch by inch. In front of him in the near darkness, he sees nobody.

He walks out and goes to the top of the stairs. Again he sees nobody. The only sound he hears is the padding of his bare feet on the stone floor. He looks down the staircase. Yet again he sees nobody. He hears no sound, either of the front door opening or closing, or of footsteps on the pavement outside.

Shaking his head and totally bewildered, he walks back to his flat. As he reaches the door, he looks down. Almost – but not quite – hidden under his doormat, which is inscribed with *AVE* facing the door and *VALE* facing the stairs, he sees a long white envelope.

He picks it up, tears it open. With the help of the hallway light that he has switched on, he begins to read the words that are underlined in black ink on a page that has clearly been torn out of a Bible.

After he has read the first few words he stops. He runs back as fast as he can into the bedroom. He switches on the main light and finds Joanna still as fast asleep as he had been before he had heard the knocking on his door. In a single violent movement he pulls back the duvet. He grasps her by her shoulders. He shakes them much more roughly than he intends.

'Wake up, Jo!' he shouts. 'For Heaven's sake! Wake up!'

She sits up slowly and reluctantly. Through the same fog of deep sleep he was in only minutes before, she sees him leaning over her.

'Whatever is it?' she whispers. 'What's happened?'

With his hands shaking, his whole body shivering, he holds the piece of paper in front of her. She glances briefly at it. Though she cannot have read more than a few words, he sees in her face – and to his great surprise – not so much horror as resignation.

'So what is it this time?' she asks. 'Tell me.'

He sits down beside her on the bed. He tries his best to stop his hands from shaking, but with limited success. With the same limited success he tries to focus on words that dance, one moment clear, the next blurred, on the page in front of him.

'If a damsel that is a virgin be betrothed unto an husband, and a man find her in the city, and lie with her, then...'

His voice suddenly dries up.

'Then what?' she demands.

'...then ye shall bring them both out unto the gate of that city, and ye shall stone them with stones that they die.'

He reads the words again to himself, tries to make sense of them. Now becoming just a little calmer, he folds the page and puts it back into its envelope.

'Another of Jack's games?' he asks.

'Of course it is. The second act of his little play. Though, if you remember the words he sent me in his text message, this isn't much more than a repeat performance.'

'Then I've got to repeat the question I asked you after you had that text message. What the hell should we be doing?'

She looks first at the envelope, then at him. She closes her eyes before she answers him. 'There's no chance I'll be able to go back to sleep after what's just happened. And I can't imagine you'll be able to either.'

She looks across at the alarm clock on his bedside table. 'As well as this, and if that's the right time, we're very close to daybreak.'

'So?'

'So shall we try to bring our stories up to date? Whatever Jack's up to is hanging over us like a gang of vultures circling over the corpse of a sheep. Who knows when in the future we'll have another chance to tell each other about the past? And what about making a pot of coffee to help us on our way?'

He makes his way to the kitchen, boils his kettle, ladles

more coffee into his percolator. While he is doing this, and before he walks back into the bedroom, he tries to think how he will tell more of his story. How he will avoid repeating too much of what he has already told her. And how he will tell it more easily than he did a little earlier.

'As the months after my return passed by, as autumn turned into winter, Erica's threats came more often than they'd ever done before. Even more often than they'd done in those weeks and months that led up to my earlier walkout.'

He remembers only too clearly some of her more dramatic explosions. Yet, although he was so shattered by them then, he is beginning to find he can talk about them now with a degree of detachment that surprises him.

'Sometimes these were threats against me. To ruin my professional reputation, such as it was, once and for all. To scar me for life by pushing a broken bottle into my face.

'Other times they were threats against herself. To cut her wrists with a blade from my razor. To put her head in the oven after she'd turned on the gas. To jump off the top floor of a multi-storey car park.

'I could, of course, have tried to discount these threats. To see them as threats made by somebody who wouldn't in any way do what she said she'd do. But I could never be sure her threats were empty. I had too much experience of threats she'd fulfilled to the letter.'

He slips out of bed, returns to the kitchen. He pours the coffee into two of his mugs and adds some milk. As he does this, some of the threats Erica put into practice flash through his mind like brief clips of films put together at random. But, as he remembers these episodes, he finds he is less and less one of the characters in a novel. He is becoming more and more its narrator.

'She never, thank God, cut her wrists. Or put her head into an oven. Or jumped off a multi-storey car park. But sometimes she clapped the palms of her open hands hard against the sides of her face. Other times she beat her clenched fists against her chest.'

He has tried to talk to Joanna before about how his wife behaved. But he has found it difficult to do this without being overwhelmed by his emotions, without fighting against tears. Now he is discovering he can tell her about this with no more of a problem than he believes she has had in telling him about her past.

As well as revealing to Joanna how he used to feel, he very much wants her to understand why he thought Erica behaved as she did. To give her his diagnosis, amateurish as it was, of her condition.

'Ever since they began, I'd been trying my best to understand what the origins of her outbursts could be. After I went back to her, and as they were happening more and more often, I thought about them longer and harder.

'As I've told you, perhaps far too often, I'd feared one of the main causes – if not the main cause – was myself. If only, I thought, I could give her the sort of life she wanted. Be the sort of man she wanted me to be. Then there'd be no outbursts, no silences, no threats. And, I hoped, no harming of herself and no bruises or scratches or cuts on me.'

He thinks back to those interminable hours of introspection when he convinced himself he was the main cause of her discontent. He thinks back as well to his hopes that, by doing more for her, he could make her happier.

'I used to phone her once, twice, sometimes more each day. From my chambers between meetings. From the court after the end of a case. When there was a film or a play that interested her, we went to see it. When she wanted to go out for a drink, we went to our local pub in Camden Town or to some wine bar or other in Hampstead.

'At weekends we went as often as we could to one of her favourite places. Places where there wasn't any stress and where I hoped she could relax. The Forest of Dean. The Peak District. The Norfolk Broads.

'Because of these efforts of mine, I was able to persuade myself I was doing something. But I felt more and more I'd be deceiving myself if I persuaded myself I was doing something that was, in any real way, helping her.

'Often our evenings at the cinema or at the theatre ended with an outburst. On our evenings at our local pub she was often silent for minutes on end. The door into her thoughts and feelings was firmly closed. And often our weekends away combined both outbursts and silences.'

He cannot in any way forget how sad and distressed he felt when so many of his attempts to help her failed so abysmally. He does, however, remember what he began to ask himself after so many of these failures. Could there, he wondered, be causes of her behaviour in which he had little part – or no part at all?

'I started to think her fragility might have been the result of what had happened to her years, even many years, before I'd met her. The result, perhaps, of some event I knew absolutely nothing about. Something, perhaps, her parents or her schoolmates had done to her. If this really was one of the reasons why she was so brittle, I hoped these memories would fade away as time passed.'

He laughs at himself as he tells her about these hopes. For he now realises he was at best deluding himself. The hopes he was raising were utterly false.

'Usually, when I thought about this, I felt I was getting precisely nowhere. I had, though, occasional and, perhaps to an outsider, blindingly obvious ideas. One above all invaded my mind more and more often. This was what had, since we'd first met, been the unthinkable.

'It was that the deep roots of what she said, including her threats of violence, had nothing at all to do with the world around her. That the deep roots of what she did, including the violence itself, were just the same. That, because of this, they had nothing to do with me. That they came, instead, from deep within her. Some powerful chemical imbalance. Some inheritance in her genes she wasn't able to control.

'And if this was so, then I had to understand something else as well. Although she'd been violent so often since that last letter of hers, she might, just might, have written what she did in completely good faith. At the moment she was writing it, she might have meant every single word!'

He remembers how this idea elbowed its way more and more to the forefront of his thinking. He remembers how angry he was with himself that he had had it so late in the day. He also recollects, as he tells Joanna, that the crucial moment in his thinking came not from his hours of introspection but from a case he had taken on.

'The client I was to represent in court was a woman in her early thirties. The case was one of persistent violence against her by her husband. What had happened to her was, I came to believe, not far from a mirror image of what was happening to me.

'Her husband's violence wasn't, as far as she could discover, caused by anything that had happened to him earlier in life. Or by any alcohol he'd just drunk or any drugs he'd just taken. Or by anything she – or anybody else for that matter – had done or not done.

'She could only conclude – as did a psychiatrist whose report I saw – that his violence was totally unprovoked and totally unpredictable. It was, as they saw it, something he'd had throughout his life. Perhaps from the moment he was born. Perhaps from the moment he was conceived.'

He realises he has talked for far too long. He fears he has made far too little sense. But at the same time he realises he is reaching the climax of his story. He hopes she will have the stamina to listen to the end.

'I had, as I've told you, begun to think the unthinkable. I now recognised it was in no way unthinkable. There was, perhaps, no better explanation than this of my wife's behaviour towards so many people, me included. And in this case, whatever I tried to do to help her would get precisely nowhere.

'But even if I was, as I'd thought for so long, one of the causes of her discontent and of her fragility? If this was the case, then by staying with her I'd be making her distress worse and not better. And by leaving her I'd be helping and not harming her.

'One evening I began to talk to her about it. With more courage than I ever thought I could summon up. And after I'd worked out exactly what I'd say. My throat was completely dry. I was hardly able to force the words out of my mouth.

'I reminded her of what she'd written in that last letter of hers. I told her she'd gone back on her word. I also told her what I would do if she were ever to go back on her word again, even once. I would, without any shadow of a doubt, leave her. And this time it would be for ever.'

He has very clear memories of every moment of this encounter. His trepidation when he began to talk. His growing determination as he continued, as he told his wife everything he wanted her to know.

'She listened to me in total silence, her body motionless, her eyes fixed on me. I finished what I had to say. For a minute or more she said nothing. Not a word.

'Then, suddenly, she hit me on my head with her clenched fists. She kicked me on my legs with her shoes. Just as suddenly, her attack on me stopped. She began to beat her fists against her own head. She kicked her feet against the legs of the table where we were sitting.

'I'd left her the first time, as I once told you, tail between legs. This time I left much more calmly. I packed a couple of bags. I told her I'd be back to pick up the rest of my things the next morning. I was as sure as I could be that this time, whether I was right to go or not, nothing she might say or do would make me go back.'

Joanna has listened to his lengthy monologue without saying a word. He has spoken it so quietly yet, to her surprise, so calmly, that she has to concentrate on his every word.

She has, throughout it, held his hand. Whenever he has hesitated, whenever she has felt he might be stopping, she has squeezed it gently to encourage him to continue. Now, however, it is clear to her he has said as much as he wants to say. She feels, she hopes rightly, that he wants her, in some way or other, to respond.

'Some of what you've just said is what you've told me already. Some of it's what you've hinted at.'

'Then,' he asks, 'do I escape the sort of cross-examination I've subjected you to on and off over the last few hours?'

'Only partly.'

'So what more can I tell you?'

'To start with, how is it you've been able to tell it all so easily? And so differently from just a few hours ago when you were about as agitated as I've ever seen you?'

'I don't know,' he replies, and she thinks she sees the beginning of a smile. 'Perhaps after I'd listened to the way you talked about your teacher-and-trollop double life I took a leaf out of your book.'

'Why did you keep on blaming yourself for so long?' she asks as she returns his smile. 'And this time can I have a serious answer to a serious question?'

'For much of the time she and I were together, it seemed only too obvious to me I was to blame. I could think of so many things I'd done, or not done, that could so easily explain what she said and did. And, when I thought along these lines, there was nobody else, absolutely nobody, who could possibly have been to blame.'

'You've told me that, if you were the real cause of your wife's condition, it would be better for her if you left her. You've told me as well that her condition could have been caused not by you or by anything in the world around her, but by something within her. And that you weren't in any way its cause.'

She pauses as she thinks how to word her next questions. 'Why did it take you so long to think differently? Why hadn't you come up with these new ways of thinking about the way she behaved years before?'

'In my work, I reckoned I could often think creatively – or at least as creatively as lawyers can. When I thought about my own predicament, though, I couldn't have thought more narrowly or unoriginally.'

'So how convinced did you become that one of the trains of thought you'd come up with was the right one?'

'I wasn't absolutely convinced. But I became more and more convinced that, even if I hadn't got to the whole truth, I was at least closer to it than I'd ever been.'

'And how difficult was it for you to recognise that these ideas were as different from each other as chalk and cheese?'

'I didn't have the slightest problem in seeing this. And, quite frankly, I couldn't be completely sure which of the two better fitted the facts. But in one case, whether I stayed with her or not wouldn't have made the slightest difference to the way she behaved. And in the other case, by staying with her I'd only have made things worse for her. I was still worried sick about what she might do to herself. The imperative to stay had, though, at least as I saw it, gone away.'

'When you talked to her that evening and gave her your ultimatum, did you try to tell her why you thought she behaved as she did?'

He shakes his head. He remembers, of all the hundreds of speeches he had prepared over the years, the one speech he never delivered. 'I'd thought about this night after night when I woke up and my mind was filled with it all within seconds. I'd even worked out what I'd say so she'd understand and wouldn't feel too hurt.

'But as soon as she started to punch and kick me, I never spoke the lines I'd worked and reworked so carefully. The curtain had gone down. The lights had gone out. The final act was over.'

'On a different tack, how sure were you this time when

you walked out that you wouldn't go back? How sure were you that, if she repeated her threats to kill herself, you wouldn't do what you'd done before? And, whether you wanted to or not, that you wouldn't go back to her?'

'I told you I knew of nothing that would make me return. I was as sure of this as I could be. And, for most of the time after I left her, for most of those days and then weeks and then months that followed, I felt I was strong enough, determined enough, to do just what I said I'd do.'

He hesitates. She sees his smile fade and his eyes wander away from her face. 'But who knows what I'd have done if one day, when my strength and determination were at a low ebb, she'd told me in graphic detail what she'd do to herself? And where? And when? Who knows, Jo, who knows?'

CHAPTER SIXTEEN

Stephen begins to climb out of bed once again in order to refill their empty mugs. Joanna holds him back, gets up herself. She leaves him with his thoughts as she makes some fresh coffee.

As well as this, she begins to ask herself how she will bring him up to date with her life story. What she will focus on. What she will mention in passing. What she will, for one reason or another, leave out.

'Soon after we first met I told you I wasn't dedicated enough as a teacher. I told you a few hours ago that, in those months after I got back from France, I still didn't feel it was my vocation in life.

'It's true that in the first couple of years after I got back I was earning more than I could possibly need from what you might, if you want to be diplomatic, call my extramural activities. But in spite of this, and in spite of not feeling it was my vocation in life, I became more and more interested and involved in my work as a teacher. Whatever might have happened the night before.

'I might be exhausted and underslept beyond belief. Yet I looked forward each morning to the day ahead. And that was even though I knew I'd have failures and frustrations piling up on top of each other. From the moment the first child arrived to the moment the last child left.

'At the end of the day, and even when I felt I'd had more than my fair share of trials and tribulations, I always felt the day hadn't been completely wasted. I persuaded myself that at least some of the boys and girls in my class had learned something from me. I also realised that I'd learned something from them. About the eccentricities of children's behaviour if nothing else.'

She thinks back to those lessons she was happy with after she had prepared them so assiduously. For these were lessons in which she knew exactly what ground she wanted to cover and exactly what she would do to bring them to life.

She also thinks back to those lessons when she felt the opposite, and when she found herself playing it by ear. For these were lessons for which – in spite of her best intentions – she was wholly unprepared.

'When the job of deputy head came up in my mid thirties I was enthusiastic – or was it misguided? – enough to apply. And, so it would seem from the result of the interview I had, I was good enough to be appointed. Then, a few years ago, the head who'd given me my very first job retired. For better or for worse, and in spite of my own reservations, I followed in her footsteps.

'So there I've sat each day. In the head's office at the end of the staff corridor. Behind a desk that's seen better days. Looking out over a playground that's not much bigger than a pocket handkerchief. There are fifteen or so teachers, almost all of them women, and four hundred or so children of all shapes and sizes, races and religions. All of them are, so I've thought to myself in daydream or nightmare moments, dependent on me. Just as, in varying degrees, their parents are.'

She reminds herself of her unexpected progress from teacher to deputy head and finally to head. She accepts she has not been the most motivating – or indeed motivated – member of her profession. She has not, as she sees it, inspired her children or her fellow teachers as a few of her colleagues have done.

But she also reminds herself – and with more than a little satisfaction – of what some these colleagues, and some of the children's parents, have told her. That her assessment of herself is quite wrong. That she is as inspirational as the best of them.

'I've had to make more decisions in this job than I've ever had to make before. And I've had to deal with problems the like of which I've never had to deal with before.

'But take me away from my daytime desk, put me in what's often labelled the matrimonial home, and you wouldn't believe I'm the same person. How I've behaved as a wife compared to how I've behaved as a head would, I suspect, excite even the broadest thinking of psychoanalysts.

'For the big decisions in life I've been utterly dependent on Jack. What colour should our kitchen be painted when it's redecorated? What sort of new sofa should we have in the sitting room? Where should we go for our next winter break?

'These have been questions to which, with absolute inevitability, he's provided the answers himself. Or, more precisely, they've been questions he's asked himself and then provided himself with the answers.

'There have been some times when I've felt more

like a member of an audience listening to his words of wisdom than his wife. When he's announced that the kitchen will be white with a hint of apricot or avocado or whatever. That we'll have a new sofa upholstered in white or black leather. That our winter break this year will be in Lanzarote or Tenerife.

'There have been other times when I've discovered by chance what he's decided we're going to do. When the decorator has arrived on the doorstep with his stepladders and dustcovers, and with the paint Jack has ordered. When the delivery men have arrived with the new sofa in their furniture van. When the postman has arrived with a letter in which I've found the tickets for our holiday flights.'

She recollects so many more decisions Jack has taken without even a pretence of consultation. And these include the time when he put their house on the market. But she decides she has told Stephen more than enough about them. She does her best to keep to herself the frustration and annoyance she has felt.

'For the little decisions in life it's been just the same. I've been just as dependent on him. Where will we go for an evening out? What music will we listen to? What will we have to eat at the weekend?

'It's been Jack who's decided we'll go to the local Odeon to watch the latest avant-garde film or the latest Hollywood blockbuster. That we'll have dinner in the Thai restaurant round the corner and eat stir-fry prawns or red beef curry.

'He's decided we'll listen in a moment of nostalgia to the Rolling Stones belting out *Satisfaction* or to Eric Clapton taking us to *The House of the Rising Sun*. That we'll have a Sunday lunch of boeuf stroganoff from the freezer or a pepperoni pizza from the nearest takeaway.

'Even for decisions on things I've always thought of as my own business and nobody else's, he's made me dependent on him. Shall I buy a Laura Ashley full-length cotton dress or a Jaeger skirt and matching jacket in the summer sales? Jack decides.

'Shall I wear my comfortable Marks and Spencer panties and bra to school? Or panties that are little more than a thong, and a bra that's more suitable for a teenage disco than a head's office in a primary school? Jack decides.'

She cannot forget those thousands of little decisions he has made alone. Again, though, she decides she does not need to trouble Stephen with every minute detail of them. Nor does she need to reveal to him the growing anger she has felt over the years at the way Jack has behaved.

'With our love making it hasn't been the slightest bit different. When? Where? How? On the floor, in the bath, in the garden? Before breakfast, after dinner, in the middle of the night? Standing, sitting, kneeling, lying flat on my back? He's decided. When he's wanted me to be quiet, he's told me to shut up. When he's wanted me to talk dirty, he's fed me my lines.

'If I've wanted him to lose his temper, I've simply had to carve out a small fragment of independence for myself. Do my own thing. But what if I've wanted a quiet life, everything sweetness and light? Then all I've had to do has been to let myself depend on him to make the decisions.'

She thinks, and with more than a little resentment, about some of his more bizarre decisions on the whys and wherefores of their love life. She also thinks, and with little less than fury, about some of the times he has lost his temper over decisions she has made.

'Part of me has been unhappy, frustrated, resentful, angry about this degree of dependence. Just as that part of me had reacted in earlier years to my dependence on other men. And it's that same part of me that's wanted to escape from it. Especially when Jack's taken control and manipulation to extremes I've never thought were possible. And this includes his surveillance of what I'm doing that we've been the victims of tonight.

'But there's another and more secret part of me. This, I've got to admit, I've often tried to hide even from myself. I have, though, given you some odd insights into already. And this part of me has welcomed at least some of my dependence on him.'

She remembers how over many years she has become more and more aware of this dual reaction of hers to her dependence on Jack. She is very clear about her desire to be more independent. She is, however, much less clear about the strength of her need to be dependent. She is, she feels, as confused now as she has been every time she has tried to dissect and analyse her reactions.

'Has it been because I've wanted, at least some of the time, to be passive? To have decisions made for me? Have I, perhaps, in some hangover from my childhood, equated being dependent with being loved?

'Whatever the reason – lurking, perhaps, in the depths of my subconscious – that part of me has welcomed my dependence on Jack. And on that succession of men before him. It's that part of me, as well, that's welcomed being at the receiving end of anything he, and that same succession of men, have wanted to do to me.

'Have I welcomed it because this violence has, in a way, been ritualised and defined? A performance in a theatre, carefully rehearsed, rather than something impromptu and uncontrolled?'

She has clear memories of the connection she has made throughout her adult life between being dependent on men and being the willing victim of their violence. She remembers she has often questioned, even agonised over, this connection. But she recognises this is a connection that, even if it explains nothing about anybody else, may explain a great deal about herself.

'Has it been because, however perverse it may seem to you, I've been excited by the forms this ritualised violence has taken? Has it been because a beating has been followed, almost inevitably, by sex? Though, if I'm honest with myself, I've got to admit something else to you. I've sometimes found as much excitement in the beating as in the sex.

'I know I'm wording all of this very badly. And I'm only too aware you've heard some of it – perhaps too much of it – already. I know as well, with these attempts to explain myself, I'm doing no more than swimming in the shallow waters between the coral reef and the shore.

'But what if I dive down into those dark waters where the reef and the deep sea meet? Then my explanations you've already had hints of may shock you as much as they've shocked me whenever I've dared to think coldly and rationally about them.'

She understands she is now talking to him about herself in ways she has never talked to anyone before. She understands as well she may do more than shock him when she completes her attempt to explain herself. But, rightly or wrongly, she decides to reveal even the most difficult questions she has asked herself: questions that have so perplexed her over many years.

'Has it been because I've needed to be humiliated and degraded? And because my way of achieving this has been by being the victim of a man's violence? Has it been because I've felt I've deserved to be the victim – echoes of how I reacted to my father's violence? Has it – as I told you in France – been because I've felt I've needed to be chastised? To do penance? To seek atonement for my sins?

'Has it been because I've found, by being dependent on men who are violent to me, I can be closest to them? Has it been, in a word, my passport to intimacy?'

During these minutes when she has told him so much about her relations with her husband, and so much more about herself, he has come to understand she has revealed more about herself than she has revealed to him before. He realises, too, that she has, by her own account, just exposed much more of herself than she has to anyone else – her husband included.

He feels it might be possible to ask her to expose more. But he understands he must avoid the style of questioning he often finds so effective in court. He recognises, in everything he says to her – and especially when she has her husband's two messages hanging over her – he needs to be sensitive in the extreme. As sensitive, indeed, as she has been in what she has asked him.

'By diving down into the depths of yourself, you've told me things you've only hinted at up to now. As well as these, you've told me things that are totally new. At least to me. And even for a hardened interrogator like me, it's difficult to ask you about what's so personal and intimate.

About what you might so very easily have kept private.'

'So do I, as you thought you might do a little time ago, escape without being questioned?' she asks him.

'If you really want to, yes. But there are just a few questions I'd like to ask you if you agree.'

'I'll do my best to answer them,' she replies. 'But you've got to understand I may say things I haven't thought enough about. Or haven't allowed myself to think enough about before now. For you it may be unknown territory. For me it may be almost the same.'

'First of all, how did you come to understand this need of yours to be dependent? And to be at the receiving end of violence? Was it slowly, over months or even years? Or was it suddenly? In a blinding flash of self-knowledge?'

'I'm not at all sure. Certainly I'd known it before you and I first met. Perhaps it began when I thought about the beatings my father gave me. Though I often tried my hardest not to think about them.

'But perhaps there was one moment some years later – again before we met – when a man I was mad about told me he wanted to cane me. I couldn't believe how much a bamboo stick could hurt as it landed time after time on my bottom. I couldn't believe how loudly I could yell in protest.

'But nor could I believe how exquisite the pleasure was after he'd thrown the cane away. Nor how loudly I shrieked with uncontrolled delight as he made peace.'

'How easy did you find it to accept that this need was part of yourself? That you weren't simply looking at somebody else who had this need? That you were looking in a mirror at yourself?'

'In the beginning, when I was still at school, it wasn't

easy. Not easy at all. I was sure nobody else was like me. I kept asking myself what was wrong with me. I thought it might be one of the trials and tribulations of growing up. A disorder as transient as teenage spots or swings of mood. I thought I might grow out of it, and one day it would be as much a part of my past as any other bit of adolescent misbehaviour.'

'And then?'

'Then I began to understand. If I did have something wrong with me, then so did plenty of other people. One of my best friends, Janet, stroking herself either for comfort or excitement in the changing room before tennis. And blushing bright scarlet when she saw I was watching her. Two of my classmates, Jimmy and Doug, kissing and fondling each other in the cloakrooms after assembly. And already bright scarlet before they saw me.

'Later still I began to understand there wasn't necessarily anything wrong with them. Or, for that matter, with me. We were neither normal nor abnormal. Just a bit different. Just ourselves. The same as liking dependence rather than independence. Being violated rather than violating. Which is, you might say, the healthier option.'

'How easy have you found it over these last few minutes,' he asks quietly, 'to tell me all this about yourself?'

'To tell you what I've told you hasn't been too difficult. True, I've told nobody about any of this before. Just as I've told nobody since then about that double life I used to lead. But once I started to tell you about my life as a tart, I didn't feel too inhibited about revealing myself to you as a glutton for punishment.

'Partly, I suppose, it's a relief to share with you what romantics might call my most intimate secrets. Partly I may be hoping you'll help me to understand better who I am and how I function. But if I had to give you chapter and verse for everything, I'd find it more than difficult. And I'd be blushing to a depth of scarlet that would make Janet and Jimmy and Doug look perfectly normal.'

'So why, when we were together before, didn't you tell me more about this?'

'For one thing I was younger. Not much more than half the age I am now. I'd had no problems at all with exposing my body. Certainly not since I was in my mid teens. But I had gargantuan problems with exposing what I was thinking and how I felt. Even to you. I didn't have the confidence I've got now. I couldn't be sure you'd keep my secrets as absolutely as I've managed to keep them.

'And, of course, I hadn't progressed very far when we first met. The real excesses all came later. When I discovered, in that double life of mine, what you might call the far extremes of gluttony.'

'How easy is it for you to understand that, in all of this, you and I are at opposite ends of the spectrum? That I'm horrified more than by anything else I can think of by being at what you've called the receiving end of violence? Just as Orwell's Winston Smith was by rats?'

'It's not too difficult for me to understand that at all. When I've been at the receiving end of violence it's been as a consenting adult. I've known what part I'd be expected to play.

'I may not have known all the lines. What happened on the night may occasionally have deviated from the plot. But I've known both the play and the other actor, or actors, in the performance. If it had been violence out of the blue, violence I hadn't reckoned on, I'm sure I'd have reacted to it with just as much horror as you've done. If not with more.'

'Aren't you sad, Jo, that I wasn't ever able to satisfy these needs of yours when we were together before? Aren't you sad I'm no more able to now than I was then? And that I'm never going to be any different from what I am now?'

'It's only sometimes I feel this need. And it's far from being the only need I feel. To be absolutely frank with you, you satisfy needs no other man I've been with has ever satisfied.

'I realised that when we were together all those years ago. In spite of everything that's happened to me over the years since then – and in spite of whatever Jack may do next – I've realised it again tonight. And at this moment, now just like then, my need isn't for a cane on my bottom but for your body on mine!'

CHAPTER SEVENTEEN

The first hints of daybreak begin to creep past the curtains of his bedroom. Stephen rolls out of bed and puts on his dressing gown and slippers. He goes into the kitchen, makes yet another pot of coffee. He recognises Joanna has taken her story up to time present. He also recognises she has taken him into parts of herself he has at most had hints of up to now.

For his part, he reckons he has no more hidden nooks or crannies of himself to expose to her. As he waits for the coffee to percolate, however, he asks himself how best he should bring his story up to date. And, as soon as he takes the mugs back into the bedroom, he launches into his account.

'In the days after I'd left Erica for the first time, I'd overnighted with friends on their spare beds and sofas. This time I did just the same. But very soon – much sooner than I'd ever expected – I found this flat on the fringes of Bloomsbury. And here I've been ever since, showing a remarkable lack of adventure or initiative. Or both.

'In chambers I carried on as I'd done before I left her. It was, though, much easier this time than it had been before. After all, it wasn't the first time I'd left her. I was, you might say, becoming an old hand at desertion.'

He remembers so well those first weeks on his own. Not weeks when he agonised in deep despair about whether he had made the right or the wrong decision. More weeks when he began, with increasing enjoyment that reached towards delight, to recreate himself. To emerge, like the butterflies he watched in Lincoln's Inn, from the confines of his chrysalis and fly free from flower to flower.

'Over the years, though by accident rather than by design, I specialised more and more in what goes under the label of family law. Most of the work that came my way was divorce. And very often it was divorce in which at least one of the parties had been violent towards the other. Even when there was no mention of it in any of the documents.

'With one of my cases a few years back, I gained a certain notoriety. The husband – my client – was a top-notch professional boxer. And a heavyweight at that. His main ground for divorce was the violence his wife terrorised him with day in and day out.

'For some of the newspapers – and not only the tabloids – this was headline news. Had it been dog biting man, it wouldn't have got even a couple of lines on an inside page of a local paper. But this was man biting dog, and they ran it for days on end and for all it was worth.

'After that case I became busier than I'd ever been. The work certainly wasn't paid as well as work in commercial law would have been. But nor was it so dry-as-dust. You've told me you were gaining insights into the eccentricities of children's behaviour in your classroom. At the same time I was gaining insights into adult behaviour – or, to be more accurate, misbehaviour. This may well have helped me to understand a little better the human condition.

And, at the same time, to understand my own.'

He reminds himself of the deep, and deepening, satisfaction he found in his work. Of how he enjoyed representing his clients as best he could in negotiations with other barristers and, if there was no agreement, in court. Of how, just as much, he enjoyed the close relationships he developed with some of those clients. Of how these became and remained, even after many years, among his best friends.

'As you know, in my early forties – it must have been at roughly the same time you were being made a deputy head – I became a Queen's Counsel. Or, as they say in the trade, I took silk. I wasn't the youngest QC, the highest flier. Nor, though, was I plodding at carthorse pace behind my contemporaries as they raced ahead in the professional steeplechase.

'I haven't been made a full-time judge as one or two of them have. I'm not sure I'd want to be one. At least not yet. But two years back, as I've told you, I became a recorder. For a month or so each year I'm a judge. For the rest of the time I'm still a barrister. Perhaps it's the best of both worlds. Or perhaps, just possibly, it's the worst.'

He thinks back with more than a little pleasure to his first day in court as a QC. No longer a junior in a major case, playing second fiddle to an established QC. Now with a junior of his own as his dogsbody.

He thinks back as well, and with just as much pleasure, to his first days as a recorder. No longer arguing his own clients' cases and refuting the cases of his clients' opponents. Now deciding between plaintiff and defendant. Bringing the adversarial process to its conclusion. Or, as he sometimes tells himself, acting as God Almighty.

'From time to time over the years, Erica's phoned me. Occasionally she's come to my chambers. Whenever she's made contact I've wondered if, at least on the surface, she'd be able to keep a lid on her emotions.

'Would she be as unpredictable and volatile as she so often was when we were man and wife? Would she be in control of herself when she began? Would she then lose control of herself? Even after all these years, I've never known.

'But what I've known for sure has been that she'd always, at greater or lesser length, work her way through her catalogue of my failings. Usually it's been with a well-trodden recitation whose subjects I've known all too well. I'd ruined her career. I'd sabotaged her friendships. I'd failed to give her the children she so desperately wanted.

'Occasionally it's been with something I hadn't heard from her for a long time. I'd deceived her about my earlier girlfriends. I'd prevented her from making a much better match. I'd never even remotely satisfied her sexual needs.

'I've also known this recitation would have an inevitable endgame. A demand for more money. That's even after our divorce settlement was agreed. It's even after she became the sole owner of the so-called matrimonial home and everything in it. It's even after I'd paid her a lump sum that ate up every penny of my savings and more besides. Yet she's wanted still more.

'I've always reminded her that the court order set out each and every one of my obligations to her. I've reminded her it was in full and final settlement of her claim. I've told her it was a done deal and I'd paid up in full. Then, with the fuse paper well and truly lit, her shouts and screams would be only seconds away.'

He has very distinct memories of what Erica has said

and done whenever she has contacted him. He has equally distinct memories of how he has reacted.

No longer has he been someone she has been able to devastate with her very first words. More he has been someone who has listened patiently to what she has had to say. Someone who has replied coldly and clinically. Almost untouched by her emotions. Almost unaffected whenever she has lost control of herself.

'Over the years she's contacted me less and less. Perhaps it's because she's come to see that whatever charitable instincts I may once have had towards her have withered and died.

'But I still see her much more often than I'd wish to. Walking here and there around Bloomsbury. And, quite often, walking past this flat whose address she knows very well from the time of our divorce.

'That's because she sold the place we'd had that she so hated. Then, for some reason I don't begin to understand, but suspect may be connected to me, she moved into a flat in Brunswick Square. Just a few minutes walk away from here.

'I've also thought about her less and less. And although the nightmare hasn't faded away, not completely, it's certainly faded. It's shadow rather than substance. Time past rather than time present.'

He explains to her how many of his memories of his past years have been relegated to the wastebin and successfully deleted. But at the same time he tells her – though he does this without explaining why – about some very special memories of times past have lived on in spite of time passing.

'In the Alps when I've been climbing part of the way

up some of the glaciers that tongue their ways down the flanks of Mont Blanc. In the Pyrenees when I've been climbing up from the valley pinewoods to the summit of Monte Perdido, joining on my way the spring exodus of thousands of sheep from the lowlands to the hillsides.'

He also explains to her that these special memories of his have lived on just as brightly and clearly when he has been backpack travelling along some of the great land routes of the past. These were routes trodden by pilgrims, soldiers, merchants and, these days, by twentieth-century tourists such as himself.

'When I've been walking along part of the pilgrimage camino to the cathedral in Santiago de Compostela. Though with no more Catholicism inside me when I've walked up the steps to its Baroque facade and into its Romanesque heart than I had when I'd left Roncesvalles.

'When I've been bussing in central Asia along fragments of the Silk Routes. Khiva, oasis city, dry-clay walls, flat-roofed houses, minarets with bands of glazed tiles. Bukhara, the Kelyan minaret, broad and built of bricks, dominating the city. Tamurlane's city of Samarkand, the grandiose ruins of the Registan and its medresas.'

Nor, he tells her, have these special memories escaped him when he has been travelling by boat along a few of the world's great rivers. Never in five-star luxury. More like a student on a shoestring budget.

'Down the Amazon from Iquitos to Manaus. By night sleeping uncomfortably on a hammock. By day sitting out on deck. Watching the rainforests sliding past unbroken hour after hour. Watching the clouds often growing in the afternoons like huge grey balloons until they burst and unleashed a violent tropical storm. And, of course, taking the photos you saw in the hallway.

'Along the Niger from Mopti, frenetically busy and reeking of drying fish. Crawling forward in an exhausted and rusting steamer. Past scrubland and near desert. Then on to the desperately decaying city of Timbuktu on the edge of the Sahara.'

He is not at all sure she has understood what, in his extremely rambling and roundabout way, he is trying to tell her. He decides to be less obscure and, in just a minute or so, to come clean.

'On most of these journeys I've been alone. On some I've been with one or two close friends. Men I'd known well at school or at Cambridge or at the bar. On a few I've travelled with a woman.

'Yet, whenever I've been on one of these adventures, wherever I've been, whoever I've been with, there's always been another traveller as a constant companion. A friend who's been as real and as special in my memory as anything I've seen, as anyone I've been with.

'Even when I've been kissing the woman I've been with as we've stood by the Atlantic on the Île de Gorée off Senegal. Even when I've been holding her as we've sat together, listening to the cracking of the ice, by the Glacier del Miage above the Val d'Aosta. Even when I've been caressing her under a torn mosquito net in a Chiang Mai hotel plagued by cockroaches.

'I may well have enjoyed these women as short-term companions. I may well have enjoyed their minds or their bodies or both. I've had to recognise, though, what was wholly obvious from the very beginning.

'The special memories have been of someone else. Of the love of my life. And she, my very dearest Jo – as

I'm sure you've worked out by now if not from the very beginning of these meanderings of mine – has been you.'

Over these past minutes, she has listened to his account – long and rambling as it was – with diminishing disbelief and growing delight. Until yesterday she had lived for twenty years with the firm conviction that, after his return from France, he had forgotten all about her.

Yesterday, however, he told her how often he had thought about her after they had parted. When he had stood in front of Botticelli's *Venus and Mars*. When he had been on the Thames towpath, in the gardens of Lincoln's Inn, along the Grand Union Canal, in Oxford, in Dentdale. She has now discovered he thought of her much, much more, and throughout the time between then and now.

'As I told you yesterday when we were in the National Gallery, Stephen, I could recreate at the drop of a hat every moment we were together. I never dared, though, to dream you were thinking about me. But so often, and so easily, I found myself thinking about you. And now I've discovered we were thinking about each other.

'I've never been on adventures like yours. They aren't exactly Jack's style. But in his business mode he's taken me to some of America's most lavish hotels. The plastic palaces of Las Vegas, Los Angeles, San Francisco.

'In his holiday mode, he's booked us into some of the world's best-known – though not necessarily best – hotels. On our weekends in Paris, we've stayed at the George V on the Champs Elysées. On our week in Venice we stayed in the Danieli. Just round the corner from St Mark's Square and the Doge's Palace.

'When we've holidayed further afield, it's been exactly

the same. The Imperial in Delhi, echoing with today's voices of Americans abroad, and yesterday's voices of the British Raj. The Winter Palace in Luxor and the Old Cataract in Aswan. Both of them overlooking the Nile. Both soaked in a century or more of history. And with the great and the good from Winston Churchill to Agatha Christie among their clientele. But wherever we've been, on business or on holiday, you've been – even if for just a moment – my companion in my dreams and my thoughts.

'In his religious mode, he's taken me to some of Europe's most memorable cathedrals and churches. Hagia Sophia in Istanbul. San Vitale in Ravenna. The cathedral in Cordova inside what used to be one of the great mosques of Islamic Spain. And they're just a sample.

'One of the reasons they're memorable for me is because they're so beautiful. They're also memorable because, under an arch, beside a flying buttress, perhaps for no more than a second or two, I remembered you.

'And wayward as I'm sure you think I've been, I've remembered you even when Jack and I have been in our most intimate moments. And here my verbal meanderings – less eloquent and more modest than yours, but at least shorter! – come to an end.'

He watches her as she sits by the side of the bed, one foot almost on the floor, the other tucked under her bottom. As she walks a few steps towards the window. As her bottom moves – deliciously, as he sees it – with each step. As she stands quite still with her back to him, her bottom no longer moving, but still moving him.

'I think, Jo, I'm as shocked and delighted by what you've just told me as you are by what I've told you. And I'm feeling as close to you now as I did that night in Giroux. After we'd slept by the fire. When we were listening together to the nightingale.'

She hears his footsteps behind her. Feels him hold her breasts again, cup them in his hands. Feels his hands again on her belly and, for a moment, fingering her navel. Feels his breath on the back of her neck. Feels the full length of his body against hers as he pulls her close to him. She turns, faces him. She wraps her arms firmly round him, pulls him close to her.

'Now,' she whispers. 'Now just like then. But, from now on, let's be sure it's not just now and then.'

He thinks back to the way she used to play with words when they were together twenty years ago, and smiles.

'I'm not *sans eyes*, *sans teeth*, *sans mind*, *sans everything*. At least not yet. But please remember this.'

With one arm round her back and the other round her thighs, he lifts her up. He lays her on the bed so her body is stretched out. He arranges her hair so it cascades over the pillow as it had done that first night in Kensal Rise.

'Then – especially when you were at your most demanding – performance sometimes exceeded desire. I could always, as they say, rise to the occasion. Now, I fear, I'm the victim of waning powers. Another Rustico I first mentioned to you twenty years ago. Responding to Alibech's surplus of lust with his own shortage of potency. Another Falstaff, whose desire always exceeds performance!'

They are woken by an explosion somewhere in the flat that could only be caused by shattering glass. They jump out of bed as quickly as she did when she heard her mobile, and as quickly as he did when he heard the knocking on his door. They race across the bedroom to the window.

Here they find nothing amiss.

With Joanna only inches behind Stephen, they dash into the living room. One of the panes of glass of the window that looks out onto Handel Street is smashed. The wooden floor, and even the carpet in front of the fireplace at the far side of the room, are littered with fragments of glass.

Almost running, he steps across them. He treads on them with his bare feet but feels nothing. Nervously, even fearfully, he peers through the hole in the window.

'What can you see?' she asks as she gasps for breath.

He looks up and down the road, still lit by the street lamps. He is searching for somebody walking or running away. He is listening for footsteps, for voices, for a car starting.

'Nothing. Not a bloody thing,' he replies. 'Nothing and nobody.'

He turns away from the window and walks back to the middle of the room. As he does this – though not thinking why – he bends down and picks up some of the larger pieces of glass. These he puts in a small pile under the broken window pane.

'Look!' she cries as she sees something that is, most certainly, not broken glass. 'Over there. By the fireplace.'

He steps on more glass as he strides over to the fireplace. From the tiles just in front of it he picks up an ornate metal cross. It is made of brass or bronze, and is almost the length of a hammer. It seems to him, however, to weigh far more than any hammer.

'This must be what broke the window,' he tells her. 'There's nothing else that could have done it. But who was it who threw it? And why?'

'I'm afraid we both know the answers. And without

giving your questions a second thought.'

They stand together in the middle of the room. They face each other, both of them holding the cross. Neither notices that the other is naked. Their faces reflect a mixture of uncertainty and fear.

'Look!' she exclaims as she examines the cross. 'Look at what's tied to it.'

He sees a piece of paper wrapped tightly and carefully round the metal. He unties the string that is binding the paper to the cross and hands it to her. She unfolds it and, in a measured voice, reads him the words she sees in front of her. These have, as with the earlier message, been underlined in black ink on a page torn from a Bible.

'If the tokens of virginity be not found for the damsel: then they shall bring out the damsel to the door of her father's house, and...'

She pauses.

'And what?' he demands.

'... and the men of the city shall stone her with stones that she die.'

'So it's just you this time.'

'No,' she sighs. 'I haven't finished.' Slowly and quietly she reads the rest of the verse.

'If a man find a betrothed damsel in the field, and the man force her, and lie with her: then...'

'Yes?'

'... then the man only that lay with her shall die.'

He takes the piece of paper from her. He puts it on the table. Now facing her again, he holds both her hands in his.

'Hell!' he blurts out. 'Hell and damnation! There's only one thing I can say. The time for talking – except for talking about what we've got to do about this – is over.

Whether we like it or not, now's the time the kissing – and everything else – has to stop.'

CHAPTER EIGHTEEN

Joanna's recollections of the last day and night squirm around wildly inside her head. They collide violently with each other. They disappear and reappear as if they have wills of their own.

She tries to grab hold of one recollection, then another. She tries to get them under control, to set them in some sort of sequence, to make some sense of them. But, however hard she tries to concentrate, she can make no order at all out of the chaos in her mind.

She knows she has to clear her head, even if not completely. She knows she has to have a chance to think, even if not nearly as coherently as she would wish.

While they are having their breakfast of grapefruit and croissants and coffee – a combination, Stephen reminds her, of what they ate after their first night in his Kensal Rise flat and after their first night in Giroux – she tells him she needs to get some fresh air. She adds that, more importantly, she needs to have some time by herself.

Her dress is still as wine-stained as it was the evening before. Because of this, he lends her some of his clothes. She puts on his college sweater – even more faded than she remembers it was twenty years ago when he wore it in France – and his equally faded tracksuit trousers. He goes with her to the top of the stairs. She kisses him, and walks downstairs.

She pulls the black front door with its broken entryphone until it is almost closed. Her shoes clatter on the four stone steps as she walks down to the pavement and onto the road. A bicycle bells rings sharply as a cyclist she has not seen swerves to avoid her. Footsteps echo behind her as she walks a few yards along Handel Street, through an iron gateway, into early-spring Saint George's Gardens.

To all these sounds around her she is wholly oblivious. She hears only her own voice, the voices of Stephen and Jack, the words of the Bible. These repeat themselves time after time, and reverberate in total confusion, inside her head.

'I can't believe I'm so deeply exhausted or so hopelessly mixed up. More so than I can ever remember I've been. Nor can I remember when the best and the worst of times have followed each other as they have since yesterday morning.

'I've been reliving in my mind those weeks with Stephen. They're as bright and delicious, in three dimensions and on wide screen, as they were when we were together twenty years ago. And, of course, I've been reliving the hell that followed. That evening when we parted at the Gare du Nord. Those months when I did whatever I could to try to put him behind me. However bizarre and ludicrous, self-inflicted and self-destructive that was.

'And, as well as reliving the past, I've just lived through a night when my body's experienced delights it hasn't known since he and I were last together. Even greater delights than it knew when I was with the most expert and experimental of sexual gymnasts.

'They're delights I never dreamed I'd experience again. Especially since Jack and I got married. Because, over the years since then, his performances have become pedestrian and perfunctory in the extreme. And, now I come to think of it, that's being more than a little generous to him!

'The delights of last night weren't only in my body. For what Stephen's done since we met yesterday morning is exactly what he did then. And it's exactly what none of that long succession of men I've known between then and now has managed to do. To fill me with delights that have reached way beyond flesh and blood.

'Even when I've been telling him about my need to be dependent, he's tried so hard to understand me and to help me to be myself. And even when he's been telling me about his need to be independent, he's always done it in ways I've easily understood. It's never been as if he's been speaking a foreign language to me.

'It's also been a night when Jack has pushed me as close to the cliff edge of despair as he's ever done. His appearance yesterday evening was bad enough. And I can relive in every minute detail every awful second he was up there in the flat. But those three messages of his, with their mixture of menace and threat, were far, far worse. Worse than anything I thought he was capable of.'

Two children are running around St George's Gardens as they chase each other. Their legs are dancing, their arms are waving, their heads are bobbing. They dash between the oblong tombs, memorials to the garden's past as a burial ground. They career round the ornate Victorian stone drinking fountain. They race in front of the yellowing terracotta statue of Euterpe, muse of instrumental music. They skip past the irises and forget-me-nots that have just begun to flower.

An old man is lying asleep on one of the wooden benches facing the lawn. His grey overcoat, faded and threadbare, is covering much of his body. His cap, stained and torn, is covering much of his face. Tattered plastic bags lie at random on the ground underneath him.

A woman is walking along the gravel path that snakes around the gardens. She walks between the bent brick walls that surround them and the lawns on which the first daisies and dandelions of spring have appeared.

When one of the children falls on the path and begins to cry, she bends down and gently puts it back on its feet. She strokes its head tenderly. She talks to it in a quiet and reassuring voice, until its tears are forgotten and it runs happily back to its playmate.

Joanna sees nothing except the images of now and then. These are thrown up onto the beach of her consciousness by the overpowering waves of her memories.

She remembers seeing Stephen looking at *Venus and Mars*. Striding towards her outside her school and kissing her on her forehead. Watching the two leaves floating past when they were together on the towpath at Hammersmith. Standing on the platform of the Gare du Nord as her train inched away from him. She remembers, too, Jack making the sign of the cross and throwing her wine over her the evening before.

'I must try as hard as I can to think about what Jack's going to do. I've got to remember there are times when he says he'll do something. When he convinces whoever he's talking to that he means just what he says. But when what he does after that is absolutely nothing.

'It's not because he forgets what he says he'll do. Not because he tries to do what he says he'll do and fails. It is, as I know full well, because he's never had the slightest intention of doing it.

'In his dealings with everybody he knows, me included, what he says is carefully calculated. Just as, almost always, his anger and violence are. And what he does to achieve his ends is meticulously planned.

'Before he does anything, he'll have made an assessment of all the risks. This'll have reached a level of detail that would probably be the envy of any professional bureaucrat. And, perhaps because of this, he almost inevitably makes the right decisions. At least the right decisions in his terms.

'My problem with him has always been to work out what he's actually going to do. And it's just this problem I'm faced with right now. Is he – as he's so often done in the past – deliberately trying to scare me? To confuse me? To lay a false trail?

'Those three messages he sent last night were all about being killed. Two of them were about being stoned to death. I don't for a moment take any of the messages literally. But I've got to think what those messages are meant to tell me.

'He knows more than enough about my past with what he's always described, after we went to see *The Glass Menagerie*, as my *gentlemen callers*. Indeed, he had a major part in that past of mine. He was, after all, one of the most regular and most demanding of those so-called gentlemen callers.

'He knows, though, next to nothing about my short time with Stephen. Except that he was the great love of my mid twenties. He's never, in all the years we've been together, found me having dinner with another man. And, even worse, in that man's own flat.'

The two children who have been playing around the tombs and the drinking fountain and the statue of Euterpe dance away noisily through the gateway at the far end of the gardens. They disappear as they run towards the nearby blocks of flats where they both live.

The old man wakes up slowly. He swivels round until he is sitting rather than lying on the bench. He bends down and painfully picks up his collection of plastic bags. He shuffles off stiffly and silently through the gateway into Handel Street.

The woman, now the only other visitor in the gardens, continues to walk round the path. She passes the cherry trees and the magnolias that are both in full blossom: bright white in a landscape dominated by bright green. She completes a circuit every five or so minutes.

Joanna has not closed her eyes. She does not, however, see the two children exit left, the old man exit right, or the woman pass in front of her. She is, if anything, even deeper into her memories than she was a few minutes ago.

She is so wholly introspective that the external world no longer exists for her. This is just as it was for her and for Stephen when they first kissed on the towpath by Hammersmith Bridge. It is just as it was when they listened together to the nightingale as they stood by the doorway in Giroux.

She does her best to push the images of now and then into the back of her mind. Instead she tries to think as clearly as she can about Jack, enigmatic and opaque as he is. She recognises the imperative, too, to think as clearly as she can about Stephen. He is, as she knows, more transparent than opaque. Yet, in spite of that, he is a man she has known for so much less time. And so much of that time was so very long ago.

'First of all, I've got to ask myself how he'll react to Jack's threats. He's told me how he used to try and protect himself against his wife's violence, unpredictable and spontaneous as it was. He wrapped himself in a defensive shell. But that was violence done to him by someone he knew all too well. And even then, from what he's said, he wasn't much good at dealing with it.

'Jack's violence, as I know better than anybody, is anything but unpredictable and spontaneous. Stephen would be about as well prepared for it as a wandering albatross over the Sahara.

'How he'd actually cope with any violence that Jack might plan for him I don't know for sure. But I'm afraid he'd be as hopeless at coping with it as I'd be at dealing with one of his wife's sudden attacks, which horrify me whenever I think about them.

'If I try to think further ahead, I'm even more unsure about what he'll want to do. Will he want to hold onto the independence he's treasured since he left his wife for the second time? An independence he may, for all I know, have been dreaming of ever since he grew up and left home if not before?

'Will he, I wonder, see me playing any part in his world? Perhaps as a fellow traveller on one of his adventures? Perhaps as a companion on a one-night stand? Or will he be content for me to disappear from his life as completely as I did after my train drew out of the Gare du Nord?

'Or, just possibly, will he want me to live with him? Some of what he's said to me since we met yesterday makes me feel he will. But for me to build a house of hopes with the bricks of a few hours together – and after we were apart for so long – would be incredibly, unutterably foolish. Even more foolish than I know I'm capable of being.'

On the north side of the gardens, on one of the branches of a plane tree whose leaves are still only a little larger than the buds they have emerged from, a grey squirrel is chattering angrily. Its tail is fluffed out and jerking. By the trunk of the tree, a tortoiseshell cat is flattening itself against the ground. It is snarling at the squirrel that is beyond its reach.

On the path that passes by the tree, the woman is walking with staccato footsteps. She is clenching and unclenching her hands. Her face is tense. Her thin lips are moving rapidly as she mutters to herself.

Joanna hears no more than she sees. Not because of the roar of jet engines as aircraft after aircraft pass over central London. Not because of the constant deep rumble of traffic along the Euston Road and Gray's Inn Road. But because she is still in her own insulated and private world. The squirrel, the cat, the woman: all these are far outside the limits of her perception.

She has already tried to think – though as she sees it far from successfully and far from satisfactorily – about what Jack and Stephen might do. But what they will actually do she can only guess at.

She knows that now, however difficult it is going to be, however painful the choices are going to be, she must put to herself the two questions she alone can answer. What is it *she* wants to do? And – which she realises is a very different and much more difficult question – what will she actually do when she has to make her decision?

'Stay with Jack? It's easy, only too easy, to make a list of all the reasons why I shouldn't stay. There's what he did yesterday evening when he came to the flat and threw the wine over me. There's what he did last night. The text message. The letter under the door. The metal cross through the window.

'There's the way he keeps so much to himself. Does so much without telling me. Even when I ask him time after time to tell me. As I was saying to Stephen, there's the way he does everything he can to dominate me. From deciding what clothes I'm going to wear to where and how and when we're going to make love.

'Then, of course, there's his violence. When it's been the opening scene of an erotic play in which I've known his lines just as well as I've known my own, I've even enjoyed it. Even when I haven't, it's still been violence I've known very well. And known very well how to deal with.

'When, though, it's been violence against people who've crossed him in some way or other? And when these are people who don't expect it and can't begin to deal with it? This I can only see as premeditated brutality.

'But as well as thinking about all the reasons why I should leave Jack, I've got to think about the reasons why I should do the opposite. To stay with him. To carry on as we've done for the last ten or more years. To inhabit the middle ground with all its predictability and all its often comfortable certainties. And with Jack's businesses going, from everything he's told me, from strength to strength.

'For one thing, it was he, and single-handedly, who rescued me from what I've very occasionally called my life of vice. It was he who set me up in a flat. It was he who provided me with everything I needed and much more. A good Samaritan to me then if ever there was one.

'He may be more in his element with an eye for an eye and a tooth for a tooth than he is with forgiving those who trespass against him. But I've got to recognise Jack's faith doesn't show itself just at a Christmas carol service or a midnight mass at Easter.

'On top of that, and especially in those early years, he's often been good fun to be with. And not only in bed. A twisted sense of humour, yes. But a sense of humour all the same. Last but not least, like it or not, for better or for worse, in sickness and in health, I am his lawful wedded wife.

'How he'd react to the prospect of a second divorce, how he'd take it out on me, how he'd screw me for every penny I've got, how he'd throw every bit of dirt he could dig up at me, I hate to think.'

'Go with Stephen? Much less than twenty four hours ago, it's a prospect I wouldn't have dreamed of in a thousand years. Now, though, it's a prospect I've got to think about as seriously as I've tried to think about staying with Jack.

'The reasons for not going with him are as clear as could be. For a start there are all of the very good reasons I've just been listing in my mind for staying with Jack. Added to that there's the absurdly short time we were together then. Weeks rather than months. And we've been together an even shorter time now. Hours rather than days.

'As well as that, I mustn't forget how, on that last day

in Giroux, we began so close to each other. And how, because of what he decided he had to do, we finished so far apart. At opposite ends of the universe. His decision to abandon me, and to go back to his wife, taken and set in concrete.

'And yet. And yet. I've got to admit to myself I enjoyed his body then more than I've enjoyed any man before or since. And the night we've just been together has made me realise nothing has changed. Nothing at all. Even after almost half a lifetime. Now just like then.

'I enjoyed being with him then more than I've enjoyed being with anybody. Boy or girl. Man or woman. After being with him again last night – in spite of the way we parted twenty years ago – I feel just the same about him now.

'From everything he's said and done since we met yesterday, I see he and Jack are exact opposites. He's as sensitive, thoughtful, considerate, gentle, understanding now as he was then. And that's only the beginning of a long list I could make if I had the time and if I could think clearly enough. Most of all, perhaps, he's treated me in ways no other man has ever done.

'Whether I'm right in thinking no man's an island, or whether he's right in saying we're all alone, I just don't know. But with him, I feel those two leaves we watched travelling down the Thames can actually float along together. And they don't necessarily have to float apart.'

'Stay with Jack? Go with Stephen? Given what I've been thinking over these last few minutes, this may seem to be the decision I've got to make. But is this really the choice I want to have? Isn't there another choice I could make if I wanted to?

'Throughout my adult life, and even when I was in my late teens, I've been dependent on a succession of men. In some ways, it's been what I've needed. In other ways, it's been what I've liked. And never, as far as I can remember, have I been reluctant to be dependent. Though some of the forms that dependence has taken have had me racing away from them at high speed.

'I can easily see the advantages there have been – and still are – of being dependent. I can also – though not as easily – see the advantages there could be of being independent. Understanding I can only fully know myself, fully develop, if I depend not on other people but on myself. Doing what I want to when I want to, and where and how. Making my own decisions for myself. Doing my own thing. Sometimes with a friend. Sometimes on my own.

'I am, after all, a mature adult whose adolescence is a very distant memory. And who's well advanced – far too well advanced for my liking – into middle age. So shouldn't I also be asking myself questions about why I should be dependent? And, just as importantly, about why I should not?

'Should I use Jack's behaviour over the years – including what he did yesterday evening and last night – to explain to myself why I'm declaring independence? Should I use Stephen's generosity to help me leap over the chasm to independence?

'If he were to ask me to be with him, should I say *no*? Or, at least, should I say *not now, not yet*? Should I tell him what I've got to do now is to find myself, be myself. And only after that, only then, to find him and to be with him? Or, by thinking like this, am I showing myself I am, ultimately, still thinking of dependence and not its reverse?

'Sitting here as I've been doing this morning, it hasn't been too difficult to think about as many of the pros and cons as I can imagine. To propose and then to oppose the motion. I admit I feel I'm caught up in a maelstrom. Though I've managed to think of some of the reasons why I'd want to do this or that.

'I can see that the arguments for staying where I am are pretty overwhelming. But in the final analysis, at the end of the day, when push comes to shove, what I'll actually do – especially when so much is outside my control – I've absolutely no idea. And...'

She feels a sharp and sudden pain as she is kicked hard on the shin of her left leg. She feels an even sharper pain as she is kicked on her other shin. A moment later, she feels a quick succession of blows as she is hit on her forehead, her nose, her mouth.

Now, instead of kicks on her shins, she feels heavy stamping on both her feet. Now, instead of blows on her head, she feels the skin on both of her cheeks being scratched and torn from her ears down to her chin.

She sees just in front of her eyes long fingernails covered in blood. She looks down and sees black boots with pointed toes and stiletto heels. She looks up and sees the face of the woman who, though she never noticed her, has been walking round and round the gardens. Eyes narrow and glaring. Lips pressed close together, pale and tight and thin. Face twisted, contorted with rage.

She feels the woman's knuckles as they hit her again and again on her cheekbones and between her eyes. She feels the woman's boots as they continue to kick her legs and stamp on her feet. She bends to one side as quickly as she can to avoid the punches. She manages, though with enormous difficulty, to stand up in front of the bench where, until this attack, she has been so deep in her own thoughts and memories.

The woman's fists now punch her on her neck, her shoulders, her arms, her breasts. Her knees jab into Joanna's thighs, her stomach, her groin. The pain of the blows on her head and the kicks on her legs has been bad enough. But the blows on her body and her breasts are unbearably painful.

She screams in agony and terror. The woman reacts by pushing her backwards with both hands. She loses her balance, falls against the end of the bench. She collapses in a heap and hardly conscious on the gravel path.

She feels more kicking and stamping on her head, her back, her behind. She hears the woman's harsh breathing above her. Then, as suddenly as it began, the attack ends. She hears the woman's footsteps on the gravel as they fade into the distance. Now all she hears is her heart thumping violently, rapidly inside her.

She edges back to the bench. She slumps across the seat. She feels the pain from the kicks and punches. They are no longer just the sharp and sudden and localised pains of each blow. They are also the dull and continuing pains over the whole of her body.

She sees the bruises that have already begun to appear on her legs. She sees the blood that is dribbling over her ankles below the places where her skin has been broken. She touches her face with the tips of her fingers. When she looks at them, she discovers that they are as bloody as the woman's fingernails were a few minutes ago.

First crawling much more than walking, then walking a little more than crawling, she moves slowly across the lawn. Up the path to the gates of St George's Gardens. Along Handel Street and back to the house where Stephen has his flat. In these few minutes, when she is fighting to stop herself from fainting, the pain is as overwhelming as it was during the attack.

But what begins to overwhelm her as much if not more is the horror of the violence itself. It was not the ritualised violence she is used to and can even, at times, enjoy. It was, rather, a brutally raw and unexpected violence. It was a violence she has never, at any time in her life, in any shape or form, encountered.

CHAPTER NINETEEN

Stephen has listened to Joanna's footsteps on the stone stairs and, for a few seconds until they faded into the distance, on the pavement and on the road below his flat. He has thought about pouring himself an early-morning glass of armagnac in the tradition of some of the peasants he has met on his travels in France.

Yet, after a debate with himself, he has decided against it – at least for the moment. He has, instead, put on the sweater and trousers he was wearing the evening before, and has made himself a cup of strong coffee. Unlike his usual anaemic cappuccinos, it has the sweetness and strength of the espressos he has drunk in bars in Rome and Florence and Venice.

He has put on one of his favourite pieces of music: the *Pastoral Symphony*. After he has tiptoed across the living room, trying to dodge the fragments of glass on the floor, he has stood for a few minutes at the shattered window. After he has looked down at the empty street, he stretches out on his sofa. His coffee is in one hand, his chin is in the palm of the other.

He, too, needs to have a chance to clear his head. He needs to think as clearly as he is able about what has happened since yesterday morning. And, just as much, he needs to think about what might be going to happen today – and beyond.

'How on earth can I make any sense of what's gone on? Might it help a bit if I try to stand back? Look at it all as an outsider might do? Set out the bare facts of the case? Tackle it as a lawyer rather than as a client?

'It's not much over twelve hours since Jo arrived here for dinner. It's well under twenty four hours since we met at the corner of High Holborn and Kingsway. In these few hours, sandwiched between thin slices of sleep, we've shared so many memories. Memories – all but one of them glorious – of our short time together all those years ago. We've exchanged as well so many memories – from the comic to the tragic – of what's happened to each of us in the years in between then and now.

'Since we met again yesterday, I've thought so much about what happened between us twenty years ago. Just as I've thought about this in all those tens of thousands of moments when she's flashed into my mind. I've thought as much about my last twenty years as at any time while I was plodding my way slowly through them.

'I've also found out more about her than I've ever found out about anybody. And that includes clients I've had who think they've exposed everything, including their most intimate and sometimes most incriminating secrets.

'We've had as well our moments of passion between these slices of sleep. Not, I'm afraid, anything like as many as we had twenty years ago. In those incredible nights with their excess of enthusiasm and their lack of moderation. In quality if not in quantity, though, as good as any we had together when we were so much younger.

'At the same time, our sleep was shattered by those three messages which, try as I might, I can't get out of my mind. Three discordant elements in last night's mixture of memory and desire we could have done without. But, whether we like it or not, they're elements that are just as much of a reality as any of our overnight lotus-eating and self-indulgence.'

Two young and buxom women who live in one of St Pancras' less decaying council estates walk round the corner into Handel Street. Each has with her a pushchair and a sleeping baby. Each is talking loudly and abusively about her husband.

Two men who have driven down from the Euston Road – taking the same route Joanna and Stephen took when they walked to his flat the evening before – turn into Handel Street. They look for a place to park the black Mercedes in which they have been travelling. The driver finds a space close by and backs the car into it.

Stephen makes himself another cup of coffee, if anything stronger and sweeter than the first. He abandons the *Pastoral* for another of his favourite pieces of music: the *Pathétique*.

He picks up Joanna's mobile which she has left on the table. He finds last night's text message and reads it carefully to himself. '*If a man be found lying with a woman married to an husband, then they shall both of them die, both the man that lay with the woman, and the woman.*'

'What is it I really want to do? Most of the time when I'm thinking about the future – and that's not at all often – I'm thinking about today and tomorrow. A bit of the time I'm thinking about next week or next month. Almost never am I thinking about the year ahead. Absolutely never do I think about the rest of my life.

'I'm feeling more tired and agitated this morning than I've felt for years. I know, though, I've got to think as hard as I can. I've also got to understand that what I think about could change my life. And, of course, not only mine.

'Do I want to stay on my own, to be independent, as I've been for the best part of the last twenty years? Do I want to keep on enjoying the natural world, as well as the company of my friends and colleagues? Drinking with them in the Seven Stars. Eating with them in Luigi's. Going with them to the South Bank and the Barbican.

'And then at the end of these evenings, after the drinks or the dinner, the theatre or the concert, walking back to my flat where I'm on my own. Master of my own destiny. Walking furthest because I walk alone.

'And do I want to keep on enjoying the company of women in brief encounters? Here today and off tomorrow. To misquote what Jo once said to me, *no sooner come than gone*. I know more than enough single men who dedicated their late teens and early twenties to precisely this. Stags in a forest at the height of the rutting season.

'As well as that, I know it's what so many married men dream of in their thirties and forties if not before. But is it still for me? I've already passed – though not very far – beyond the threshold of my fifties. I may not have reached my declining years. I may be able to avoid them for a time. I've got to recognise, though, that these declining years are staring me in the face.

'Do I want Jo to be the latest in that succession of one-night stands? Nights which are, I've got to admit, less frequent and less immoderate these days than they were a few years back.

'Would she follow on a couple of months – or is it a little more? – after Sharon the solicitor? Not the most memorable of my overnight adventures. Yet not by any stretch of the imagination the least agreeable. Would she precede – after who knows how long – whoever the next consenting adult female may be?'

The two women saunter with a total lack of urgency along Handel Street. They stop for a moment below his flat. One is complaining in a quick-fire succession of expletives, nothing deleted, about her husband's demands, as unremitting as they are unorthodox.

The other complains with equal vigour about the wealth and variety of excuses her husband gives her to avoid performing what she clearly sees as his matrimonial duties. Between bursts of raucous laughter and an exchange of more rich expletives, each tells the other how lucky she is, and they walk on.

One of the men takes a cigar from a silver case in his jacket pocket. The other takes a packet of cigarettes from the dashboard of the Mercedes. Both light up and, as the two women pass them, they exhale small clouds of smoke. They watch the movement of the women's substantial rumps with a combination of professional detachment and uninhibited lust.

Stephen finishes his second cup of coffee, and enjoys the strong aftertaste in his mouth. He listens to the sadness of the strings in the *Pathétique*. He gets up, walks into the kitchen where he has left the sheet of paper he found in the envelope outside his front door during the night.

As with the text message, he reads it to himself: '*If a*

damsel that is a virgin be betrothed unto an husband, and a man find her in the city, and lie with her; then ye shall bring them both out unto the gate of that city, and ye shall stone them with stones that they die.'

'Do I want to be with Jo? Till death or divorce do us part? True, I now know just how easy she was with her favours after she got back from France. But, in spite of what she says, I do feel I'm in some ways responsible for what she did. And, after she's been so open with me, after she's told me so many of her secrets, I also feel I can trust her. As well as that, she was as faithful to me when were together as I was to her.

'As for me, and if I were to play fair with her – which is what I'd want to do – those brief encounters I've indulged in for so long would have to become part of my past. I'd have to lose the company of those women – which in any case hasn't been a particularly distinguished part of that past. But I certainly wouldn't want to lose the company of my friends. Nor, I'm sure, would I have to.

'We'd simply have an extra stool for her at the bar. Make an extra place for her at the table. Get an extra theatre or concert ticket for her. They'd take to her – and she to them – without a moment's hesitation.

'Much more important, I'd be reunited at long last with the great love of my life. With the woman who, when we were together twenty years ago, I'd dreamed of being with for the rest of my life. Until I abandoned her that evening at the Gare du Nord.

'I'd be reunited with the woman who's excited and delighted me more than any other woman – even Erica in those early halcyon days in Cambridge – has ever done. As close to heaven as Erica in those last years was to hell.

'But whatever it is I might want to do, the biggest question has to be what she herself might want. Which, for all I know, may be what she's thinking about right now. We were, after all, together for such a short time. It was almost half her lifetime ago. And she was so very young.

'Why would she want to be with me? When my best years were then? And when I've got so little to offer her now? She'd be trying to drive a car whose engine needs a major overhaul. Whose gearbox needs to be replaced. More a candidate for the scrapheap than a desirable model in a used-car showroom.

'And that's not all. I've got to accept, as I'm sure she does, she's a married woman. She must have had good times with her husband. And, for all I know, she still does. If she were ever to think about leaving him for me, she'd have to think again and again. She'd have to weigh in the balance not just the bad times she's told me about and that I saw for myself last night, but those good times as well.

'Why should she give up the certainties of her life with her husband for the uncertainties of a new life with me? Why should she choose to walk into the horrors of separation and divorce, just to finish up here with me rather than in her own home with him?'

The two women stop again at the end of Handel Street before they walk on towards the Brunswick shopping centre. Talking so loudly that the two men can still hear them, they fantasise wildly about the prowess of the lead characters in their favourite soap operas. They endow them with phenomenal attributes, with superhuman stamina and with breathtaking powers of inventiveness.

In this exchange of erotic daydreams, their husbands are forgotten as completely as are their babies. These continue to sleep soundly in spite of their mothers' performances, one soprano, the other contralto.

One of the men takes a last drag at his cigarette. He drops it onto the pavement and grinds it on the stone slab with the sole of his shoe. The other throws his cigar, though it is far from finished, into the gutter. Here it lies, still smoking, among an assortment of street litter.

They walk up to the steps where, a little while before, Joanna walked down on her way to St George's Gardens. They stand, talking in low voices, by the black front door.

With the caffeine already doing its work, and with the *Pathétique* reaching one of the movements he most enjoys, Stephen walks over to the table. He picks up the final message that Joanna unwrapped from the cross. He unfolds and flattens it.

He reads it slowly to himself. '*If the tokens of virginity be not found for the damsel: then they shall bring out the damsel to the door of her father's house, and the men of the city shall stone her with stones that she die. If a man find a betrothed damsel in the field, and the man force her, and lie with her: then the man only that lay with her shall die.*'

'There is, I'm sure, only one sensible and rational path for me to take. Only one course of action any lawyer would advise his client to follow. And that's to stay on my own. Yet whatever Jo decides, whatever I decide, we're still faced with the threats her husband has made in those overnight messages.

'It's obvious to me, as I'm certain it is to her as well, that he doesn't mean to do what the messages imply. Stoning to death in Old Testament Palestine may have been common practice. But, between Bloomsbury and St Pancras in the first years of the twenty-first century, it doesn't seem the most likely of scenarios.

'What, though, is he trying to tell us? Are his messages just empty threats? The words themselves are full of menace. But is the meaning behind the words nothing more than histrionics? Or should we assume the worst, and then work out what to do?

'Jo will, I'm sure, have much better answers to all these questions than I've got. But if I can think clearly now, at least when she comes back I'll be able to help her to come up with best possible answers. And with these answers, we'll be able to make our decisions.

'If he does plan to do something, what will it be? Will he agree to have her back, but on condition she never sees me again? Will he throw her out and divorce her? And make sure the settlement leaves her on the breadline? Will he, in some way or other, be violent towards her, and not necessarily play by the Queensberry rules?

'And what about me? By looking at those photos of me yesterday evening, he'll have worked out I'm a lawyer. So will he try to damage whatever reputation I have? Tell his story to a tabloid at one extreme or the Bar Council at the other? Or tell it to both?

'Will he try to damage my flat? After all, he's already broken a window. Will he try to damage me? From the experiences of clients I've acted for over the years, as well from what Jo has told me about him, any of these could be on the cards.

'If he does do something to take his revenge, when will it happen? Will his response be as quick as it was yesterday evening when he came here? And as it was last night with his messages? Or will he hold back? Delay his response? Aim to give me, to give us both, a false sense of security? Make us more anxious and more uncertain about what he'll do? I haven't the slightest idea.

'How will Jo deal with whatever he does? She reacted extremely badly yesterday evening when he came to the flat. But she's lived with him long enough to know something of how he behaves. And to predict what he might do. If she can't cope with him, nobody can.

'And me? How will I manage? Will I be as useless as I always was when Erica launched one of her attacks out of the blue? Will I do better because, from what Jo's told me, nothing he ever does is off-the-cuff and everything's carefully calculated? Or, precisely because I've got no experience of anyone behaving like that, will I do even worse than I did with Erica?'

He hears three sharp knocks on his front door, then a short gap, then three more.

'It must be Jo!' he thinks.

He is more than delighted she is back. She has been away for well under an hour. But he has so wanted her to return, so wanted to look at her again, so wanted to embrace her again, so wanted just to be with her again.

He walks as fast as he can along the hallway to the door. With his heart beating fast and with a broad smile of welcome, he opens it. Instead of her, however, he sees two men standing beside each other in front of him. They are dressed in dark suits, white shirts, sombre ties. There is not a trace of a smile between them.

One of the men is enormous, less in height – though he is much taller than Stephen – than in the formidable breadth of his body. It is, moreover, a body that asserts its power even in those few motionless moments before he steps forward.

The other man – the smaller of the two though still larger than Stephen – he recognises at once. He is the man who visited them the evening before. Who threw the wine over Joanna. Who must have been responsible for the three overnight messages. Who over the last minutes has been one of the main objects of his concerns and uncertainties. This man is, without any doubt at all, her husband.

'*Thy kingdom come,*' he says in the deep voice that Stephen remembers from yesterday evening. '*Thy will be done, in earth as it is in heaven.*'

Before Stephen can move, before he can do anything to resist, the big man puts his hands firmly on his shoulders. He spins him round like a parent playing with a young child. He frog-marches him along the hallway and into the living room, dictating where and how fast he goes. He is a puppeteer determining every movement of his puppet.

With his hands still on Stephen's shoulders, and without displaying the slightest effort, the man pushes him onto his knees. He holds Stephen down with one hand on his back. With the other hand he lifts a dining chair away from the table and places it with the side of its seat inches from his face.

Effortlessly, he pushes Stephen forward so that his chest and stomach are across the seat. He pins him down with one foot on the small of his back. He leans over him, holds his arms, ties each of them tightly above his wrists to two of the chair legs.

Still standing beside Stephen, he bends down. He ties his legs above his knees, and just as tightly, to the other two legs of the chair. Finally, he puts a white handkerchief across his mouth and ties it behind his neck.

Stephen tries as hard as he can, but with not the slightest success, to move his arms, his legs, his body. He can move only his head, and that only a little. When he lifts it, he sees just a yard or so in front of him the black shoes and grey suit trousers of Joanna's husband. He tries, too, to shout his protests. Because of the gag he can only grunt.

He hears a match strike. A moment later, he smells cigar smoke. He hears the man above him breathe in deeply and then, slowly and deliberately, breathe out. He watches the husband's feet as he walks unhurriedly towards the broken window and, just as unhurriedly, as he turns round.

Give us this day our daily bread, and forgive us our trespasses,' he says as he stands by the window with the broken pane, '*as we forgive them that trespass against us.*'

The big man puts down his cigar, still alight, in an ashtray he finds on the sideboard. Stephen feels him take hold of his belt and the top of his trousers. He feels the man's knuckles on his spine, bone against bone.

He feels the front of his trousers tight against his stomach as they are torn away from his waist, as they are pulled down over his behind. Though he cannot see them, they then lie, together with his pants, on the floor around his knees.

The man picks up his cigar, breathes in the smoke yet again. After a few moments he blows one smoke ring. This is followed by a second and a third before he returns it to the ashtray. He puts a hand into one of the side pockets of his jacket where he finds what he is looking for.

By turning his head to one side, Stephen sees the man's legs only inches away from him. With no idea what is happening, and with no idea of what is about to happen, he watches the man take two short paces back, and stand with his feet a little apart. He hears a sharp intake of breath.

'*Lead us not into temptation,*' intones the husband from the window he is still standing beside, '*but deliver us from evil.*'

Stephen feels a sudden, terrible, dreadful pain. It is as if a poker has been pulled red-hot from a fire and dragged at high speed over his backside, branding him like a Texan steer. In spite of the gag he cries out, a strangled shout of horror and disbelief.

He feels the impossibly sharp pain again as another blow cuts into his flesh. A third, then a fourth blow slash across his skin, cutting even deeper than the first two blows have cut.

One blow relentlessly follows another. New cuts cross cuts that have already been made. The blows are so sharp, so frequent, that the pain soon becomes far greater than anything he has experienced at any moment in his life.

At the same time, where most of the lashes have landed, he begins to feel numb. What are now most painful are the new cuts across flesh where no blow has fallen before.

The whipping goes on, blow after blow after blow. He feels his heart racing even more out of control than it has been since the two men arrived. He sees a chaos of stars swirling around in the blackness in front of him. He hears a high-pitched ringing in his ears. Swaying on the edge of consciousness, he hears the voice of the husband from the far side of the room.

'*For thine is the kingdom, the power and the glory, for ever and ever.*'

Almost nonchalantly, the big man rolls up the horsewhip he has been holding. He puts it back into his jacket pocket. He picks up his cigar again and inhales deeply. After more deep breaths and more smoke rings, he stubs it out in the ashtray.

Then he kneels down, and reaches the finale of his act. Adding insult to injury, he shoves the end of his cigar as far inside Stephen as he can, so that only a couple of inches stick out between his buttocks. The final indignity. The ultimate humiliation.

'*Amen*,' concludes the husband.

He walks away from the window, treading on some of the fragments of glass and breaking them into smaller fragments. He strides across the room and passes Stephen without a second glance. He goes over to the pile of CDs. He works his way through them, slowly and deliberately, and puts one of them on.

As the *Requiem Mass* – the same music Stephen had remembered when he had sat by the Seine twenty years before – blasts out of the loudspeakers at full volume, they stand in silence. When it reaches *Kyrie eleison* they make the sign of the cross. When the choir begins to sing *Dies irae* they shake hands.

Leaving the door ajar, they stroll casually out of the flat together. They walk slowly down the stairs and out of the house. As if they have not a care in the world, they stand on the pavement beside their Mercedes. Before they turn the car round and drive off, one lights another cigarette, the other another cigar.

For Stephen, the awful pain of the cuts across his

behind and of the cigar inside him remains, as does the numbness. But, as he edges back towards consciousness, as the ringing in his ears and the stars in the blackness begin to fade, he begins to feel a quite different pain.

He has, more times than he can remember, experienced his wife's violence. That violence was wild and unexpected, and ended as quickly as it began. He has never, though, experienced anything like this brand of violence: calculated, cold-blooded, without emotion.

He lies helplessly across the chair, more a trussed chicken than a Queen's Counsel. His trousers and pants are still on the floor around his knees. His bottom with its attendant cigar is exposed, both comically and pathetically, to the elements.

He realises to his horror and despair that this violence has devastated him more profoundly by far than any of the violence his wife inflicted on him at any time in their marriage.

CHAPTER TWENTY

In spite of how bad she is feeling, Joanna remembers the entryphone is broken and the front door is not locked. She pushes it open, and crawls on all fours to the foot of the stairs. She stops to recover her breath. She succeeds, though with great difficulty, in standing almost upright.

She begins to climb. For the first few tortoise-slow steps she clings to the stair rail with both hands. She goes up one step at a time, displaying all the uncertainty of a toddler in its first walking days.

A chorus of pains floods around her and pours over her. The treble of the surface pains on her arms and legs, on her back and stomach and face. The tenor of the pains deeper inside her. The echoing bass of the pains in her mind. The stairs sway wildly in front of her. She has no clear sense of what is above or below her.

She falls down heavily on her knees, adding yet another pain to the chorus. She climbs the rest of the stairs – a succession of stone steps that seem to her as she looks up them to be impossibly steep, and to be rising endlessly above her – on her hands and knees.

At the top of the stairs, and now completely out of breath, she stops. She tries to stand again but fails. Still on her hands and knees, she crawls along the corridor towards the flat.

Almost beyond the limits of exhaustion, she inches past the door she does not notice is partly open, and moves into the hallway. At last, she tells herself, she has reached the flat.

'Stephen!' she calls in a voice that is more than anything a weak and almost silent croak. She hears nothing in reply.

'Stephen!' she calls again, her voice just as weak.

From the living room next to the hallway she hears a moan, then a strangled voice that is whispering her name. Not noticing any of the broken glass that is still on the floor, she crawls into the room. When it stops revolving around her and she manages to bring it into focus, she freezes in disbelief.

'Good God!' she cries.

She sees him bent over one of his chairs. Though his sweater is covering his back, his trousers are round his knees. Even more bizarre, she sees his bottom, as bare as the day he was born, and criss-crossed by long, red weals.

From some of these weals, especially where they cross, she sees trickles of blood. These have dribbled down the back of his thighs. They are now congealing, like drips of drying gravy that have spilled down the side of a saucepan. Most bizarre of all – though the absurdity of it escapes her – she sees the end of a cigar hanging limply between his buttocks.

She is not much more conscious than she was when she collapsed on the gravel path in St George's Gardens. Her body aches and throbs as much as it did on her journey back from the gardens to the flat. She understands, however, that – at least for now – his needs are greater, much greater, than hers.

She scrambles to him across the floor as quickly as she can, though more crabwise than straight. She kneels beside him, unties the gag that is over his mouth, puts her arms round him.

'What in Heaven's name's happened to you?' she whispers with her voice breaking. 'And what can I do to help you?'

He turns his head towards her by twisting his neck round as far as he can. He sees by his side a shape that is at first blurred, then clearer as his eyes begin to focus.

'The story of what happened can wait,' he answers, his voice as much a weak and almost silent croak as hers. 'For now, Jo, just untie me. But before you do that, can you get out whatever's stuck up my backside?'

She squats down on the floor, still not noticing the broken glass. Her fingers have little of their feeling. Her hands have begun to shake. In spite of these difficulties, she manages to get hold of the cigar and pull it out of him. She throws it across the room into the fireplace.

One by one, and after several false starts, she unties the four knots. As each length of rope falls to the ground, she sees the deep, white channels they have left behind on his arms above his wrists. Even deeper and whiter are the channels she sees on his legs above his knees.

He lifts one hand off the floor, stretches it little by little. He clenches it, stretches it again. He lifts his other hand and does the same. He lifts his left knee off the floor, straightens his leg. He bends it, straightens it again. With all the speed of a sloth waking from its sleep, he repeats the movements with his right leg.

'Now,' he appeals to her, 'help me up.'

She gets unsteadily to her feet, steps behind him. She puts her hands under his armpits, does her best to help him to stand. He tries to get up, but has too little strength. He collapses onto the chair, dragging her down with him. She is now back on her knees, with her body on top of his.

'Let's try again,' she suggests, in a voice that is becoming a little stronger.

'Give me a minute or two,' he gasps. 'I'm still far too weak.'

He moves his arms and legs again, now just a little more easily than before. With her standing in front of him, and with his hands round her neck, he tries again. He reels drunkenly to the left and then to the right. She braces herself for a second fall.

This time, though, he succeeds in keeping his balance. With his trousers now round his ankles, he rests his hands on the back of the chair. He looks more like a patient on his first walk after major surgery than a moderately fit man hardly turned fifty.

'What's the damage?' he asks.

She moves round the chair, stands behind him. She inspects his bare behind once again. 'All I can tell you is you've been given a beating the like of which I've never seen in my life. Either on me or on anyone else.'

'Bloody hell!' he hisses. 'And what was it that was hitting me?'

'From looking at the marks and the cuts, I'd say it was done with a stick or a whip rather than a belt or a strap. What's for sure is that you won't be able to sit down comfortably for days. And it'll be much longer than that before the cuts completely heal.'

'Be an angel and pull my trousers up,' he sighs. 'You've told me more than enough.'

She bends down, pulls his pants up to his waist. She

bends down again, pulls up his trousers. She does up his belt and his zip. As he continues to stand behind the chair, she puts her arms round him to comfort him. She rests her head on his shoulder.

He, in response, strokes her hair, kisses her head. He turns to look at her and, for the first time since she came back to his flat, sees her face. He is horrified by what he sees. For it is masked by bruises that are turning yellow and purple, and by scratches that are still open and red. He cannot begin to believe – just as she could not believe a few minutes ago when she found him tied to the chair – what he is seeing.

'What the hell, Jo! This can't be true,' he exclaims. 'It can't be. It can't have happened to you as well.'

He lifts his hands to her face. He strokes it as tenderly as he can with his fingertips, kisses it.

'So they've gone for both of us.' He pauses as he recalls one of last night's messages: '*If a man be found lying with a woman married to an husband...*'

'That's how it looks,' she replies. She hesitates for a moment as she searches her memory: '*If a damsel that is a virgin be betrothed unto an husband, and a man finds her in the city...*'

'What are we going to do?' he asks as he tries, though with great difficult, to think more clearly.

'One of us – or even both of us – may need to go to hospital. But first let's see if we can repair some of the damage ourselves.'

She takes hold of his hand. Like two long-term inmates of an old people's home, and trying to avoid the fragments of broken glass on the floor, they shuffle slowly across the living room, through the bedroom and into the bathroom.

Both are still more than a little unsteady on their legs. Both are still feeling more pain than they have felt at any time of their lives. Both are still hopelessly disoriented by what has happened to themselves and to each other.

Without saying another word, and with much more difficulty than he has ever had in undressing her before, he takes off most of her clothes. With great care, he uses a flannel he has soaked in warm water to wipe the blood from her face and her legs. He dries her gently with his bath towel, dabbing rather than rubbing her. Using some cotton wool from his bathroom cupboard, he puts some ointment on her cuts.

After she has undressed him and, using the same flannel, has washed the blood from the cuts on his bottom, she uses the same ointment on his wounds. They wrap themselves loosely in towels. A little less hesitantly and uncertainly than on their journey to the bathroom, they hobble back through the bedroom and collapse on the sofa.

'Who was it who came here?' she asks him, though fearing she already knows the answer.

'There were two of them. One I've seen before. And you know him infinitely better than I do.'

'So it was Jack. Just as I thought when I saw you tied to the chair.'

'The other man, the one who gave me that thrashing, I've never seen in my life before. And I never want to see again.'

'I've got no idea who that could be. I can only think it could have been one of the men Jack calls his business associates. Or, though you'll never believe me, it could have been one of the men he knows at his church.'

'Is that why he was thrashing me at the same time Jack was reciting *The Lord's Prayer*?'

'It could well be. Whatever else he may be, and however difficult it may be to believe it, Jack sees himself as a deeply religious man. Nothing would be more his style than to give his act of retribution a Christian façade.'

'He may think he's got God on his side. He may think he's another Raskolnikov who's above and beyond the law. Or could he be reckoning I'll respond by doing nothing?'

'He'll have made a careful calculation. It's what he always does. I'm sure he'll have worked out from the photos of you he was looking at here last night that you're a barrister. And that you're a QC. He might even have found out from his contacts – and he's got them everywhere – exactly who you are and what you do.'

'I suppose he'll also have worked out that the very last thing I'd want is the publicity I'd get if I went to the police. And if he finished up telling his story in court. Even if he was on a criminal charge.'

'He's as good at knowing what people will do and what they won't as he is – in his terms if not in yours or mine – at being a good Christian.'

'So was what they did to me the main course of his retribution? Or was it just the starters, and with more to follow?'

'Right now I'm not sure about anything. This included. But from what I know of Jack in his revenge mode, it could well be that he's done as much – or as little – as he wants to do.'

She stops as a profusion of thoughts flounder around in her mind. A small smile flickers for a moment across her bruised face.

'And he might even decide to practice a little of what he preaches. In spite of how he's behaved, he is, after all, meant to forgive those – like you and me – who trespass against him.'

A little less awkwardly than when they came back from the bathroom, he limps over to the kitchen. He makes a pot of coffee that is even stronger than the coffee he made for himself earlier on. He pours it into two mugs. He adds more than a double measure of armagnac to each mug. Finally he limps back to her on the sofa.

'What about the attack on you?' he asks. 'Was it by the same man who gave me my thrashing? Was Jack there in attendance?'

'I never saw Jack. And it couldn't possibly have been the same man.'

'Because?'

'Because it wasn't a man who attacked me. It was a woman.'

He shudders. His face contorts. 'Oh Christ!' He stares at her sharply and demands: 'What did she look like?'

She hesitates as she tries as hard as she can to recall those few seconds when she saw her attacker. 'Middle-aged. Medium height. Brown hair. Or that's what I remember. But what I can't forget, what I'll never forget, is her face. Overwrought beyond belief. And I can't forget her eyes either. Glaring so fiercely at me.'

He slaps the palms of his hands on his knees with a force that shocks her. He makes a noise halfway between a grunt and a groan.

'Whatever's wrong?' she asks.

'Jo, I jumped to a conclusion a few minutes ago. But, from what you've just told me, I'm as sure as I can be I was completely and utterly wrong.'

'What do you mean? What conclusion? And why wrong?' she asks him in a voice full of uncertainty.

'I thought what was done to you and what was done to me were connected. Last night's messages put into practice. Jack's retribution.'

'But?'

'But your husband had nothing to do with that attack on you. Absolutely nothing. From what you've just told me – about what the woman looked like and what she did to you – it had everything to do with my ex-wife.'

She looks at him, amazed and at the same time bewildered. 'How can you be so sure?'

'I know that look on her face only too well. And with those kicks and punches, she's done to you exactly what she used to do to me.'

'But isn't it too much of a coincidence?'

'Not if I remind you that the flat she moved to is only a short walk away from here. And I've often seen her in this neck of the woods. Even in this very street. Not if I remind you she knows I live here. Not if I tell you I've seen her staring up at these windows.'

'You could have reminded me of that again before I went out,' she replies with what is almost a laugh. 'After all, forewarned is forearmed.'

'My fault,' he admits as he drinks the last mouthful of his coffee and armagnac. 'I'm to blame for this if not for much more.'

'But what next?' she asks. 'It's a question you asked me about Jack. Now, from everything you went through when you and she were man and wife, it's a question I'm asking you about her.'

'When the magma builds up in the volcano, as I've told

you far too often since we first met, there's no knowing what she'll do. But, from what I know of her, it's more than likely she's done her worst. The volcano has, after all, erupted.'

He stands up, again a little more easily than before. He carries their mugs into the kitchen He pours some more coffee and – just as liberally as before – he adds some more armagnac.

As he returns and sits down beside her, he finds to his great relief his head is beginning, even if only marginally, to clear.

'What happens next doesn't only depend on what Jack – or Erica for that matter – decides to do,' he begins. He is thinking far more slowly than he usually does. But he is still managing to put his thoughts into some sort of shape.

'What do you mean?' she asks.

'We could, I suppose, go to the police. After all, we've both been assaulted. And there's no doubt who were responsible. But what I'd lose by doing that is all too obvious. Just as what I'd gain is extremely uncertain. As well as that, though Erica wouldn't have the slightest idea of what the consequences of her attack on you might be, I'm sure you wouldn't want the headlines any more than I would.'

'So what should we be doing now?'

He hesitates. He is sure what he would dearly like her to be asking him with this question. He is, however, far from sure that this is what she is, in fact, asking him. At the same time, he is very unsure how to answer her.

'You could walk cap-in-hand to Jack. Admit you've sinned. Ask for his forgiveness. I could carry on as I've been doing. Making sure, though, that the lock on the front door gets repaired. And making quite sure my next overnight visitor is rather better briefed than you were.'

'Is that all we should be doing?'

He is still unsure of the answer she is looking for, and of the answer he should give her.

'We could get away from London for a few days. Perhaps back to Dent where we went for that first weekend of ours together. Perhaps back to Giroux. Though without the endgame at the Gare du Nord. Or, of course, we could go somewhere we've never been to before.'

She looks at him, directly and quizzically. After a small smile has played across her face for a few seconds, she slowly shakes her head.

'I don't just mean what we should do today or tomorrow or the day after that.' She pauses, looks searchingly into his eyes. She draws in her breath. 'I'm asking myself – and asking you – what you and I should do from now on. In the long term. Into the distant future. For the rest of your life, and for the rest of mine. And whether we should do any – or all – of it together.'

'That's just what I was trying to think about after you'd gone out earlier on. Until your husband and his strongman turned up on my doorstep.'

'And that's exactly what I was trying to do in the gardens. Until your ex-wife attacked me.'

He now thinks he understands what she meant when she asked him what they should be doing. But for him the priority now to know what she has to say, and to be sure what she wants to do.

'So what thoughts did you have?' he asks her. 'And what did you decide you'd do?'

'I tried as best I could to think rationally and sensibly

and clearly. I tried to weigh up all the pros and cons.' She tells him everything she can remember about the thoughts she had as she sat on the bench in the gardens. About whether she should stay with Jack. About whether she should leave him for Stephen. About whether she should be on her own.

'And your conclusion?' he asks, trying – though without much success – to hide his anxiety. 'What did you decide?'

'If I'd been able to keep on thinking, stirring the conflicting ideas around in my mind, testing them as best I could, making some sort of sense of them all, I might, just might, have come to a conclusion. But before I'd got very far, your ex-wife made sure I didn't get any further.'

He smiles at what she has just told him. For a brief moment, he even laughs. 'It's extraordinary, Jo. I was trying to think in just the same ways you were thinking. Calmly. Objectively. Standing outside myself looking in. Acting the advocate for both sides of each option before becoming judge and jury.'

He explains to her, telling her as much as he can recall, what he saw as the arguments. For and against staying on his own. For and against being with her if she'd have him.

'So?' she asks when he stops and leans forward to pick up his mug of coffee and armagnac from the floor.

'It's exactly the same story as yours. When the knock came on the door, I was still trying to get my ideas into shape. I was, to be honest, as uncertain about what to do as I'd been when I started to do my thinking. Thanks to your husband and his friend, I never reached my summing up. Let alone my verdict.'

They have migrated from the sofa, where they have

drunk more mugs of coffee and armagnac than either can remember. They have sat down in the two easy chairs by the fireplace where they found the metal cross and the final message a few hours ago.

'After what's been happening to me since we met yesterday morning,' she tells him, 'I've been feeling so totally and hopelessly disoriented. I've had so many emotions crawling over each other inside me like worms in compost. I'm sure anybody with any sanity or good sense would tell me it's absolutely the wrong time to make the right decisions. But...'

The cuts on her face will not form scabs for many hours. The bruises both on her face and on her body and legs will not fade for many days. Some cuts are still weeping. Some bruises are still growing. But now she has become almost oblivious to her body. She is oblivious even to the pains she has been feeling so acutely.

The world outside her mind has receded even further than it did when she was sitting on the bench in the gardens. Her focus has narrowed, sharpened, and excluded everything except her thoughts about her future. What was uncertain has receded, evaporated. What is certain has grown and taken shape.

'... I'm just as sure there are times when what's rational and sensible has to be pushed from the centre of the stage into the wings. When what my heart tells me is right is, indeed, just that. When my gut reaction is the best reaction. When instinct has to rule. And when, by giving my emotions free rein, I see absolutely clearly what I should do.'

His heart beats more quickly. He looks at her. He is still not sure what she will say. He is hoping against hope she will tell him what he wants more than anything in the world to hear.

'On this,' he tells her, 'I couldn't agree with you more. And it's exactly how I've reacted to everything that's happened. But what is it you're seeing so clearly?'

'Before I was attacked I was overwhelmed by uncertainties. Now these uncertainties have gone. Storm clouds blown away by the west wind. To my surprise and astonishment – and even though it may seem far too hasty – I've reached total certainty. A cloudless sky and blue beyond belief.'

He is now even more anxious for her to tell him what she has decided to do. 'Yet again, Jo, I couldn't agree more. And, like you, I'm as sure now as I was unsure then. But what is it you're so certain about? What is it you're seeing in that cloudless sky?'

'Whatever he says, whatever he does, whatever threats he makes, I'm leaving Jack. I can't ever forget what he's done. Or forgive him for it. Though I should, perhaps, be grateful to him for showing me so convincingly that he and I live in such completely different worlds. As, I suppose, we always have.'

He knows now she has eliminated one of her options. But he does not yet know which of her other options she has chosen. 'So what will you do? Declare independence? Go off on your own? Do your own thing at long last?'

'My head's been telling me that's exactly what I should do. And that it's what I should have done years ago. But my heart's singing a very different tune. It's telling me quite the opposite.'

At last – and to his immense and boundless joy – he believes he knows what she will tell him. He still, though, cannot be completely sure. 'And what does your heart tell you, Jo?'

'That, although we've been together so little time, and although I'm sure we haven't heard the last of Jack or of Erica, I'd be utterly insane to throw away a chance of happiness the like of which I've only known once before. A chance that, if I don't grab hold of it now, I may never have again. Quite simply, it's the chance...'

Her blush spreads rapidly across the whole of her face. In spite of the scratches and the bruises, this blush gives it a greater radiance than he has ever seen before. '... the chance, Stephen, to be with you.'

He leans over to her and puts his arms round her. She, however, looks at him with mock severity, and pretends to scold him.

'Over these last minutes, you've been acting true to form. You've been asking question after question about what I've been thinking. About what I've been feeling. About what I've decided to do.

'All you've told me are your arguments for and against staying on your own. For and against being with me. And adding for good measure that you're as sure now as you were unsure then. So what is it you're so sure of now? And don't you dare give me some lawyer's answer!'

His behind is no less damaged than it was immediately after his thrashing. Yet his aches and pains are, like hers, almost outside the range of his perceptions. He, too, is focussing with a precision he hardly believes he is capable of on his future – and on hers.

'It's as if you and I have learned the same lines of a play. And I'm the echo of what you've just said. It's as if those two leaves we talked about all those years ago are still floating down the river side by side.'

She looks even more sternly at him, and with as much

ferocity as she can muster. 'You're not even beginning to answer my question,' she teases him.

He does his best to look sternly back at her, and with equal ferocity. 'Given you're a married woman. Given I'm so far past my prime. Given we met each other again less than twenty-four hours ago, and after a gap of twenty or more years. Given all that, the only rational choice is to stay on my own...'

He leans over and, trying his best to appear patronising, pats her on her knee. '... though with you as a very welcome visitor here from time to time.'

'And the irrational, the intuitive choice? If you've managed to think of one?'

'The intuitive choice is one I've made in the aftermath of that thrashing. And perhaps because of it.' His voice breaks with the intensity of the emotions that engulf him. 'It is, whatever Erica or Jack may try to do, however hasty we're being – and, of course, if you're sure you'll have me – to be with you.'

They stand up at the same moment. They hold each other as tightly as when they were in bed together the night before. They look searchingly into each other's eyes. They recognise with delight the delight they both see and both feel. They kiss each other for longer and with more longing than they have ever kissed before.

'I can see us walking through a minefield without a mine-detector between us. And with blindfolds on us both.'

'Are you thinking of Erica and Jack?' she asks as they stand close together, still in an embrace.

'Of them and what they might do to us, yes. They are, though, only the most obvious of our problems. And, perhaps because of that, they're the easiest to deal with. There are, so I reckon, mines that are much more lethal. And with much bigger explosive charges.'

'Which are?'

He presses his lips together, narrows his eyes. 'We haven't seen each other for twenty years. We know so desperately little about who we are now. Whether we like it or not, we're not the same people we were then. For all I know, you may be almost as set in your ways as I am in mine.

'You may not have set off on your downhill journey yet. But I'm certainly on the slippery slope of decline and fall. And I'm sliding all too close to the bottom for comfort.'

'Not yet,' she reassures him. 'Not yet. And even when you really do think you're in decline, even when the evidence of your decline is staring you in the face, remember this quotation that's just popped into my mind. It's those last few lines of *Ulysses*.'

'Then do your best to console me with them.'

'For a start, you may not be *that strength which in old days moved earth and heaven*. You may even be *made weak by time and fate*. But you're still in so many ways, as I've seen for myself since yesterday morning, *strong in will...*'

He puts his index finger against her lips to silence her. His voice grows in strength with each word as he delivers the final line: '... *to strive, to seek, to find, and not to yield.*'

'But I've got another offering,' she tells him. 'Written well over a thousand years ago. The work of an Anglo-Saxon poet after his side's defeat at the hands of the Vikings ...'

'... and I'm sure,' he admits, 'it's something I don't have the slightest idea about.'

'*Our resolve must be stronger, our hearts must be bolder,*

our courage must be greater...' She lowers her voice to a whisper. '*... as our strength fails us.*'

They begin to choose each word they say to each other with great care. They are very aware that what they say now may well affect the rest of their lives.

'Growing old. That's only one of the problems we'll have to face.' She hesitates before she goes on. 'Shall I be able to help you to explore that natural world of yours even more passionately than you've done up to now? And even when I know less about it than almost anybody I know?'

'Shall I be able to help you to explore your poetry to new depths? Even when I know so little about it myself?'

'Shall I be able to help you to satisfy your need for independence? Shall I, if I have to, be able to let you enjoy the fleshpots of Bangkok and the wastelands of Mongolia without me?'

'And shall I be able to satisfy that need you have from time to time to be dependent? When my instinct and reason unite in an unholy alliance to tell me to help you to be the exact opposite?'

Each listens carefully to everything the other says. With each word they hear, they do their best to work out what exactly it might mean.

'Shall I be able,' she asks, 'to understand your belief that we live, as you once told me, in island universes? On islands in a vast ocean that can move no closer to each other?'

'And shall I be able to understand your belief that no man is an island? That, whether we like it or not, we all depend on each other?'

Each looks at the movements of the other's face. Each

searches for even the slightest change in the expression of the other's lips, brows, above all eyes.

'Shall I be able to share your pessimism?' she asks. 'Shall I see us as the successors in miniature of that hugely long list of lovers? Orpheus and Euridice. Helen and Paris. Troilus and Cressida. Dido and Aeneas. Abelard and Heloise. Othello and Desdemona. Romeo and Juliet. Performers in tragedy. Fated for disaster.'

'Just as importantly,' he responds, 'shall I be able to share your optimism? See us as pale imitations, but triumphant for all that, of Beatrice and Benedick. In conflict until they found they were in love. And until he declares *Peace! I will stop your mouth*, and kisses her?'

'So very many questions, Stephen.'

'And, Jo, so very few answers.'

Their eyes are still meeting. Each still registers every nuance in the other's face. More than ever before, more even than when they first kissed on the towpath, more even than when they listened to the nightingale, the outside world has receded. At this moment, the only world that exists for them is their own.

'Shall we,' he asks, 'be able to live life more fully? To give every one of our senses fuller rein? To explore new worlds together – worlds we've never explored before on our own?'

'Shall we be able to create for each other spaces where we can be spontaneous?' she asks in reply. 'Where we can experience unexpected delights?'

'Shall we be able to help each other, at least from time to time, to avoid moderation? To go for excess?'

'Shall we be able to persuade each other to spend more time doing less? To float as well as swim? To find joy in doing nothing?'

'Shall we be able to grow old together just a little disgracefully?' he replies. 'Even to wear purple?'

'Shall we be able - at long last - to be like those two leaves we looked at together on the river? But forever floating together, never torn apart?'

So remote are they now from the outside world, they have no sense at all of how immoderate and extravagant, how absurd and ridiculous, their dialogue would sound to anyone who might overhear them. The only sense they have is of each other.

They look long and hard at each other. They look long and deep into each other. Each sees what the other is now. Each remembers what the other was then.

'Shall we be able, Jo, to put the times before then, before we first met, and the times between then and now, onto the backburners of our memories?'

'Shall we be able to remember then, Stephen, with its agony that came at the end and its ecstasies en route? But at the same time shall we be able to live for now? And for all the times there'll be from now on?'

'Shall we really be able to survive together for the rest of the time we'll share on this earth? For better or for worse? Till death us do part?'

'Shall we ever be able to survive the strain of being together full time? Day after day? Week after week? Month after month? Year after year? Whether we like it or not, a life sentence if ever there was one!'

As he first did outside her school before their walk by the Thames, he holds her hands in his. He brushes her forehead with his lips.

'Who knows?' he replies. 'Who knows? But let's give it a try. Let's do our level best. And not, as you once said, *just now and then*!'

THE END

Printed in Great Britain
by Amazon.co.uk, Ltd.,
Marston Gate.